TO LOVE AGAIN

Geneviève Montcombroux

ISBN 978-1-987946-40-6

Cover: mmontcombroux

Published by Solitude Publishing

solitudepublishing@gmail.com

To Bruce
With love, Ma

CONTENTS

CHAPTER ONE

Vanessa screamed as the snowmobile bore down on her, a flash of shining black and swirling snow. With

a split-second to spare, she leaped to the safety of the boardwalk. Her foot slipped, and she landed hard on her backside.

F rom this unglamorous position, she saw the driver turn his visored head toward her. Only a suit of silver and black registered in her mind, stunned by the shock. She hated snowmobiles with a passion. No, she didn't hate snowmobiles as much as the snowmobile drivers, like the idiot now barreling down the town's snow-packed street.

Where were the cops when you needed them?

Thankful that no one witnessed her inelegant performance, she got to her feet and brushed the powdery snow off her clothes. Relieved that only her pride had been injured, her anger flared at the driver, now out of sight round the corner. *Damned, inconsiderate, thoughtless, speed-crazy idiot.* Her brain ran out of invectives. *Snowmobiles! Give me a team of sled dogs, any day!*

She paused in front of the trading post at the end of the block and looked up at the false-front that belonged to another era. A rustic sign read *Pathfinder Outfitters*–Everything You Need for Your Wilderness Experience. Vanessa knocked the snow off her boots against the wrought-iron scraper and went in.

The door swished shut behind her. An intriguing mix of leather, pine resin, and cedar assailed her nostrils. She penetrated the interior crammed with every conceivable variety of outdoor equipment. A couple of browsing customers acknowledged her with polite nods.

A sales clerk came from behind a counter. "Hi, can I help you?"

"Thanks. I'd like to look around first."

"Go right ahead, ma'am. Ask if you need help."

A colorful rack of postcards reminded her that her parents might enjoy a glimpse of the magnificent Yukon scenery. Right now, her number one priority was to buy winter clothes, check out the sledding gear, and order a supply of dog food.

Through an arch, she entered an even larger room. Racks of heavy parkas vied for her attention. A display of eye-catching bead-embroidered mitts tempted her, lovely but not practical. Insulated boots, fleece jackets, thermal underwear and more crowded the shelves. The store appeared to have everything she'd need to survive her first winter in the backcountry. Climate here in the Yukon was an altogether more serious matter than back home among the gentle hills she was used to.

A hot-pink parka spoke to her. She picked it up and draped it across her front. The cushiony thickness of the material promised comfort even in the deepest cold. She dropped her shoulder purse to the floor and shrugged off her anorak to slip her arms into the parka. Not bothering to close the zip, she held the garment closed and struck a pose worthy of an accomplished model in the full-length mirror.

At that moment, she saw the reflection of a man standing right behind her. Their eyes met and locked for a brief instant. A smile came to the most sensuous pair of male lips she'd seen in a long time.

An imperceptible inclination of his head expressed his approval. "Pink suits you."

The vibrant voice and the manly cut of his jaw sent a ripple of excitement through her. She then froze. His outfit! He wore a trim silver and black one-piece snowmobile suit.

His smile inched wider. "I came to apologize, but you did jump out in front of me."

He spoke in such a self-confident manner that Vanessa wanted to scream all over again. She controlled herself, but her words shot out, anyway. "Jump out? I did no such thing!"

"Sorry, sweetheart, but the way you launched yourself off that boardwalk, I'd swear your mind was on another planet. If I hadn't swerved, you'd have two neat snowmobile tracks right across that gorgeous body of yours."

Heat flushed her cheeks. "Don't be so insulting! And don't call me 'sweetheart'."

Unruffled, he propped an elbow against the top of a rack. "You must be new around here. In this town, everyone knows the snow-mobile rules."

The upward curl of his lips and the crowfoot creases at the corners of his penetrating eyes showed he was enjoying himself at her expense! Yet, come to think of it, he was right about one thing. Out in the street, she had her mind on other things. Although her overall per-ception of snowmobile drivers remained the same, she admitted that this particular driver might not be as reckless as she initially thought. Just possibly.

"Excuse my outburst. I guess I may have been distracted. Thanks for not running me over. I'm not used to snowmobiles driving down the main street." She removed the parka, went to replace it on the rack, and promptly tripped on the purse she had dropped on the floor.

He steadied her by the arm. "It seems you still have your mind elsewhere. Our sharp northern air must be making you a touch light headed."

The warmth of his fingers zapped through the woolen sleeve of her sweater. Twice now, she had embarrassed herself in front of him. She frowned and gave him a quick glance. Thick black hair framed the rugged planes of his face. Another thrill ran down her spine. Nobody had a right to be that handsome. Then she remembered the breath she held. She let it out with an audible whoosh.

He picked up the offending purse and handed it to her. "Just visiting?"

His devastating smile played havoc with her nerves. "No. I've recently moved here. I intend to stay." She struggled to keep her voice even.

The man reached out his hand. "Then let me be the first to welcome you to Donek. I'm Brett Lancaster. I operate Wolf Hollow Lodge down on Eagle Point."

A flash of recognition animated her features. So, the swanky-looking resort she passed on her way home was his! That made him her closest neighbor, albeit some two miles distant. She steeled herself. His smile and his casual, assured way of speaking grated on her nerves. She shook his hand. His touch felt warm and pleasant. "I'm Vanessa Riley. I own a little cabin in the woods."

Brett kept her hand trapped for a moment longer than was necessary. "Very witty, Ms. Riley. I like your wry sense of humor. Have you found what you're looking for?"

"You mean, here in the store? Not yet. But I'm confident that the place carries what I need. You see, I wasn't so spaced out that I didn't read the sign over the entrance."

"As I said, you look great in that." He motioned with his chin to the pink parka still draped over her left arm.

Again, she struggled to remain calm under his steely gaze. His dark brown eyes seemed to undress her. She didn't enjoy the feeling.

"It's too dressy for me." She hurriedly threw the parka over the rack for the clerk to rehang.

"If there's anything you can't find, ask Patrick, Patrick Corrigan. He's the owner. If it's available, he'll get it for you. Here, follow me and I'll introduce you."

Vanessa walked with him to the back of the store, conscious of a disturbing quiver somewhere deep inside her. A feeling she had not experienced in a long time, not since her husband's death.

Brett Lancaster was by far the best looking male she had ever encountered. Not the kind she expected to find in this backwoods location. His broad shoulders stretched the snowmobile suit. He walked with the ease of a conditioned athlete, yet his manner was that of a successful businessman.

Brett thrust his head through an open doorway. "Patrick, you old dog, come out and meet Donek's newest citizen, and by far, its prettiest." He gave Vanessa a knowing wink.

Patrick Corrigan, a bearded bear of a man, shuffled out of his office, a sheaf of papers in his hand. He represented the type Vanessa expected a wilderness outfitter to look like. She imagined he'd much sooner be out shooting white water rapids than cooped up in a messy office writing purchase orders.

Brett made the introductions. Patrick shook Vanessa's hand.

"I'd like to order some dog food," she said.

Patrick nodded. "We have a good selection on the other side of the store."

"I don't use commercial kibble. I need frozen meat packs for my sled dogs."

He looked at her, a twinkle in his eyes. "So, you have a dog team? We can provide you with any equipment or supplies you need."

For several minutes, she and Patrick discussed the needs of her dogs. Brett remained silent.

When she turned to look at him, his eyes were focused on her. Patrick's hearty clap on Brett's shoulder jerked him out of his reverie.

"Well, folks," the storekeeper said. "It's been nice chatting with you. You'll have to excuse me. I've got a stack of orders to make up before closing time."

Vanessa smiled at him. "Thanks for your help, Mr. Corrigan. Mr. Lancaster, you'll have to excuse me, too. I've got shopping to do."

A flicker of disappointment crossed his features. "Please call me Brett. Donek's an informal town." His aura of calm assurance returned. "Drop by the lodge sometime. I'd love to show you around. Now that we've got an adequate snow pack, I'd be happy to take you on a tour of the countryside... by snowmobile."

Vanessa laughed. "After my narrow escape in the street, I'm not sure I want to trust my life to one of those machines."

"You're safe in the hands of an expert."

"You obviously consider yourself in that category. Thanks, I'll consider your kind invitation, though it'll have to wait until I get myself settled in. Right now, the cabin is full of unopened packing cases."

"Let me know if I can help."

Vanessa watched him stride to the door, half expecting him to look back at her.

He didn't.

She returned to select clothes, but her concentration was shattered. Without a second thought, the pink parka went into her cart. Images of Brett Lancaster darted through her head. Somehow, his presence heightened the feeling of elation that had enveloped her since her arrival in this magical territory.

Her dream was beginning to come together. Her parents and extended family expressed horror when she'd first announced her plan to relocate to one of the remotest corners of the country. *You must be out of your mind*, they'd said, *quitting a well-paid job and pulling up roots to live in the wilderness with your dogs*. Adding that the notion of setting up a dogsled tour business in the wilderness was pure folly.

After her husband's premature death, family and friends had rallied around her, and for that she would always be grateful, but they didn't understand her need to escape the memories. Nothing could deter her. After that, they gave their grudging approval, certain she'd be back within a few short months.

What was the point of dreams if you didn't act on them? For so long, she'd shared Walter's passion for sled dog racing. Racing! Everything had been geared to racing. The memories brought a sharp pain to her heart. Not the organ beating within her, but in that undefinable area that hurts more than a flesh wound.

She closed her eyes. The image of her laughing husband half-turned to blow her a kiss as he sped out of the yard on the sled runners behind sixteen Alaskan huskies flashed before her eyes.

That day, the team and its driver never came back. Thin ice in the center of the lake had given way. Walter drowned trying to save his dogs. No one ever discovered why such an experienced musher had ventured on the lake so early in the season, just after freeze-up. Some locals noticed snowmobile tracks on the dogsled trail and reckoned the team had gotten spooked and bolted across the lake. Whatever the explanation, fate had snatched Walter from her, leaving her traumatized and broken.

For the four years following the accident, she lived on auto-pilot. Fellow racers came to buy her remaining dogs and, sadly, she let them go. Only later, when the sharpest of the grief receded, did she realize how much she missed her dogs. Her life hadn't stopped because her beloved husband was dead. She acknowledged the need to do something for herself, something with dogs. Not racing. Racing belonged to Walter.

Her dream took root when someone told her about some Arctic dogs being discarded by a party of modern-day explorers, with the rider that, while they were friendly with people, they were *not* pets. Nor were they were racing dogs. These from the polar north were working dogs. They lived outside in all weathers and loved nothing better than running and pulling a sled. They would be ideal for the idea germinating in her mind.

Only her grandmother, who delighted in taking contrary views to the rest of the family, understood her yearning for renewal, for adventure. Secretly, she'd handed Vanessa a large check.

"You can't give me all that money, Nana."

"It's your share of the inheritance, sweetie pie. I can do what I want with my modest fortune. You'll be able to buy that cabin and the land you've talked about. With a roof over your head, you're halfway to success, and I'll enjoy seeing the money put color back into your cheeks."

Walter had taught her how to manage a kennel of dogs and how to survive in the wilderness. Together, they used to go on long training trips. Winter camping held no secret for her. The moment she had set foot in this Yukon valley the previous summer, she knew she had found her dream home. Huge rocks, streaked with pink and greenish veins, that had centuries past tumbled down onto the shores of the lake shimmering in the sun, stood guard on one side of her yard. The scenery took her breath away. The peace of the evergreen forest was a soothing balm for her wounded soul.

Patrick Corrigan's baritone voice broke into her jumbled thoughts. "Are you into racing?"

She shook her head. "I don't race. I'm setting up a dogsledding tour business. I spoke to the local chamber of commerce last summer. They were very encouraging. It seems no one else offers what I'm proposing."

"You're right. We've got lots of mushers in the area, but everyone's sights are on racing, or rather, the prize money that goes with it. Considering the number of tourists that come to Donek, you should have no trouble finding clients."

Vanessa's face lit up. "You really think so?" The only thing that made her happier than talking about her dogs was to be out sledding with them.

"Absolutely. Brett Lancaster has a huge tour business. He attracts a slew of people happy to experience the wilderness by snowmobile." He laughed. "You won't be competing with him. Your dog teams will appeal more to the eco-tourist. These days, so many folks want to get back to nature, at least during their vacation. We're getting more guiding requests from environmentalists than from hunters and fishermen. People have cottoned on to the idea that observing and photographing wildlife is more fun than shooting or catching them."

"That's encouraging."

"You're in luck. This year we've had a good snow cover for a couple of weeks now."

Pleasure lit up her features. "I heard about the big storm that started the season."

"That was quite something! How many dogs do you have?"

"Ten so far. My lead dog, Lulik, is about to have pups. So she'll be out of commission for a while."

Patrick's pale-blue eyes twinkled. "As soon as my boy learns you have dogs, he'll be over at your place in a flash."

"He's quite welcome. How old is he?"

"Seventeen. He's nuts about dogs. Not only will he beg you for one of your pups, he'll want to work for you. He's already helping some of the other mushers."

"I'll be needing help once I get going."

"How about I put up a poster in the store, right next to the cash register? Like that, everyone who comes through will know you're offering excursions. What's your outfit's name?"

"I thought of calling it Tapiskoot Tours."

"Tapiskoot? That sounds like a native name."

"It's a Cree word I picked up when I attended a pow-wow in Manitoba. It means 'The Old Days', as in the good old days."

Patrick nodded. "Tapiskoot. That's a sharp handle for a dog touring business. We have some native and Metis guides in the area who'd love to work for you."

"Good. I still have a lot to learn. Nature here is so much wilder here than back East."

"And you're wise to respect it. Where do you come from back East?"

"New Brunswick."

"Plenty of snow out there."

"Yes, but it doesn't last long enough, and it's not dry like here. That's why I wanted to come to the Yukon." Her other reason, like being as far away as possible from the place of her husband's accident and all her well-meaning relatives and friends, she kept to herself.

Patrick's eyes sparkled. "Right. We have abundant snow, not to mention the scenery of winter and summer. How did you find about us?"

"I researched the internet. Donek was listed as a tiny settlement with a big tourist industry."

"That's sums it up, yet it isn't so tiny anymore. Even though it is growing, everyone knows and cares for their neighbor. I'd better go and take care of your dog chow order."

Vanessa paid for her purchases and thanked him again. She couldn't help noticing the wistful sadness that crept into his eyes. She had met men with eyes full of the regret of lost dreams. That strengthened her determination to achieve her own.

She had a gut instinct that Donek was where her dream would become reality. Already, in the few days she had been here, a sense of tranquility had settled over her. For the first time, the ever-present pain that welled up whenever she thought of her husband had lessened.

Now and then, a nagging fear crept into in the back of her mind. What if she failed? Scenery and a pristine environment were cold comfort if she couldn't pay her bills. But she'd succeed. Of that, she was sure. She wasn't so sure about her reaction to handsome Brett Lancaster.

Chapter Two

A quick twirl of a platinum blond tress to ensure it emphasized her appeal. Ingrid, the manager and hostess of Wolf Hollow Lodge, smiled at the eager guests taking their places at the lunch table. A man came up to her and handed her a small gift box.

"My wife and I want to thank you for making our stay so great."

"Thank you. It was my pleasure. I hope you'll come back."

"We certainly will. Ah, I see our driver is here to take us to the airport."

"Have a pleasant journey."

The door closed after the couple. A half smile on her lips, Ingrid entered her office on one side of the lobby. A shadow detached itself from the behind the door. She gasped and dropped her present.

"Dan, you scared me!" She took a deep breath. "I told you not to come here. It's too risky."

The swarthy man sat in the chair behind her desk. Elbows on the desk, his fingers forming a steeple, he frowned. His silence unnerved her.

Then he spoke. "Where's the cake?"

She trembled and dug her long fingernails into her palms to keep cool. "Still in the shack. I couldn't go across."

"You fucked up that whole deal."

"I told you. We've got to keep low for a while."

"The boss won't have it."

"You better believe me. Cops have been patrolling the lake."

Anger put an edge to his voice. "What's that has to do with it? You never go by the lake."

"The new neighbor has moved in. I couldn't go across."

"You stupid or something? Sleep with the guy, get him drunk, but get across. Right now you've got two hours to get the parcel on the road, or else you won't be managing this fancy resort much longer."

"Brett has been watching who takes snowmobiles and has the guys keeping tabs on the gas, too. I wouldn't be surprised if he was suspicious. One of the guides has already reported unusual snowmobile traffic."

"To whom? Brett or the cops?"

"I don't know, both maybe. I have to lie low."

"As in sleep with him?"

"What?"

"I know you!"

"You're the one who made me come here."

"Because your dear, so-called brother had the good idea of starting an adventure business. Very practical."

"But now the passage is closed."

"Get us out of this bloody mess." Dan stroked his chin. His knitted eyebrows deepened the frown.

"It's not my fault!"

"Are you're chickening out? We don't need crybabies with us."

"I told you, I want out."

A sinister smile played on Dan's angular features. "The answer is no. This is an ideal setup and you're useful. That is when you don't bungle the job. You're a partner, whether or not you like it."

The sarcasm in his voice sent icy shivers down Ingrid's spine. "You said it'd only be for a little while. I've done it long enough. I quit."

He drummed his fingers on the desk. "Nobody quits. The cops'll haul your ass back to Michigan if they found out who was the hit-and-run driver that killed that retired chief of police."

Ingrid paled. Her stomach clenched. Her nails dug deeper into the palms of her hands.

"So, what ya waiting for? Get the delivery done!"

"But..."

"No buts. You got two hours. We can't wait forever. It ain't safe."

He brushed past her and out the door, disappearing silently.

As soon as he'd gone, Ingrid's panic set in. Always conscious of the presence of guests, she smoothed the skirt of her dress and repined her hair. She steeled herself to walk normally through the lobby, then rushed to her room. With trembling hands, she pulled on her snow-mobile suit. At the kitchen door, she shouted, "I'll be gone for a while, Mike." Without waiting for the assistant manager's reply, she took the back steps to the snowmobile garage. Heart racing, she crept to the window of the shop and peered inside. The mechanic wasn't there. Relieved, she eyed the powerful, yellow Polaris Rush-Pro. Good thing that everybody believed she didn't like riding snowmobiles, not even as a passenger.

Despite her agitated state, she took care to check the gas and oil. Her helmet strapped on, she climbed on the machine. The engine roared to life. She couldn't take the chance that the new neighbor could be away and she had no time to phone first to make sure. She had to go around the lake and through town.

The snowmobile bounced over the rough snow in the ditch. *Dan Cipolla, I hate you. HATE YOU! I should never have listened to you.* After Dan had given her a Lexus, he had suggested a trip to the States.

A kind of honeymoon, he had said. Although he had given her the car, he was in the driver's seat all the way there. They had a great time and, with fine clothes and jewelry, she believed life was finally smiling at her. On the way back, she took the wheel. When dusk was falling over the land, at that time when shadows were gray and headlights useless, she hit a man walking on the shoulder of a rural stretch of road.

Her scream had woken up Dan. She'd wanted to get out and call the police on her cell. He pushed her in the passenger seat and after checking there was no one in sight, had burned rubber all the way to Pete's garage.

Dan told her he acted in order to save her from going to prison. The next day in the motel, she had learned from the TV that the victim was the county's former police chief out walking his dog. The police were searching for a black Lexus driven by a woman. Apparently, someone in a house a little farther down the road had seen the car speed past. Though how that person could have seen who was driving when it was almost dark remained a mystery, or maybe not if they had a security camera.

Holed up in a motel room, she had lived in fear for a week, getting meals delivered. Then Dan came back with her Lexus. It was now green and had different plates on. "The guy's dead. It won't make any difference whether or not they know it was you," he had told her. But she detected the threat in his voice.

Ingrid bitterly regretted having told him about Donek. Especially after Dan ordered her to get a job at Wolf Hollow Lodge. She hadn't seen Brett, who was technically her step-brother, for ages. They were not related by blood and had little in common. Her mother married his father when she was six. Her new step-father already had a son from a previous marriage. Brett, who was already twelve, took only a moderate interest in his new sibling. However, she had been sure he wouldn't turn her down in her time of need, and he hadn't.

The 'slow down' sign at the entrance of town jolted her out of her somber reminiscence. She prayed she wouldn't meet Brett in town and would be back at the lodge before he did. Careful to take the designated trails and streets along the edge of town, relief flooded her as she joined up with a snowmobile trail. Her sporty Rush-Pro literally flew over the groomed surface. In an hour, she would reach the shack. Then she'd have to come back the same way, before the two hours were up to put the package in the tool and maintenance shed at the back of the lodge for the next mule to carry it on. She hadn't been able to figure out who that was, perhaps a guest. By now, she knew only too well Dan never made idle threats. Why the hell did she still love him? Or did she?

Ingrid had just enough time to change back into her dress before Brett entered the front door of Wolf Hollow Lodge. He dumped a heavy carton of freeze-dried chicken à la King on the bench in the entranceway. She watched him unlace his boots and kick them off. As a second thought, he picked them up and lined them up with the guests' boots in the tray under the bench. He then carried the box to the kitchen. She mentally braced herself for an uncomfortable few minutes ahead and joined him.

The shack was on the new neighbor's land. She'd have to push Brett to obtain permission from the neighbor to use the path across his land. If it came to that, she'd rather sleep with Brett than the unknown owner of the disputed land, though she didn't fully understand what it would achieve.

His eyes met hers. "You're back! You seem to have taken your time collecting the mail and that small order from the store. Did you get delayed?"

"Huh..?"

"Never mind. How were things in town?"

"In town? Oh, just fine."

Relief flooded over her. At least he hadn't seen her on the snow-mobile. Putting on a show, Ingrid rolled her eyes and folded her arms. "What an enlightened conversation we seem to be having! If it wasn't zero degrees out there, I'd say you have a touch of the sun. While you were out enjoying yourself, the Pearsons phoned to say there'll be two more in their party than the original booking. I figured we could put the new couple in the north bunkroom."

"No problem. Can you deal with it?"

"Of course I can. Don't I always? You know, Brett, I don't believe you've heard a word I said."

Brett dragged his fingers through his hair. "Sorry, Ingrid. I've got something on my mind."

"That's easy to tell. What's wrong?"

"Nothing, really. I was just thinking about, er... the plans to expand the lodge." He glanced through the open door at the empty dining room beyond. "We need more seating space."

He took a step toward the stairs that led up to his office on the mezzanine.

Ingrid laid her hand on his sleeve. "Why can't you tell me what's bothering you? You know I'm here to help."

"I don't want to trouble you with my problems. Just take care of the guests. It's a job you do better than anyone else."

"Thanks for the compliment." A hint of sarcasm sharpened her tone. "That's why I run the lodge for you. We could be more than partners, you know. Business partners, unless..."

"My dear, it's out of the question. I don't want to discuss that or anything else right now."

Ingrid bit her lip, smudging her meticulously applied gloss. She kept her hand on his sleeve. "All the same, we're good friends, aren't we? Even though we are not blood relatives, we still are brother and sister. That must count for something, no?"

She undulated her hips to catch his attention. Her fitted, white crepe dress with a silver filigree design shimmered in the sunlight that streamed down from the tall windows. The dress looked out-of-place amid the pine-clad walls and rustic lodge furniture.

Brett wasn't to be distracted. "You're talking about those innocent days at home. Of course it counts. That's why you're working here."

Ingrid flinched. She didn't like being reminded of her employee status, even if she directed the staff. Her eyes flashed fire. "Tell me I'm sentimental, but I've always loved you, Brett."

"May I remind you it was you that ran away from home? I can't forget mom's distress. She had a heart attack because of you. I put everything aside and went home. She'd been a wonderful step-mother to me. I was angry at you, even more, because after I tracked you down, you didn't bother to come home when she needed you."

"I was young and foolish back then. Things are different now. I'm mature."

"Sure you are. Your pursuit of fame and fortune with some Adonis who had dropped into town didn't work out, so you came waltzing back to me, like the *Merry Widow*, only not as wealthy. I gave you a job. Don't expect anything more."

Ingrid pursed her lips. "By the way, our new neighbor moved in."

"Really?"

"Since you weren't successful in buying that track of land, you now need to put on your Sunday best manners and go and ask the guy if we can still cross his property to access the snowmobile trails on the north side, like we did with old Ed."

"I guess you're right. It still bugs the hell out of me that some jerk from down East could snitch that parcel from under my nose."

"How come you didn't manage to buy it when it came on the market? You should have offered more money."

"I did and still lost out."

"The old coot who was selling it didn't have all his marbles. He should have been put in a home."

Brett frowned. "Edmund was okay and still is."

"While it was alive, he treated that old donkey of his like a family member! Just about had it sleep in the house."

"I see anything wrong with it. Treating the animal well, that is."

Ingrid again rolled her eyes, then glanced over her shoulder. A party of boisterous guests was invading the dining room. "I'd better see about the clients."

Brett used the distraction to take sanctuary in his office. The soft yellow glow from an antique lamp reflected off the wood paneling and contrasted strangely with the cold blue light coming from outside. The window gave him a sweeping view of the lake, its limpid waters now locked in ice.

Disjointed thoughts ran through his head. He slumped into a chair. His mind switched from Ingrid to the woman he had met in the store. Her lovely face danced before his eyes. She disconcerted him in ways he didn't want not to think about right now. He shuffled a stack of papers on his desk, then leaned back in his chair and chided himself for behaving like a love-struck adolescent. At thirty-four, getting dreamy-eyed over a pretty girl was not typical of his no-nonsense approach to life. What had she thought of him? He laughed. Most likely, she hadn't given him a second thought.

But he couldn't help thinking about her.

CHAPTER THREE

V anessa parked her pickup next to the log cabin. Her cabin!
Before going indoors, she walked the few paces to the edge of
the steep slope, studded with pines, that led down to the shore of the
lake. Through the screen of branches, snow crystals winked at her in
the sun like a million diamonds. She reveled in the simple beauty all
around her.

On the opposite shore, a line of dark coniferous trees pointed
into the clear sky. Only the crosshatch of snowmobile tracks on the
snow-covered lake and the distant whine of engines marred the serenity of the scene.

Her deep sigh of contentment morphed into an actual shout of
happiness, much to the delight of the dogs, who stood waiting faithfully against the fence of their enclosure to greet her return. She
couldn't resist petting each one, even though she had spent more than
an hour that morning caring for them.

She tried not to let the hateful snowmobiles diminish her love for
the land. It was an annoyance she'd have to get used to. Just as in summer, when the lake would be alive with powerboats and float planes.
Yet the magic of the primeval wilderness beyond compensated for any
irritation brought on by the internal combustion engines. Nature's
healing presence was everywhere.

The wilderness stretched for miles, and many smaller lakes nestled among wide valleys. Behind her extended the vast wildlife reserve and the hilly Aishin Forest. To the north lay private land. A sense of well-being enveloped her. She had everything she needed to be successful.

Whilst lost in the harmony of nature that permeated her soul, a soft wet nose came and snuffled her fingers. She looked down to find a very pregnant Lulik demanding attention.

"Well, old girl, you want to come into the cabin? Are you about ready to deliver those pups, by any chance?" The dog thrashed its bushy tail against Vanessa's legs and waddled with her to the door of the cabin.

The two-roomed log structure was simplicity at its finest. One end contained the bedroom, the other doubled as a large living space and kitchen. Log walls, darkened to a rich brown, soaked up the heat from the wood-burning stove and maintained the cabin's interior at a comfortable, even temperature. A couch, two armchairs, draped with colorful afghans, and a bookcase furnished the living area of the room. It was home, and it suited Vanessa perfectly.

In the corner by the door, she'd constructed a puppy pen lined with newspapers and a blanket to provide a space for Lulik and her expected pups. Vanessa checked the dog had ample food and water. The mother-to-be showed her gratitude by promptly curling into a ball and falling asleep. Since the birth would probably not happen until the early hours of the morning, Vanessa left the dog alone and went out to do some exploring before sundown.

Her aim was to hike around the perimeter of her land, some ten miles, which would take her maybe three hours. She strapped her boots into snowshoes and set off toward the north. In the summer, she had made only a brief tour of inspection with Edmund. Now that she knew firsthand what it meant to have pride of ownership, she wanted to become fully acquainted with her personal piece of wilderness. Now and then a marker showed where her land and that of the neighbor met. The neighbor being Wolf Hollow Lodge. No habitation nearby. After an hour of breaking trail through deep snow, she stopped to examine the topography, and frowned.

On her north boundary lay a parcel of land belonging to Wolf Hollow Lodge. On the west side, her land abutted against the park reserve and the Aishin forest, with acres and acres of untouched forest. Vanessa recalled Edmund saying there were miles of trails in the Aishin forest. Multi-use trails. This meant trails heavily used by snowmobiles and sometimes a skier or two.

She heaved a sigh. Those machines were everywhere. On the positive side, though, the trails would be well packed and she could use them.

On the south side of her property lay Wolf Hollow Lodge, owned by Brett Lancaster, the man who had almost run her down in the street. The man she found so fascinating when she had met him in the store.

Mystified, she narrowed her eyes. The road ended at her cabin. Therefore, her land was sandwiched between Mr. Lancaster's properties all the way to the lake. Her land effectively blocked him from gaining access to his other parcel of land and the Aishin network of trails. At the municipal office, they had told her that motorized vehicles were prohibited in the reserve, but her dog team was welcome, as long as the dogs wouldn't chase wildlife. She had reassured them her dogs were always hitched to the sled.

It reminded her of another parcel of land that she had considered close to the territorial capital of Whitehorse. Other than by a lake, the only access was through a private property. The owner wanted to charge a toll for the use of his road. In addition, it was in a sub-division with rules and regulations about owning a dog team. She had abandoned it as a possibility and had driven on all the way to Donek. The government offered crown land for sale, providing its use would respect the land and benefit the community, either with vital agriculture or an eco-tourist destination. Semi-retired Edmund had succeeded in buying this eighteen-hundred acres parcel to preserve its unique biodiversity and prevent the snowmobiles of Wolf Hollow from riding through it, indiscriminately. He had cut a network of trails to favor wildlife and plants which required an edge to grow.

This real estate oddity puzzled her. Why hadn't her neighbor bought this land rather than the inaccessible lot to the north? Unless he had purchased the northern parcel after Edmund had bought his. Whatever it was, it didn't concern her unduly.

Her attention was drawn to a line of tracks in the snow a few feet away. She stooped to take a closer look. The round prints lacked claw marks and had been made by an animal with furry pads. They led toward a thick clump of pines. A lynx? Goose bumps crept over her skin as she skirted the trees to see if the animal was lurking there. The lynx, if it was one, had disappeared. She breathed a little easier. After all, lynx were very shy creatures and unlikely to hang around when they sensed a human. Or were they?

Hardly ten paces farther on, Vanessa had the impression that she was being followed. Taking care not to make any sudden movement, she looked over her shoulder. Behind her, standing in her own snow-shoe tracks, stood a large canine, its ears fully erect.

"You're no ordinary dog." She caught her breath. "You're a wolf! A grey wolf."

A pair of almond-shaped amber eyes fixed her intently. Tufts of hair from below his ears gave him an imposing, almost disdainful air. His long bushy tail hung at rest and his brown coat streaked with black shone in the sun that now dipped low above the ridge.

"You're a truly magnificent creature!"

The wolf cocked his ears at the sound of Vanessa's gentle voice.

"I get it. This is your territory and you're escorting me." Any sense of fear she might have had vanished in the contemplation the proud animal, steeped as it was in myth and plenty of misunderstandings. Her Cree friends had told her many stories, but had insisted that wolves do not attack humans, despite what was shown in *Little Red Riding Hood* and other tales of popular fiction.

She didn't know how long she and the wolf remained motionless, politely staring at each other. After a moment, the wolf appeared satisfied with its appraisal of the human and slipped noiselessly back into the dense forest. She felt a pang of regret when she watched him go and thought of all the ills humans had inflicted on this majestic animal over the years, out of ignorance and unfounded fear.

Vanessa emerged from the trees and stood by the frozen shoreline of the lake. In the dwindling October daylight, the snowmobile tracks leaped out at her, like so many slash marks. Most of them appeared to come from and return to Brett Lancaster's lodge. They also appeared to give a wide berth to the cove bordering her land. Her nose wrinkled in renewed disgust. That was one kind of machine she could happily live without. How could anyone admire the utter stillness of the back-country from the seat of a raucous machine?

In her admittedly biased opinion, the world would be better off driving teams of dogs. Definitely better for the environment. Maybe, with the changing climate, fossil fuels being targeted as the villains, snowmobiles would disappear to be replaced by dog teams... What a dream!

By late afternoon, dusk wrapped her cabin in violet shadows. In the north country, winter came early, as did the night. Vanessa removed her snowshoes and hung them on a peg by the door. After caring for her dogs, she went indoors and prepared a hot meal for herself. A few remaining shipping cartons stood by the bedroom door, awaiting her attention. Today, she had little inclination to unpack. Tomorrow would be soon enough. She took out the large-scale map of the area and spread it out on the dining table to familiarize herself with her new surroundings. More particularly, she wanted to see exactly where the boundaries of her land and that of Wolf Hollow Lodge intersected. Too bad the price to pay for this ideal situation was the lack of reliable cell phone coverage. It also meant no 3-D maps on the internet except along the Alaska Highway, which, before the move, she had followed on her laptop.

Only minutes into her study of the map, a chorus of dog howls warned her of a visitor's approach. When she opened the door, the very man who had occupied her thoughts for much of the day stood on the porch steps.

"Mr. Lancaster, what a surprise!"

Brett froze. He opened his mouth to speak. His jaw sagged, and his eyes widened in surprise.

"Vanessa!"

She couldn't help smiling at the look of amazement which spread over his tanned face. For a moment, he lost the overbearing attitude which had so unnerved her that morning.

"You live here?"

"Of course I do."

"I was expecting..."

"A man?"

"Well, yes." He lost some of the superior brashness he'd displayed that morning.

"You're pretty sexist, aren't you?" She spoke with a smile, but with a touch of disdain. She was enjoying his discomfort. It was a small revenge for her earlier humiliation.

"Don't be too hard on me."

She waited patiently, enjoying his discomposure while he tied himself in knots.

"I only meant... I never imagined you were the new owner of Ed's—."

"I told you I had a little cabin in the woods."

"Are you married?"

"What's that to you? Look, while we're standing out here, my precious heat is escaping into the frigid night. Come in or go away, but don't stand on the doorstep."

The breadth of his shoulders shrunk the room. He unzipped his parka.

"You haven't answered my question."

"No."

"You mean no, you've not answered my question or, no, you're not married?"

Vanessa let him decide. He followed her inside and closed the door behind him. "You're not married, I take it."

"Now, why would you jump to that conclusion?"

Brett pulled off his heavy parka and threw it, along with his hat and mitts, onto a chair. He shifted his feet uncomfortably, the way a man does when a woman outsmarts him in a verbal exchange. He glanced at her hand. "You're not wearing a ring."

"With having to handle dogs, I wouldn't wear any kind of ring. It's not practical. But, as for your shrewd observation, I am no longer married." Her voice dropped a notch. "I am a widow."

"I'm sorry. You look too young to be widowed."

She looked away. "Widows come in all ages." A silence stretched for several long moments until she added. "An accident."

"Recently?"

She heard the concern in his voice. "Five years ago."

Vanessa looked at her dog lying on the floor, suspicious eyes fixed with on the visitor. She turned back to Brett.

He caught her movement and looked down. "You live on your own?"

A sarcastic reply came to her mind, but she smiled instead. "And they say women are the curious ones! To answer your question, I share the place with ten friends, males and females."

Her remark caught him off guard.

"Ten?" He cast a glance around the room.

His look of surprise made her laugh. "Yes, ten. You must have seen and heard them out in the yard."

"Your dogs!"

"Who else did you think I meant?"

Brett raked his long fingers through his hair.

"No, no. I was just wondering, that's all. It's customary to welcome neighbors."

"Have a seat."

She perched herself on an armchair. She enjoyed his discomfort and knew the effect she was having on him. Her green eyes, flecked with gold, and long, curly brown hair had distracted more than one a man before him. In her younger days, this inexplicable feminine power had embarrassed her to no end. Then Walter had come along and she never looked at another man again.

Her bantering tone carried a thinly veiled hint she had no intention of being swept off her feet by mere masculine good looks. Brett avoided her eyes by visually inspecting the cabin's interior.

"You've made the place look mighty attractive. Your predecessor lacked your flair for design."

"The old cabin's warm and comfortable, and that's all that matters."

His unease suggested he wasn't here for a purely social call. She let the conversation lapse before asking, "Was there something you expressly came to see me about?"

"I may as well tell you up front I had tried for years to buy this parcel of land from Ed. I'm still baffled by how you managed to get your hands on it."

"I'm sorry my good fortune caused your disappointment. I bought it fair and square on the open market. My agent must have been more skilled than yours, that's all. He introduced me to Ed. That's all." She got to her feet. "Could I offer you coffee? I just made it."

"Thanks. I take it black."

Vanessa rolled up the map and threw it on the couch.

She busied herself with the coffee, all the while casting discreet glances toward him. His every gesture made his powerful muscles ripple under the fine wool of his sweater. She filled two mugs from the enameled coffee pot, blackened by many campfires, and handed him one.

"Smells heavenly. Did you get to meet old Edmund?"

"I met him once when I came to view the property. He showed me the miles of trails he had cut so he could walk his donkey. It's just ideal for me and my dogs."

"Everyone calls him Ed the Hermit. He's leading the Preserve the Environment League."

Vanessa smiled. "I know. He told me. I'm going to join."

"The old fool didn't want to put the donkey down."

"He isn't a fool and you should admire him for taking care of his lifelong animal friend, even if the poor donkey could no longer carry wood back to the cabin."

A small shake of his head was Brett's only comment.

From a tin box, she put a handful of cookies on a plate and watched Brett out of the corner of her eye. He moved to the table. She had to admit he was one hunk of a man. He literally dwarfed the cabin. Her heart gave a flutter. No man since Walter had ever set her blood tingling in her veins, as was happening now.

Brett took a sip of coffee and set the mug on the table. "I don't know if you are aware of it, but I own the land immediately to the north of yours."

"I saw that."

"I have trails to reach the designated snowmobile trails in the Aishin Forest."

"So I gathered. Interestingly enough, I was just examining the map when you arrived."

"I was wondering if we couldn't strike a deal."

"A deal?" The presence of this gorgeous man in her own cabin affected her strangely, though the alarm bells in her brain didn't prevent her from feeling the disturbing sensations. The fact he had tried a number of time to buy the property that was now legally hers put her on the defensive. With an effort, she kept the emotion out of her voice. "What kind of deal do you have in mind, Mr. Lancaster?"

"How about if we drop the formality, Vanessa? The name's Brett."

"Yes, of course. We had a somewhat unorthodox introduction."

"How about we put that incident behind us?"

"Consider it forgotten. I was asking what kind of deal you were thinking of."

"Nothing complicated. As you have noticed, my land bookends yours. To resolve the problem, I'm asking you to agree to continue to let my guests cross your land to get to mine and the designated trails in the forest. Ed didn't make any objections. Ideally, I'd like to either widen the existing trail or, better still, cut a parallel trail to make them both one-way. It's safer like that."

He took a sip of coffee and sank his teeth into a cookie.

Unsure of how to reply, Vanessa greeted his proposal with a stony silence. She cringed at the thought of fast moving machines disturbing her and the dogs at all hours of the day and night. Her apprehension was valid. There was always the risk of an accident should her dog team meet a snowmobile on the trail on her own land! Her mind flew back to Walter's team, spooked by snowmobiles.

"You're talking about the trail that runs just behind the cabin?"

"Yes."

"I can't agree with that."

Brett blinked. Both surprised and annoyed, he slicked his hair back. "A couple of narrow trails about two miles long wouldn't take up much room in your eighteen hundred acres. Naturally, I'll pay compensation."

"It's not a question of money or space. Snowmobiles are potentially dangerous. I have to think about the safety of my dogs."

"The safety of your dogs? I don't get it. What danger would there be?" He leaned forward, a smile on his face, yet a hard edge to his voice.

"In order to train my dogs, I'll be using the meandering trails Edmund established through the woods. Where the trails cross the one you propose, there's always the chance of a collision. If one of my dogs is running loose, there's no saying what might happen."

Annoyance briefly darkened his features

"Ed had no problem with that."

"Stopping a donkey on a dime is a lot easier than stopping a team of dogs hooked up to a sled."

"What do you do with your dogs?"

"I train them. They have to run regularly. Therefore, I need the trails on my land."

"Are you training for racing?" His eyebrows went up.

"No, touring."

He leaned forward. "What do you mean by touring?"

A Cheshire Cat smile came to her lips. "I'm setting up a business offering dogsledding excursions."

"Dogsledding excursions?"

Vanessa stared at him. He stared back with the blank look of an alien from Mars.

She maintained her smile. "Surely, you don't see us as business rivals? Our respective operations are entirely different. You use snow-mobiles. I take tourists by dogsled into the wilderness. Some of them might like to learn to handle the team on their own, or go skijoring."

"Or what?"

His incredulous look would have been funny had it not been such a serious issue.

"You've lived a sheltered life. Skijoring is a person on skis, while being pulled by one or two dogs."

Vanessa's heart pinched. She disliked this confrontation over her dining table. This was not how she envisioned starting her new life in Donek. Surely, he wasn't bitter over her refusal to let him cross her land? She saw a shadow flit across his face.

"Is that some newfangled kind of sport?"

"Hardly. The Norwegians invented it several centuries ago. It came on this continent more recently. Just over a hundred years ago." She concentrated on not showing her merriment.

"I've never heard of it."

"I'm not surprised if you always see the world from a snowmobile seat. Come and try it sometime."

She detected a fascinated look in his eyes.

"Do you think you're going to get tourists to come ride your sled?"

"Of course. Many people are getting worried about man's impact on the environment, with pollution and climate change. Dogsledding is the ideal means of transport. No atmospheric or noise pollution, if you discount a little excited howling."

She immediately realized she had just accused him of being part of the problem.

He frowned. "You're insinuating that my snowmobiles are polluters."

"I wasn't trying to point fingers, but in truth, they are among the biggest polluters."

He shook his head and absently stared toward the back of the cabin. "Let's not start on that. Changing the subject, you realize that backcountry tour guides are always men."

"So what?"

"Clients need to feel safe. They have to have confidence in those leading them. All round the world, men perform that role."

"What nonsense! Men dominate because that's how patriarchy works. That's changing. Besides, women have a better safety record than men." She curbed her mounting anger. Obviously, he deliberately provoked her in an attempt to reassert the domineering arrogance that had marked their earlier encounter. He was not the first man to tell her she was encroaching on male turf.

"You reckon you're going to get enough clients to make the business pay?"

"Eco-tourism is growing in popularity everywhere. So, yes, it will pay. Travel by dogsled will give tourists an opportunity to enjoy nature without contributing to the degradation of the environment. No gasoline engines spewing out noxious fumes. I'm sorry to say you can't claim that for your snowmobiles."

"Ouch!" Brett gave himself a mock stab to the heart.

"Sorry to be so blunt, but burning fossil fuels do all kinds of harm."

A skeptical look spread over his face. "Tourists are usually business people with little time to spare. They want to get out onto the land to see something of the wildlife."

Her voice rose despite her self-control. "What a joke! Let's be honest. How much wildlife can you see from the seat of a speeding snowmobile? Any self-respecting animal would be long gone at the first sound of those noisy things."

Vanessa watched him rub his chin. That the discussion wasn't going in the direction he wanted was plain from his attitude. He was virtually squirming in his seat.

She pressed her point home. "When was the last time you were out on your snowmobile and saw a wolf?"

"You won't see any at this end of the lake. It's too close to the settlement."

"I hate to contradict you, but I saw one just this afternoon."

He just about jump up. "Where?"

"Right here on my property, no more than a few hundred yards from my cabin door. After all, the wildlife reserve is our western boundary."

Brett's face expressed utter disbelief. "I think you are mistaken. Even if there were wolves, they'd be soon driven out by the barking of your dogs."

Something akin to a condescending smile floated on her lips. "You're wrong. My dogs don't bark. They howl. That makes them second cousins to the wolves. No wild canine is going to be intimidated by them. In fact, they will sing along with them."

He pushed back his chair and crossed his legs, body language that Vanessa read to mean he wasn't convinced and he was prepared to argue. She resigned herself to spend the evening debating the merits of sled dogs over snowmobiles.

"Now look, I'll pay you well for the right to cut the trails I need. You've got to realize it's the only way I can get access to the fifty-odd miles of trails on my land, plus the public network of trails on that side."

"Why can't you go around on the lake?"

"It's a long detour, and it isn't reliable. Even in the depths of winter, there are times when the ice isn't safe around the point. There can be open leads in the ice."

"Of course, besides freezing and breakup, there is ice movement on an enormous lake. Like it does on sea ice. I've learned to recognize the ice. My dogs can handle it. Instinct, you know. Of course, snowmobiles don't have that essential quality. Maybe you should learn the ice patterns."

"That was the reason Ed let me cross his land."

"Actually, snowmobiles appeared to have been crossing everywhere and spoiling this beautiful piece of land with its rich biodiversity. That's why he bought it, since the Territory's Land and Property Department declined your offer to purchase. Being a kind soul, Ed allowed you one trail."

He grasped his head in both hands. "You're impossible."

"There must be another way to get to the forest." Stubbornness also was part of her character. When she was in her right, nothing could make her budge an inch.

"In order to be safe, I'd have to go through town and around the lake. That's a long way over the bridge at the narrows. A twelve-mile detour."

"Or about five minutes, the way I've seen the snowmobiles whizz by. Also, if other snowmobile riders see an unmarked trail, they'll come barreling down to explore it."

"I could put up signs."

"As if that'd stop them." Vanessa rolled back her eyes and wondered why the man was so pig-headedly difficult? "You must be aware that for every respectful snowmobiler, there are two who ignore private property and caution signs."

Brett shrugged. "Then I'll need access in the summer to maintain the trails on my land and help with the Aishin network."

"Don't tell me you don't have a boat for the canoeing part of your business." Vanessa didn't like being pushed, and Brett was being very pushy. His voice alternately caressed and coerced her. His stubbornness irked her. No matter how convincing his arguments, she stood to lose too much. An inner voice willed her to remain calm.

"A boat is just not practical. I use some heavy equipment. I'd need a barge and tugboat to haul it by water."

"Or a truck going by road. I've given you my reasons. I'm sorry you can't see things from my point of view. Besides, in summer, I'll be running with my dogs over my woodland trails." She smiled at him. She hated to pit herself against a neighbor, but safety and privacy were not something she'd compromise on. "Then I see no alternative but to blast the rocks and prolong the road." "What?" "As you have noticed, the road stops at your property.""Before I purchased the land, I had a talk with the mayor. He told me the road had come under discussion at council meetings. The resolution passed at unanimity that the municipality would not ever extend the road. The expense alone is way beyond what they can afford. Besides, the province flatly refused permission on the account of the environment damage it would cause to the eco-system on land and in the lake."

"I know. Then I will propose to pay for it myself."

Vanessa shook her head and bit her tongue to prevent herself from saying anything disparaging. "You do realize that first they would have to conduct an environmental survey, then they would have to expropriate a ribbon of my land. Of course, I'd put up objections and before you know it, there would be thousands of environmentalists protesting. It will drag you through the courts for years. Are you sure you want that?"

Brett gave a sigh of exasperation and bit his lower lip. He got to his feet. Though Vanessa knew he must be angry and frustrated, she had to admire the way he masked his emotions. But only just. In that respect, they belonged to the same school.

"I see. But I haven't said my last word." With a moment of hesitation, he held out his hand. "No hard feelings, I hope. The invitation for a grand tour on one of my evil snowmobile still stands. If you intend to take tourists out, you'd better get to know the lay of the land. Once you're away from what little habitation there is around Donek, you're in true wilderness. Between here and Alaska, there's nothing but a vast expanse of empty forest and mountain."

Vanessa accepted his hand. The touch sent vibrant tremors through her. She promptly pulled back. He was burning her skin. They exchanged smoldering looks.

"Thanks, I'll keep your invitation in mind." Her voice quavered for a second before she could control it.

"Goodnight, Vanessa."

"Goodnight... Brett."

She saw him to the door and waited while he pulled on his coat and gloves. He raked her from head to foot with an unfathomable look. Vanessa wondered if he was about to reopen their inconclusive discussion. Either that or kiss her.

Brett grinned again and walked out into the starlit night. A cloud of warm air rushed out from the cabin and condensed like a magician's cloak about his shoulders. Vanessa shut the door and leaned her back against the rough planks. She listened to his retreating footsteps across the yard. A couple of dogs murmured as he passed. The sound of his truck starting, the crunch of tires on snow, and he was gone. Darkness swallowed the sounds. All that remained was the infinite silence of the untamed North.

A mood of acute dissatisfaction settled over her. Thanks to that stubborn streak of hers, she had earned the animosity of her closest neighbor. She had no doubt he'd soon be back to try to sweet-talk her into granting his request. His invitation was simply a not-so-subtle ploy to get her to capitulate. If she did, his detested snowmobiles would make her life miserable. Too many unhappy memories associated with snowmobiles crowded her mind. As to build an extension of the road, she needed not fear. It would never happen. She lifted the curtain to glimpse the rocky promontory bathed in moonlight. His visit alone damped her earlier high spirits. "I'm sorry, Mr. Lancaster, I'll be on my guard around you. This is one battle you will not win. Not even if you deploy all your manly charm."

A vigorous panting from the corner of the room snatched her attention from her neighbor's unsettling visit.

"Lulik, my princess, are you about to have those babies of yours?"

At Vanessa's words, the dog swept the floor with her tail and panted harder. Delivery was imminent. Vanessa continued to talk to her dog while getting the kitchen scale and cutting a bath towel in four.

She crouched next to the dog. A few minutes later, the first pup appeared. Lulik promptly licked it clean while the squirming pup bawled with all the strength of his new lungs. As soon as he was liberated from the sac, he crawled toward the nearest teat. The miracle of new life never ceased to amaze Vanessa.

Soon, another pup made his entry into the world. Vanessa picked up the sleepy firstborn, dried him completely and put him on the scale. Woken up, the brown-reddish male, with white around the eyes, squirmed, seeking his mother.

Lulik completed the toilet of the second pup, who wouldn't let go of her teat. Vanessa wrote the date and hour, the weight and markings of the pups. She was proud and happy. Two more males and two females were born at regular intervals. She couldn't have asked for a better birth. Her future team of six, all of them strong. Their little stomachs replete, they fell sound asleep.

An hour later, Lulik stood and nudged the blanket around her offspring to make a nest, and asked for the door. Vanessa let her out, knowing she wouldn't go far from her pups. She put a clean blanket into the makeshift pen. She had hardly finished, than Lulik was furiously scratching the door. The new mother bounded to the enclosure and lay next to her pups with a satisfied sigh. Vanessa placed a bowl of broth in front of the mother. "Have a drink, Lulik. Your pretty little pups need your milk and you need water to make it. Tomorrow you can have a big bowl of meat and corn."

Without getting to her paws, the dedicated mother avidly lapped the warm liquid. A smile flickered over Vanessa's lips. *Brett Lancaster would have me committed if he saw me talking to my dog.* Brett again! Such a brief acquaintance, and yet he was occupying so much of her thoughts. A shiver ran down her back. Why did he have to be so drop-dead handsome and evoke so many unwanted reactions in her? She shook herself to chase him from her mind and went to bed, hoping to catch a few hours' sleep.

***

On the way back home, Brett berated himself for being such an idiot. He, perfectly at ease in any situation, hadn't managed to string two coherent sentences together. An unusual roiling continued in his stomach. He'd done his best to keep his eyes off the slim body outlined by a tight sweater and an old pair of jeans, yet his brain had registered every minute detail. The reason for his visit vaguely came back to his befogged mind. His mission had been to persuade the new owner to agree to his continued access through her property. In that regard, he had totally failed. The image of the pink lips devoid of makeup haunted him and made him uncomfortable. It couldn't go on. It was only the novelty of a beautiful woman. Tomorrow, he would have forgotten her. At least, that was what he told himself.

Chapter Four

Next morning, Vanessa was up early and went to check on her new family of pups. Afterwards, assured that they were well cared for by the mother, she placed a thermos of hot chocolate and a sandwich in the sled bag. When the long night was giving way to daylight, she entered her coordinates into her Global Positioning System, pocketed the map and went out to harness the dogs. Since the team had not been working for a while and would be excited, she took the precaution to weight the sled with a couple of the large ornamental stones that decorated her porch.

Coming down the steep slope to the lake was akin to an acrobatic performance at high speed. The exuberant dogs took the tortuous path at full tilt. With both feet on the brake, Vanessa clung on, thankful she had waited until the darkness lifted. She vowed next time she'd have them run around the whole Tapiskoot property before pointing them down the slope.

Once on the lake, the dogs continued to pull hard and fast. Fortunately, at this hour of the morning, the snowmobilers were all still asleep.

"Take it easy, Vercors! Steady, old girl."

Her lead dog glanced back and tried to slow the pace, but the rest of the team was pressing hard from behind. Vanessa gave them their head, hoping that they would burn off their surplus energy before reaching the trees on the far side.

"Vercors, Haw! Haw!" Vanessa urged her leader to swing left toward the forest trails.

Vercors obeyed and turned. The others fell into line behind her. Less rambunctious now but with plenty of power in reserve, they swept up the opposite bank, through a gap in the woods in one long graceful motion, hitting the steep gradient at a brisk pace before falling into their cruising speed on the level.

Intoxicated by the varied landscape of forest, clearings, frozen streams, filled with the brilliance of thick snow, Vanessa knew the deepest of contentment. The blue sky frolicked between the gaps in the pine trees, only to surge in its full glory in the quiet clearings filled with untrodden snow. She found the pristine beauty utterly enchanting. The sun, too, played hide and seek among the branches, and scattered a shower of glitter on the wind-carved snow.

Not long after reaching the top of a crest, Vanessa heard the unmistakable whine of a snowmobile engine coming up the slope behind her. As a precaution, she pulled her team off the trail and buried the snow hook to anchor the sled. Next, she fastened a line from the sled to the closest tree. This done, she went to the head of the team and gripped her lead dog and its companion by the collar. Her dogs were not used to snowmobiles, and she didn't know what their reaction would be when meeting this noisy machine.

A minute later, the snowmobile came into view. To her relief, the driver saw her and slowed down, coming to a halt a few yards away. He killed the motor and removed his helmet.

"Vanessa, what pleasure meeting you again!"

"Hello, Brett."

"So, these are your famous huskies?"

"All of them except my top female, who just had pups."

"Pups? More dogs?"

"They're needed for my business."

"These guys look well behaved."

She nodded. "I'm impressed that they're not fazed-out by the noise of your engine." She cast a disparaging glance at the sleek snowmobile. She got the impression that he wanted to start a conversation. The dogs lay down, not a bit bothered by the commotion.

"Going far?"

"As far as the park limits. Then I'll head back home."

"And how long will that take you?"

"About an hour. Maybe a little more."

"I must remember that sled dogs don't travel fast. I could make that in ten minutes."

The tone was slightly mocking.

"Trying to impress me? Of course they are slow. They don't have a fossil fuel engine to propel them. I'm not pushing the dogs. This is only a conditioning run. Because of the move, it's been a while since they've been out like this."

"Well, I hope we'll meet again. Enjoy your outing."

"Thanks." As an afterthought, she added, "You too. Bon voyage."

An enigmatic smile floated on his lips. "*Touché!*"

He replaced his helmet, started the engine and set off, leaving a cloud of snow hovering in the air where he'd been. The rider and his iron steed soon disappeared beyond the trees.

Vanessa remained motionless, watching the plume of ice crystals settle on the snow. How handsome he was when he laughed. She scolded herself. It wasn't appropriate to succumb to a man's charm when all he wanted was a passage across her land. She reminded herself of the reason she'd come to this lost corner of the Yukon; to find peace and embrace her destiny. The wild land, her dogs and the hope of a small business were all she wanted from life.

It was Vercors and her favorite companion, Cousteau, who stretched and yawned and made the first move. This chance meeting with Brett stirred Vanessa's residual anger from the previous evening. She reminded herself she needed to take a firm grip on her emotions to curb such thoughts.

On her return to the cabin, she found a truck parked in her yard. A lanky youth with dark blond hair sticking out below a baseball cap was perched on the tailgate. He jumped down and came forward to hold the dogs. Quietly, he walked next to Cousteau, who immediately began sniffing him up and down.

"Hi, I'm Alden Carrigan. My dad told me you had a team. He didn't tell me they were beauties. I've never seen such great-looking dogs." He bent down and scratched Cousteau behind the ears. The dog responded by licking his hand. "I came to take a look-see for myself. I hope you don't mind."

"No, of course not, Alden. You're welcome."

"May I give you a hand to unharness them?"

"I'd appreciate that."

With a sureness that seemed bred in the bone, Alden transferred the dogs from the sled to their pickets inside the temporary enclosure, giving each dog a pat as he did so. He didn't waste time chatting except to ask their names.

"Do you want me to set up a gate to the pen?"

"That would be nice. The problem is that the nuts and bolts have been lost in the move."

"Don't worry. I'll find what's needed and I'll come back tomorrow to fix it. I imagine you'd prefer to let the dogs loose in the pen, right?"

"I'll let them loose only when I am with them until the pens are permanently built in the spring."

While he busied himself with the team, Vanessa fetched the food she had prepared that morning. With economical moves, Alden helped her distribute the broth after the dogs finished their food. He then collected the bowls.

"I can wash the bowls if you like. Do you have more dogs than these?"

"I have some brand new pups. Do you want to see them?"

She easily guessed that Alden didn't dare ask the question burning his tongue. He almost dropped the bowls to do a little dance. "You bet!"

"Come on inside."

"Thanks." Vanessa opened the door and invited Lulik to go outside, but she refused.

"She doesn't know you, so she's not moving away from her pups."

Alden took a piece of dried meat from his pocket. "May I..?"

"Lulik is a sucker for treats. After that, she'll accept you, no problem."

The dog sniffed the tasty morsel, the hand that held it and up the sleeve. Finally, she delicately took the treat and swallowed it after a quick chew. Only then did she come out of her pen to inspect the visitor. Seemingly satisfied he posed no threat, she rubbed herself against his thigh, then went to the door. As Vanessa turned to open it, Lulik rushed back to her pups, nosing them gently into a pile of squirming fur. She returned to the door, looked back once more, and ran outside.

"See, you've been adopted. She's given her permission for you to look at her babies. She wouldn't have gone out otherwise." While talking, she tethered the mother outside the door.

Alden bent over the blanket that Lulik had formed into a nest for her young. Vanessa picked up a warm pup and placed it in his hands. They took the pups one by one to pet them and whisper to them.

The teenager's gentle manner struck her. "Of course, their eyes are not yet open, but they can hear, though not for the first three hours after birth. It's good to socialize them at the earliest possible age."

Lulik came back in and began licking her pups. When each one was properly washed and accounted for, she arranged them all back in the nest.

"It's strange to think a dog knows how to count," Alden said.

"True. If we kept hold of one, she'd know."

"Ms. Riley, can I ask you something?"

"Call me Vanessa. Everyone does. What do you want to ask?"

"Vanessa, that's a nice name. Would you sell me a pup? It's my dream to have my own team one day."

"I think I could give you one, providing your parents agree."

The young man's face lit up. "My dad was very impressed when he met you. Now I see why. My mother doesn't want animals in the house."

"A sled dog lives outside."

"I know, and I'll try to convince her. She doesn't believe I'd be responsible enough to look after a dog. She keeps telling me that when I go to university, there'll be nobody to look after my dog and she wants nothing to do with it."

"Too bad. I can see you really love the dogs. You have a natural way with them. Lulik accepted you on the spot. That's proof. She's very picky who she makes friends with. But it's true you have to think about your future. Nowadays, to succeed in life, a person must have a lot of education. The world and society have changed since the days when a willing worker could become a successful businessman. But that doesn't prevent you from having a couple of dogs. You'll simply have to make arrangements for the care of them."

The adolescent's face had saddened, but now lit up. "I'd really like to study and become a vet, but it takes a long time and a lot of money. I've been saving, but it won't be enough, even with the scholarships I'm sure I'll get."

"Maybe there are private scholarships you could explore. I could help you with that. In the meantime, send your application to the veterinary school before all the places are taken."

"You're so nice. I was going to give up, but you make me think. I'll send the forms tomorrow."

Vanessa smiled at Alden's unbounded enthusiasm.

The young man turned his attention back to the litter. "Can I come and help you with the dogs? Dad tells me you're going to offer dogsled tours."

"That's correct. And yes, I'd welcome your help whenever you're free."

"I'll be here every day."

"Hey, what about school?"

"I have time after classes and at weekends."

"I seem to remember your father saying you work at the store. I'd hate him to be mad at me for luring away the hired help."

The youth's mobile face went serious again. "I can do both. I really hope to have a team of my own someday."

"Since my business is not yet up and running, I couldn't pay you. Not at first, anyway. Let's say that you'll give me a hand when you're not needed at the store. The moment the tourists start coming, I'll be in a position to offer you a wage. How about that?"

"That sounds great, Ms. — I mean, Vanessa."

"As for the pup, I'm not in the business of selling puppies. You can choose one from the litter when they're a bit older as a reward for helping me."

"You mean it?"

"Absolutely."

His face fell. "Since my mother won't allow me to have a dog, could my pup live here, with you, and I'd come every day to train him?"

"That's possible."

"I'm finishing school ahead of time." For her benefit, he added. "At the end of the semester in February. Afterward, I could rent a cabin until the fall when I'd have to leave for college."

"I hope it won't be necessary and your mother will see that you are managing well. In any case, your pup can live here as long as necessary."

Joy returned to his face. "Thanks. These aren't just any ordinary huskies, are they? They're nothing like the dogs the racing mushers I've worked for had."

"That's very observant of you. Mine are different. They are freighting dogs from the high Arctic."

"Wow! Like the Canadian Inuit sled dogs the polar explorers used?"

Vanessa admired the young man's lively intelligence. In her experience, few people knew what type of dog was used in polar exploration, or even that dogs were used at all. "A couple of years ago, a party of explorers made a crossing of the high Arctic. On their return, they sold off their dogs. That's how I acquired these."

Alden's eyes widened in shock. "How could they have simply got rid of their dogs after they'd traveled so far with them?"

"Unfortunately, that's how it is. Racing mushers are no different. Once their dogs can no longer run, they get rid of them."

"Lucky for these dogs you were there to buy them."

"Inuit sled dogs can be exasperating at times. They love nothing better than a good scrap, though they're always well-mannered with people. They are not house pets, though. Next time you visit, we'll hitch up a couple of sleds and you can come with me for a run."

"Thanks, Vanessa. That's great! And thanks again for the offer of a pup."

All smiles, Alden drove off home. Vanessa found the boy's enthusiasm infectious. That's how she had been like at his age. She walked to the pen and petted each dog. Yes, coming north had been the right thing to do.

A sense of peace settled over her. Happiness was enveloping her little log cabin and with it, her heart. She was finally letting go of her burden of grief. Once more, she felt young and ready to take on the future, even though alone. Donek was a healing place. Reality was even more beautiful than her dream. The region was magnificent in its wild glory. Storekeepers and others she had met had welcomed her.

Thoughts of how close she was to success sent a rush of adrenaline through her veins. In the cabin, her future team was lustily showing signs of being as strong and robust as the dogs now lounging on the flat roofs of their houses. The only looming shadow was when she thought of Brett Lancaster, but she banished it from her mind. True, he had been amiable. She surprised herself by thinking how nice it would be to have him as a friend. She straightened. Because of their differences, there was little hope of that happening. And there was no way she would let herself be taken in by his charm. What he wanted was unfettered access to her land. Her land, now her most cherished possession. She could never let that happen.

Chapter Five

It was still dark when Vanessa woke up under the comfortable duvet. How temptingly decadent it would be to remain in its delicious warmth. Unfortunately, the wood stove needed to be reloaded. She braved the chill to put logs on the fire. After she dressed, she made herself a substantial hot breakfast. In a happy frame of mind, she went outside to prepare the dogs for a run.

Later, on the trail, Vanessa sang to encourage the dogs. They seemed to like the sound of her lilting voice. Her team, detecting the closeness of home, put on an extra spurt on the uphill slope to the cabin. When the sled burst into the open space in front of the cabin, she spotted a truck. Visitors were fast becoming a regular feature.

"Hi Vanessa!" Patrick Carrigan climbed out to help her unhitch the dogs. "Here, we'll give you a hand with your team."

Vanessa looked up. A man got out of the passenger side with the easy grace of an athlete.

"Vanessa, meet Marcel Morris, one of the best guides in this neck of the woods. I thought you might enjoy talking to him."

Marcel reached out his hand. "Pleased to meet you, Vanessa. I've already heard a lot about you."

She took his hand and perceived in his voice the measured tones of a man who spends his time alone in the wilderness. "And now my reputation's shot! Seriously, though, I'm pleased to meet you. Maybe you can give me some useful pointers."

The two men approached the dogs and had them sniff the back of their bare hands.

"Let me picket the dogs first. Oh, the gate is hung!"

Patrick nodded. "Alden dropped by during his lunch break to set it up."

Between the three of them, it took no time to unharness the team and lead the dogs to their pickets in the enclosure. They gave each dog a bowl of water.

"Would you like to come in for a hot drink?"

"An offer a guy couldn't refuse," Patrick said. "That is, if you're not too busy. We didn't call first."

"No problem. Come and see my new pups." Her face glowed with pride.

Just as Alden had done before them, the men crouched on the floor to examine the newborn pups. Lulik, however, refused to leave her young and growled a warning.

"Funny, she didn't act like that with Alden."

Patrick gave a proud smile. "My son has a real knack with animals. All he talks about is becoming a vet."

"Our present vet would welcome another vet. With all the mushers in the area, he's hardly home," Marcel said. "Did you meet Dave Roberts yet?"

"I did. He's planning a visit to get acquainted with my dogs."

"He's a good man."

While coffee was brewing, Vanessa glanced at her guests seated at the table. The guide's lean features were bronzed from exposure to the sun and wind. His high cheekbones betrayed his native ancestry, tempered by well-trimmed brown hair and beard. A pair of light brown eyes looked in her direction and sparkled with an infectious laughter. He appeared not to have an ounce of fat on his wiry frame. In contrast, Patrick's florid features had softened over the years. Marcel was the kind of man she immediately felt at ease with.

Vanessa poured the coffee. "Please help yourself to cream and sugar and tell me your visit is purely social."

"Did you have another sort of visit?"

"Unfortunately, yes. My neighbor wants to buy me out."

They snorted.

"Lancaster is still miffed that old Edmund refused to sell to him. Ed the Hermit has no love for snowmobiles," Patrick said.

"But he allowed Mr. Lancaster's snowmobiles to cross his land."

"Diplomatic concession, until he succeeds in getting the snowmobiles banned."

"It might come sooner that we expect with the climate changing so fast and rules to lower CO_2 emissions," Marcel said. He raised his coffee mug to his lips and took a sip. "Like Patrick said, I'm a guide. He told me you're going to offer sledding excursions. I'd be happy to offer you my services."

"I'm delighted. As soon as I get my business organized and running, I can foresee the need for one, two guides, even. I saw you're used to handling dogs."

"I was told I drove a team before I could walk."

"That's as strong a recommendation as any."

He gave a good-natured laugh. "Seriously, as soon as I finished school, I returned to the land of my maternal ancestors. We had sled dogs."

While Vanessa was listening to Marcel, she could feel Patrick's gaze boring into her. Once or twice she glanced at him and met his eyes for a fleeting second before he averted his. He, too, had the robust build of an outdoorsman, but inactivity had added extra padding to his girth.

Patrick must have read her mind. "Sometimes I wish I hadn't settled down to run a store. I miss paddling untamed rivers and snowshoeing the back country."

Marcel nudged him in the ribs. "Why don't you come out with me from time to time? You've got employees to do the work for you."

"Thanks, but as I said before, with wife and kid, it isn't easy to take off for a week or so."

Marcel nodded. He'd probably heard the same argument many times. He pointed a finger toward the yard and looked at Vanessa. "You're going to need more dogs than those. It'll be awhile yet before you can hitch up these pups."

"True. I've been told of a team coming up for sale."

"Where from?"

"The high Arctic. I've already made contact with a reliable Inuit hunter."

Patrick nodded. "If you need to go, don't worry about who will take care of this place. Alden is eager to help out. He was so fired up when he came back from seeing your dogs. Never seen him like that."

"You're right. He does have a natural affinity for them."

"Talking about your proposed business," Marcel said. "One piece of advice about winter excursions is always to keep your clients warm and dry. Like that, you'll have happy customers and they'll spread the word."

"Thanks for the tip. I've got some experience, but still have a lot to learn. Fortunately, I'll have time to practice. It'll be a while before the first paying customers actually arrive."

"Don't be too sure. Word has a way of getting around. You may find yourself overwhelmed with inquiries," said Patrick. "How are you getting on with setting up your website? Did you get connected to Wolf Hollow satellite tower?"

"No. And after our disastrous meeting, I'm not sure I want to depend on him. But I can't afford a professional to work it remotely at the moment. I have a landline telephone."

"I'll give you the coordinates for the region's internet provider. They can connect you over the phone. You don't have to ask Lancaster."

"The internet will be slow and irregular, however," Marcel said. "Not the best to run a business website. I can't see Lancaster asking for more bandwidth to share with you if he is trying to get you out of here."

"Tell you what. I will include a page on my website for Tapiskoot. Reception is good in town, mind you, so I'll just forward the emails. And I'll print them to make sure they don't get lost."

"Thanks for adding Tapiskoot onto yours."

"No big deal. It is in the town's interest to see you succeed. I'll set up a booking calendar, like I have for the boat rental business."

"I don't know how to thank you."

Embarrassed, Patrick shook his head. "We small business people must support one another. The more successful your business is, the better it is for mine."

Marcel nodded. "Way to go, man."

They chuckled. Lulik came to sniff at the hand Marcel was dangling from his chair. She let him scratch her under the chin and went to inspect Patrick. The two men moved toward the pen. This time, the mother made no objection to letting them look at her pups, but she stood guard.

Vanessa looked on. *Big rugged men have soft hearts. The exception was her neighbor, who had a cash register where his heart should be.* "So, Patrick, you really think my business will take off?"

"Absolutely!"

The two men laughed and pulled on their coats, ready to go. Lulik ran to her pups and appeared to count them by nosing each one.

Alone once more, Vanessa took out her account book and opened it on the page showing her current balance, not in the red yet. She estimated that if she had enough bookings to keep her present team fully occupied, she'd break even before Christmas and maybe have enough left over to justify the purchase of additional dogs. It represented a sizable expenditure. Then she'd need a guide. To ward off the fear of failure that hung like a cloud over her, she drummed on the table with the end of her pen. "This has got to work out. It has to!"

Chapter Six

The din of howling dogs outside heralded a visitor. Vanessa ran to the window in time to see Brett get from behind the wheel of his truck. The somber expression on his face was a sure sign he wasn't coming for a social visit. Her brain sounded a call to battle stations. Yet another skirmish in the war between them.

She paused a moment to compose herself before answering his knock. "Hello, Brett."

"Those dogs of yours make a hell of a racket!"

The visit was not off to a proper start. "They are my early warning system. You can't say that of your snowmobiles." Vanessa made a sweeping gesture with her arm toward the inside of the cabin. "Come in."

She wondered why he was such a grouch he didn't even give her a polite greeting. She closed the door. "So, what brings you to my humble abode?"

Brett growled something she didn't catch.

"Why don't you take off your coat and sit down?"

"I can't stay long." Nonetheless, he unzipped an expensive-looking parka and hooked it over the back of a chair. "I just came to ask you something."

"If you wanted to speak to me, why didn't you just phone? Or isn't the lodge equipped with such modern devices yet?" Despite her bantering words, she felt awkward. It pained her not to be gracious. She didn't mean to be sarcastic.

"Ha, ha, very funny."

She scooped up her books and dumped them on the kitchen counter. "Could I offer you something to drink? Coffee, tea, arsenic?"

A smile darted across his lips. "I'll settle for coffee right now, thanks. Tell me, do your dogs also bark all night long?"

"If a wild animal were to stray into the yard or if an intruder comes during the night, they'd get quite vocal but, except for the hypothetical intruder, they quickly settle down again. If you've noticed, as soon as I opened the door, they stopped. Why do you ask?"

"My guests at the lodge have complained that your dogs keep them awake nights."

"That's absurd! The lodge is too far away, with dense forest between us, for your guests to be disturbed. You don't keep the lodge windows open in the dead of winter, by any chance? You said your guests, but what about you? Do you hear my dogs at night?"

Her spirited rebuttal flustered Brett. He chewed the inside of his cheek. His initial resolve appeared to melt away.

Vanessa insisted. "Well, did they? Did my dogs disturb you personally?" The gaze of her green eyes plunged into his.

He looked away and appeared to shudder. "I must sleep like a log."

"And I presume these guests of yours also complained about the idiots drag racing on the lake at two in the morning?"

"You must be imagining things." His tone grew heated. "Drag racing?"

"Or a pretty close imitation of. A person would have to be either dead or stone deaf not to hear them. They must have kept all the inhabitants of this side of the lake awake."

For a moment, Brett lost his composure. He stiffened. "Okay. I grant you that a few of the town's hotheads let off steam occasionally, particularly on Saturday nights. But that's not usual. However, I'm told the dog barking goes on every night."

Vanessa's irritation turned to anger. The man was stubbornly insisting on something of which she knew was blatantly untrue. "You say you *were told*."

"Yes."

"And my dogs were barking?"

"That's correct."

"But you personally heard nothing?"

"My manager told me."

"Then they weren't my dogs."

"Of course, they were yours."

"My dogs are Canadian Inuit sled dogs. I told you before, they don't bark. They howl." Chin raised in defiance, she watched his arrogance deflate.

He looked befuddled. A dull anger was mounting within her. What was he trying to do? She had already spoken to the two nearest neighbors, both a little over two miles away and closer to the lodge than her. They, themselves, kept big outdoor dogs who were capable of making quite a racket. When she asked them if her dogs' howling were disturbing them, they'd laughed good-naturedly at her concerns. After all, this was dog mushing country.

She waited for Brett to say something. When he didn't, she continued. "What about your other neighbors' dogs? Some are closer to the lodge than I am. Are they also complaining, or are you also complaining about them?"

Brett leaned back and squirmed in his chair. "Ingrid, she's my manager, told me about the guests' complaints. The comfort of my clients is of prime importance. Wolf Hollow Lodge is noted for its luxury."

A note of finality crept into Vanessa's voice. "My dogs howled last night, but only last night, for ten minutes. That's all. Some wolves were close to the cabin. Did you or your guests hear them?"

"Wolves again?"

"Yes, wolves, an entire pack, believe it or not. They probably strayed from the park. Unless they came to investigate this new pack on their territory. They recognized the howling and must have been satisfied it was no threat because they didn't hang around long."

Brett pressed his eyes closed and let out a long breath. It was several moments before he again spoke. "You realize you'll never make enough money giving dogsled rides. Tourists will be scared off by any talk of wolves."

"You and I obviously hold differing opinions on the matter. More and more people are becoming aware of the environment and the need to protect it to keep the balance of nature."

"What wolves have to do with it?"

"They're an essential part of the ecological system. To be balanced, nature needs every species at every level. When things get out of balance, you get explosions of undesirable species, be it plants or animals. It's the survival of our planet we're talking about."

"You talk like old Ed. I like nature alright but I also have to make a living. Now, with snowmobiles, it's different. People like power and speed. They pay big money for tours. You can't expect the same from a bunch of dogs."

"Obviously, my clients will be people who love to take things slowly and quietly. Don't underestimate the attraction. Many people have a lot of feelings for a *bunch* of dogs, as you so eloquently put it." She got up to remove from the oven the loaf she was baking. A tantalizing aroma filled the air. "Care for some fresh bread straight from the oven?"

Brett nodded. His annoyance visibly slipping away.

Vanessa could have taken a smug pleasure of having beaten him twice already in this battle of wits, but deep down she regretted having to waste so much time and energy on arguing. She plunked a board and the warm bread in the center of the table and stood over him, holding the bread knife. "Maybe you don't trust me with this knife. Perhaps you'd prefer to cut your own?"

The provocative words forced a smile from his lips. "I'm sure you're quite handy with that knife. Cut me a slice. Did you give any more thought to the request I made the other day?"

"There's nothing to give more thought to."

"What if I settled for just one trail and routed it as far from your cabin as possible?"

"That would change nothing. I gave you my reasons for not allowing it. And since you can get to the forest and to your land by going around town when the lake isn't safe, I see no reason to entertain your proposal any further."

"Driving in the ungroomed ditches is too rough for snowmobiles."

"My! That's the first time I've heard that your machines have limitations."

"From the lodge, I can't skirt to the south or I'm into the wildlife preserve, where snowmobiles aren't allowed."

"I'm sorry you have a problem. There's really nothing I can do about it. I'm not about to change my mind."

"Excuse me for saying so, but you're being extremely stubborn."

"If I appear to be, I've got good reason to be."

They glowered at each other over the cut loaf of bread. A wisp of steam from the hot loaf rose in the air. After a few seconds of stand-off, Vanessa caught his gaze traveling from her hair cascading over her shoulders and down her body molded by her green wool sweater. She blushed at the frankness of his look. The fine hair on her skin bristled and a wave of awareness hit her. It couldn't be. She hadn't felt anything like it since Walter.

To shake it off, she slathered butter and strawberry jam onto a doorstep-sized slice of bread and handed it to him. Vanessa watched his white teeth bite into the bread. His eyes half-closed with sensuous pleasure. He finished the slice with obvious satisfaction and smiled in appreciation.

"You make good bread. I'll say that much. I could use your talents up at the lodge. To come back to the problem, could we work together to find a solution?"

"Yes, as long as it doesn't involve crossing my land or blowing off rocks."

He got to his feet. "I can see when I'm not getting anywhere."

Lulik growled as he inadvertently came too close to her pen. He looked down. "Oh! You've got pups."

"That's my new team in waiting."

"Mind if I take a look?"

His abrupt change of mood surprised Vanessa. "Not at all."

Brett went up to the barrier. The mother dog came and rubbed herself against him and put her paws against his knees. In disbelief, Vanessa watched this impeccably groomed man in a fine woolen sport suit kneeling next to her dog, then crawl into the pups' enclosure. He gently picked up a blind, wriggling pup. This man, who ten seconds ago was driving her mad over a ridiculous dispute, was now handling Lulik's pups with infinite tenderness. To add to her dismay, Lulik licked his ear.

At long last. he emerged from the pen, somewhat disheveled, and casually brushed off his pants.

Vanessa made a peace offering. "You're welcome to come and see them anytime you wish."

"Thanks. I couldn't resist. They're cute. Then, so is the owner."

She pursed her lips and chose not to comment.

"Tell me, why do you hate snowmobiles so much?"

Pain washed over her. "Snowmobiles used to harass dog teams back home. Although no proof, just a couple of tracks, it appeared that it was this type of harassment that led my husband to lose control of his sixteen-dog team. The lake's new ice in the center didn't hold."

"What happened to him?"

"He drowned with the dogs."

A silence stretched between them. She exhaled a loud sigh.

His face contracted. "I'm sorry. I wish I knew words to ease your grief."

His parka half undone, he left. Heart beating a bit faster, she watched him walked to his vehicle. He'd come ready to do battle and was going home with dog hair on his clothes.

***

Brett kicked off his snow boots at the entrance of the lodge. His eyes surveyed the common room where Ingrid, as supremely elegant as always, was entertaining the guests. His mind compared her to the woman he had just left, standing in a simple log cabin amid a sea of pups. Vanessa was down to earth and close to nature in a way Ingrid knew nothing about. Yet few women of his acquaintance could match Vanessa's disarming simplicity, or her beauty. He winced ... or that rapier-quick mind of hers.

He no longer knew where he stood. Ingrid had insisted the clients had complained about the dog barking. He had now learned Vanessa's dogs howled like wolves. He, himself, had heard no howling, but occasionally he did hear the snowmobiles on the lake late at night. With two miles of woodland between the lodge and the cabin, he admitted it was most unlikely that anyone could hear the dogs to the point of disturbance.

In front of Vanessa, he'd lost his grip. Her lips, pink, yet without makeup, stirred desires he never thought of with Ingrid. Legally, she was his step-sister, and he had always seen her as such. His mind compared the two women. The one he had just left with her closeness to nature and practicality, and his manager, who had no idea about nature or much else.

He reached his office unnoticed and lost himself in a daydream.

CHAPTER SEVEN

S hortly after breakfast, Vanessa received a phone call from Patrick to say he had lined up her first clients. A man and woman were booked for a short tour on the following day. Thrilled by the prospect of actually launching her business, Vanessa quickly harnessed the team. Exploring the trail Marcel had recommended to her was her priority, to avoid surprises.

Her dogs were now accustomed to their new surroundings and loved to race down to the lake and across the expanse of level ice, without breaking their stride, until they fell back into their usual pace. She would explore the reserve later. The network of trails in the Aishin Forest made it easy to navigate. Today, Vanessa directed them over a trail to a small lake. They leaned into their harnesses on the uphill. On either side, a jumble of stones was piled up one upon the other, like discarded children's toys. On the steep uphill slopes, she pedaled the sled with alternating feet. Not because the dogs needed help, but it kept her feet warm.

They had barely arrived at the top of a ridge and had stopped to rest that she heard a snowmobile grinding its way up the slope behind her. "There's no getting away from those things!"

As she had done on the first occasion, she secured her team off the trail and held Vercors and Cousteau by their collars. She waited for the machine to overtake her. When it broke from the trees, Vanessa saw it was not one but three machines. The first one was pulling a laden toboggan, the others carried two riders apiece. She had no difficulty in recognizing the leader as Brett. He waved to her and slowed to a crawl to pass her team. To her surprise, the other two machines halted and cut their motors. The riders, two men and two women, dismounted.

"So that's how you walk your dogs!"

She laughed. "It is indeed."

"We watched you cross the lake. You were really moving back there," said one of the men. "These huskies sure can pull."

"Thanks. I'm very proud of my team."

"I'm Harold Glover. This is my wife, Liz. These other two are our friends, Dee and Lance Palmer."

"Pleased to meet you. My name is Vanessa Riley."

Liz, a woman in her middle years, stepped closer to the dogs. "May we pet them?"

"Go ahead. Let them sniff the back of your hand first. Then tickle them under the chin. They're friendly enough, but a little wary of strangers. They won't bite ever."

While the visitors fussed over the dogs, Vanessa peered toward the trail where Brett had vanished, probably unaware that his clients had stopped. A few moments later, however, he came roaring back down the slope, stopped a few yards away and strode toward the group.

He removed his helmet. "What's happening?"

"Your guests got distracted," Vanessa replied. Now he was going to be furious with her. "They wanted to pet the dogs."

"But it isn't..." He swallowed the next words.

Brett's displeasure was obvious, and Vanessa easily guessed his thoughts. She bit back a retort. Liz broke the awkward silence. "Tell me, Vanessa, would you mind awfully giving us a ride in your sled?"

"Liz, you can hardly abandon the snowmobile in the middle of the trail," Brett said. His voice was level, but Vanessa heard his displeasure all the same.

Liz appeared unruffled by his brusqueness. "That's no problem. Harold drives it anyway and I'll ride in the sled. That's if this young lady agrees." In her expensive leather snowmobile suit, the woman had the air of a woman whose husband panders to her every whim.

"It's fine by me," replied Vanessa. She flashed Brett a disarming smile.

Brett threw up his hands. "I'm not objecting to you taking a sled ride. Only, it travels so slowly, we'll never make it to the picnic site before lunch."

With a diplomatic look on his features, Harold snapped his fingers. "Now that's something I hadn't thought of. The cold has given me the appetite of a horse, and I wouldn't want to miss the gourmet lunch our hostess has packed for us." He turned to Vanessa. "Where can we get hold of you, so that we can arrange a later outing, paid, of course?"

"My business is called Tapiskoot Tours. I'll give you my phone number." Vanessa pulled out her notebook and pencil, making a mental note to act on those business cards she planned to have printed. Under Brett's baleful glare, she handed Harold a slip of paper. "Give me a call and let me know when you want to go." She raised her eyebrows at Brett in a blatant act of defiance.

The tourists bade her a cheerful farewell and climbed back on their machines under Brett's disgusted look. Vanessa waited for the sound of the engines to fade into the distance before putting her team back on the trail. After their brief rest, the dogs ran with enthusiasm. She had to keep them in check so they wouldn't use up their energy too fast.

She completed her training run and headed back home. She gave water to the dogs and finished her chores. Not a minute later, Brett's truck rolled into the yard.

"It must be at least three hours since we last met." Her laughter echoed back from the trees. "Come in out of the cold."

He followed her. "I just dropped by to tell you I take a dim view of you trying to steal my clients and sabotage my excursions. They talked about nothing but the dogs."

At that moment, Lulik came and nuzzled his hand. He reached down and scratched the dog behind the ears. Vanessa assumed his anger was not too deep if he could still pet her dog.

"Steal your clients? Be reasonable, Brett. I did no such thing. Do you think I flagged down those people and forced them to stop? I was off the trail to let you all pass."

Brett brushed aside her objections. "Those people are only here for a short stay, as it is, and now they're going to waste a whole day getting dragged around by some dogs."

"You just said it. They're on vacation. Surely, it's up to your guests to decide how they want to spend their time, no?"

"We have plenty of activities for them to choose from up at the lodge."

Vanessa put on the kettle to boil. "Obviously dogsledding is not one of them. And as you saw, people are fascinated by the dogs." She couldn't help tease him. "Maybe it's something you should consider."

Her argument was logical. His lips tightened into a thin line.

"Look, this is getting crazy. I'm prepared to make you a very generous offer."

Vanessa groaned. She knew what was coming next. "Are we back on the same old subject?"

"You already know I tried to buy this piece of land. Since you snatched it from under my nose, I'm prepared to take it off your hands at whatever price you care to name. I'll cut you a check right this minute."

She glared back at him, her eyes wide in disbelief. Her heart pounded madly. Worry or anger had etched shadows on his lean face. For a moment, she saw a side of him she hadn't seen before. She gritted her teeth. "Sorry. Tapiskoot is not for sale... at any price."

"Don't you understand what I'm saying?" His voice rose a notch. "I don't care what you paid for the land and the cabin, but I'll make sure you get a handsome profit out of it. Like that, you'll be able to get yourself an even better place elsewhere."

Her heart churning, she looked straight into his eyes and carefully articulated. "The answer is still no."

"Try to appreciate my problem. Your property lies smack in the middle of mine and it's impacting on my business."

"Sorry for that, but I had nothing to do with the layout of the various parcels of land."

"Don't you understand what I'm saying? Whatever you paid for it, I'll give you twice as much. You'll be able to buy something much better suited to your needs."

"You, however, don't seem to realize I've grown attached to my little corner of the Yukon. Besides, there's nothing else for sale in this area, and it's very doubtful the government would open up more crown land."

"If you agree to sell, I'll help you find something else. True, there's nothing already established on the open market. There's never much land for sale outside the designated areas, but there are always people wanting to sell privately. Trust me. I've got connections."

"Trust you? I'm sorry, I don't think I want to right now. Not that I don't understand your predicament or appreciate your offer. The bottom line is that I'm staying right here. There is no way I am selling or giving you the right-of-way across my land. That's final."

Brett sucked in a sharp breath. "Okay. I get the message, loud and clear. Let's forget it."

He took a step closer, his look so intense it mesmerized her. For one breathless second, her lips trembled. He wouldn't dare kiss her, would he? That iron resolve of hers may not extend to her emotions. Deeply disturbed, she summoned her last memory of Walter. It didn't appear. She'd never even looked at a man before. When she met someone, her love for her husband would always surface and she'd find the other man lacking. Yet the man in front of her blotted out all her thoughts.

The magical spell that hung over them was broken when Lulik anxiously jumped up and put her front paws on Vanessa's chest.

"Goodnight." Brett's stilted voice sounded strangely formal.

Vanessa had no time to watch him drive away. The sound of the phone sent her scurrying back inside. It took her a moment or two to realize that it was Harold Glover, one of the clients she was accused of stealing, calling to arrange a picnic outing for him and his wife the day after next.

***

Vanessa's very first clients, the ones arranged for her by Patrick, proved to be a young, newly engaged couple, as enthusiastic about the outdoors as herself. To be out with them was more like a vacation than work, especially when the three of them picnicked on a snow-covered ridge. They had brought their skis and wanted to try skijoring. Vanessa gave them Kissimi, a strong and reliable female, well able to lead a skier, and her daughter, Ilak, who would happily follow her mother. Vanessa had as much fun as her clients.

***

Harold and Liz arrived early the next morning. Not content to be carried along in the sled, they, too, wanted to learn about the dogs. The couple bombarded Vanessa with questions about the dogs' origins and their traditional role with the Inuit people of the Arctic, and how she had become involved in this life.

Harold, with all the savvy of a shrewd businessman, listened to Vanessa outline her dreams for Tapiskoot, nodding his approval from time to time. "You've got a pretty good head for business, young lady. When we have time to talk more, I'll give you a few suggestions on how you can refine those ideas of yours."

"Thank you. I'd welcome your advice. For this outing, I suggest I show you how to harness the dogs and give you some instruction on handling the sled. Then you can drive my small sled with three of my most reliable dogs hitched up. I'll drive Liz in the larger toboggan sled."

The trip passed without the slightest problem. Her clients were enchanted and promised to come back.

When the team was unhitched, Liz opened the trunk of her car. "I hope you don't mind, but we brought the dogs some bones as a reward for all their hard work. May I hand them out?"

"With pleasure. Only watch out. The dogs get very excited about food. They're not too fussy about what they sink their teeth into. I'd hate for you to lose a finger."

Liz laughed. "I understand. I'll be careful" She went about her task talking to the dogs and distributing the treats. As if they knew the kind woman was also clueless, they sat and took the treats delicately.

Harold led Vanessa aside. "I want to thank you. I've not seen my wife this happy in a long time, not since our daughter was killed in a car accident. Seeing her radiating joy is all because of you. Listen, I run an investment consultant business and I deal with companies large and small on a daily basis. I know why some succeed and some don't. If you like, I'll write you up a blue-ribbon business plan."

"That'd be too much work for you."

"Nonsense. Believe me, the surest way to guarantee the success of an enterprise is to have a sound organizational plan, covering everything from your mission statement to projected revenues. It'll help you attract capital. I can arrange that for you, too, if you like."

"That's very generous of you, Harold. I have some savings and I was aiming to buy another team of dogs later."

"Hang onto your savings. It would make better fiscal sense to acquire those dogs right away on credit. I'm confident that when word gets around, you're going to be swamped with clients."

"Thanks. I'll give some serious thought to your advice."

Vanessa watched them go, not believing how a chance encounter was about to give a boost to her business. She was always ready to take up a challenge. For now, she spent the entire evening writing letters and pondering on what Harold Glover had said. Next day, after a good night's sleep, she gave her dogs a rest and drove into town to restock her provisions.

At Pathfinder Outfitters, she bought a plentiful supply of dehydrated meals in preparation for the long tour she and Marcel intended taking to familiarize her with the area.

She was idly browsing in the book section when she found the aisle blocked by an elegant, immaculately dressed, platinum blond woman. The look of pure venom in the woman's eyes instantly put Vanessa on her guard. She smiled and stepped aside, but the woman made no move to let her pass.

"Vanessa Riley?"

Vanessa's first impulse was to make a rude reply at being addressed in such a coarse manner. Instead, she swallowed her pride. "That's me."

The woman raked her eyes over Vanessa's trim figure. "I'm Ingrid Lancaster. I run Wolf Hollow Lodge."

The haughty tone rubbed Vanessa the wrong way. She straightened her spine. "Pleased to meet you." Was she Brett's wife? There has been no mention of a wife.

"Are you the woman with the dogs?"

Vanessa understood the woman's tactics. Ms. Lancaster knew perfectly who she was. "I happen to have dogs and I suppose I am a lady, though myself, I never use the term." Vanessa had no intention of being put down by the woman.

Ingrid looked taken aback. "Mr. Lancaster was supposed to tell you that your dogs upset our guests. Maybe you don't realize these people are important executives and corporate CEOs. They come up here to relax."

Vanessa remained unmoved by the outburst. "So you're Brett Lancaster's manager. Don't worry. This problem has already been settled with Mr. Lancaster, because they weren't my dogs that you heard, Ms. Lancaster."

"That's what *you* say. I suggest you shut your dogs up and stop annoying the lodge's guests. The barking is intolerable."

"My dogs do not bark, ma'am."

"Don't be stupid. All dogs bark. I heard them all night."

"Not my dogs. They don't bark. They howl. They howl like wolves."

Satisfied with her riposte, Vanessa watched Ingrid's face dissolve into white fury. The woman had said Mr. Lancaster, not *my husband,* as would be expected if she were a wife. Trouble in paradise?

"That's what I said. I don't bother with the terminology. They howled all night."

"You heard a pack of wolves."

"I can tell the difference between howling dogs and wolves."

"That's rich. For your information, not even the experts can tell the difference."

The woman was losing her poise. An acidic comment was on the tip of Vanessa's tongue. She was spared further anguish by the appearance of Patrick.

"How nice to see you two ladies have already met!"

His sarcasm wasn't lost on them. Ingrid snorted in an undignified manner.

Patrick remained unruffled. "I'm glad you came in, Vanessa. I want to show you all the inquiries I'm receiving for sledding excursions."

As much as Vanessa would have liked to nail Ingrid and her sharp tongue to the log walls of the store, she was grateful for Patrick's timely intervention.

The store owner motioned Vanessa into his office and closed the door. "I heard. Don't let Ingrid get to you. She isn't the easiest person in the world to deal with. Frankly, I don't know what Brett sees in her."

Mention of Brett brought an unexpected flush to Vanessa's cheeks. Come to think of it, the two were well matched. Both dressed more fashionably than anyone should in a place like this, and both were unabashedly outspoken. "She's good-looking."

"And frostier than the water in Donek Lake." Patrick pulled a folder from his desk.

"Underneath, she's probably a very nice person." Vanessa sincerely wished to believe that even Ingrid must have a positive side to her character.

"She came back just over a couple of years ago. I can't say she's well liked. One thing I will say for her, the lodge runs better since she came on the scene. Under Brett, it was a pretty slack operation. I never thought he'd take her on. But he has always had an eye for a beautiful woman."

"Are they married?"

"Hell, no. She's his sister, sort of. A sister by marriage. Her mother married his father, and each already had a child."

A somersault of joy flipped in her stomach and left her puzzled at her reaction. Patrick motioned her to take a seat. He pulled up his chair.

"Isn't Brett a good manager? He strikes me as a capable person."

"He used to race. Got lots of trophies. His strong suit is taking clients out. He doesn't give much thought to the problem of management. Ingrid is an expert in that department. We all go back to high school days. We were the Canoe Gang, with Marcel and Stefan Browne. He's a Metis guide too. Spent more time out of school than in." He chuckled. "We'd snowshoe all over in winter. Little Ingrid hated being left behind and tagged along as best as she could."

"And canoe in the summer?"

"Until the ice was too thick to be broken. Brett went on to college." Patrick passed a hand over his face.

Vanessa understood he didn't. "You did well, though. This is a superb store."

"Yeah, well, I had to get married."

It was time to change the subject. "Brett wants me to sell him my property."

"I'm not surprised. He's been after it for a long time. You didn't agree, did you?"

"No. And I won't, even if I have to go to war over it." Mentally, she added, *against that hellcat manager he's got, too.*

"Good for you, Vanessa. If you need to expand and get more dogs to handle your growing business, let me know. Maybe we could work out some partnership arrangement."

Vanessa smiled. Patrick was awkward at expressing himself, but she was sure he meant well. "That's the second offer of help I've received in twenty-four hours."

"Oh, who made the first?"

"Harold Glover, one of Brett's clients."

"That figures. He's a regular visitor and one of the wealthiest guys I know. He could bankroll both of us ten times over and still not notice it. If you get help from him, you'll be in business, big time."

"That explains the advice he gave me."

"I had in mind a more modest help. Helping to buy half a dozen dogs or so, for starters."

Vanessa made a fast appraisal of the situation. Instinctively, she didn't want financial ties to anyone. That would complicate any business relation.

"I don't see why we couldn't have a business arrangement. You can be my booking agent and provider of guides and equipment. Despite Harold's generous offer, I'd prefer not to borrow money. I'll use my savings to buy a new team."

"Great! I'll handle the bookings and your advertising. It goes hand in hand with my enterprise. We'll build your business between us. By the way…"

"Yes?"

"About Ingrid. I heard her complain. Ignore her. And ignore Lancaster too."

"I'll try my best. Are we going to formalize our business partnership?"

"Absolutely. It's in our best interest to have everything spelled out. I'll get on with a contract. I'm used to those with my many suppliers."

During the drive home, Vanessa mulled over the unpleasant encounter with Ingrid Lancaster. The woman and her sour disposition she could handle. What she was less sure of was her own emotions when it came to Brett. As for Patrick, he obviously had his reasons for telling her to forget him. But he was a married man and out of bounds, and definitely not her type.

Deep in her heart, she knew she could no more forget Brett Lancaster than prevent the snow from falling, as it was now, from the leaden sky.

Chapter Eight

Alden leaped out of the truck. "Great news, Vanessa! My dad said it was okay to dog sit while you're away overnight and any time that's needed."

"Did your mom agree too?"

"She did after I told her that the pups' mother has to be let outside in the morning and two or three times during the evening. She even said it'd be better for me to stay in your house too, so I could keep the fire going so the house wouldn't freeze."

"Excellent. Without your help, I'd have to come back tonight. I've written out the instructions for feeding the dogs."

"Thanks. I'm coming straight after school and I'll bring my homework. I'm more than ever determined to get ahead and finish school early."

"Smart of you. And don't forget to get up in time for school tomorrow. Talking of which, you'd better get a move on, or else you'll be late for your first class."

Alden climbed into his truck just as Marcel turned into the yard.

He got out of the cab and watched Alden drive away. "I've never seen that young fella look so pleased with himself. And he loves helping at the races."

"He's thrilled to be given full responsibility for Lulik and her new litter."

"He's a good kid."

"I don't have to be back tonight, now."

A knowing look came over his handsome face. "I didn't doubt he'd get permission. Okay, ma'am, are you ready to go? Let's hitch up the teams."

Between them, it took no time to prepare for their departure. Vanessa checked each item of equipment and each package of supplies against the list she had drawn up. She then she assured herself that Lulik had enough water to last until Alden's arrival. The pups were growing by the minute. Their eyes were now open. By spring, she'd be able to take them for short outings in the sled to get them used to the routine.

"Ready, Vanessa?"

She grabbed her GPS from the table. "Ready!"

"Oh no, you're not taking that."

Taken aback, she looked at him. "But…"

"You've got to learn the lay of the land and how to find your way without those gizmos, because when the battery freezes, you're on your own."

Vanessa looked at the offending object in her hand. "But it also saves lives when people are lost."

Marcel smiled indulgently. "I didn't say it didn't, just that you need to know how to find your way without. It's not entirely reliable. People have been known to drive onto dead-end roads, especially in the mountains where satellite reception can play tricks on technology."

It made a lot of sense. After all, people had tramped the wilds long before the GPS was invented. She tossed it on the table.

"Right. Let's go."

Marcel broke trail with his sled and she followed with the smaller sled. Once across the lake and into the reserve, trails were not marked, and from time to time, non-existent, but Marcel had no difficulty finding his way. To Vanessa, one part of the forest looked identical to another. With Walter, they had always followed designated, well-marked trails. Under Marcel's tutoring, she began to notice subtle differences in the terrain.

"The beauty of a pine forest is that the trees aren't usually tightly bunched together, so you can meander through them and make your own trail. Watch where they are taller. It means less undergrowth and easier going."

"I'm still not sure I'd find the same way back."

"You'd have your tracks."

"Suppose it snowed; how do I find my trail?"

"Learn to read the land between creeks and mountains. Take note of the shape of rocks, their location on the landscape and the odd twists of some tree trunks. File landmarks in your head."

"I know it's not enough, but I do pretty well orienting myself with the sun and my watch."

"I saw that. Congrats! Not everybody can do it. When there's no sun, a compass is an ancient, simple device which can be relied on." He grinned. "So that's permitted. I can't insist enough that a GPS is a great tool but never rely totally on technology while in the wilds. Don't forget about the short hours of daytime up here. You don't have sun all day."

"I won't. Actually, if I can't find my way, I'll rely on my dogs to get me home."

Marcel laughed heartily. "They will, of course. Okay, take the lead."

Vanessa hoped she wouldn't get them hopelessly lost. Their path lay over a frozen lake and back into the trees. At intervals, and without stopping the team, she checked her route with her compass. Traveling was anything but dull. They climbed past chaotic rocks, crossed a small lake, and followed a portage path. An overflowing joy accompanied her. Where larches interspaced the spruce, mule deer watched with cautious curiosity the passage of the sleds. Occasionally, a hare in white winter garb would dart out in front of the team. The dogs, eager for sport, would put on a spurt to catch it and Vanessa would have to call out to bring her team back into line. Not that the hare was in any danger. It ran faster than the eager dogs.

Two hours later, she ordered a halt to rest and water the dogs. The humans, too, welcomed the chance to warm up with hot chocolate and eat a bite.

"Am I still on track?"

"Couldn't have done better myself."

"I'm beginning to get an idea of the mountain country. It's so different from New Brunswick."

For a few minutes, the pair remained silent, content to enjoy the exhilaration of the outdoors.

"Did you hear that your neighbor Lancaster, is collecting signatures on a petition?"

"Brett? A petition? What for?"

"To force you to get rid of your dogs on account of the noise they make."

"You've got to be kidding. The lodge is two miles away. Who'd sign such a petition? We have all but two immediate neighbors."

"I don't rightly know, considering the number of mushers that live in the area. Actually, the thing is in his name, but it's that gal Ingrid who's organizing it. Have you met her?"

"I've had that displeasure." The news of the petition both surprised and shocked her. "Lancaster is pressing me to sell my land to him. I didn't think he'd stoop so low."

"You know him, then?"

"Yes, sort of. We've met."

"I see a dreamy look in your eyes. You keen on him?"

"Marcel! What do you think I am? The man is trying to run me out of business."

Marcel combed his fingers through his short beard.

"But you think about him."

"Not in the way you're implying."

"I'd prefer if you thought about me."

Vanessa burst out laughing. "I don't intend to think about him or you."

"Do you have a secret admirer?"

A haunted look came to her eyes. "Not since my husband passed away. I don't need one. My dogs keep me company. And I have my dream of establishing my business."

"Dreams are poor company at nights." His warm grin was inviting.

"Be serious, Marcel, or you'll be making the trip back on your own."

"Couldn't a guy try his luck?"

"Keep your distance." Her curt reply stated all that needed to be said about her feelings.

"Okay. I can take a hint." Marcel's hearty laugh dispelled the momentary tension. "How about hitting the trail again?"

"Fine by me. I'll take the lead again."

She gave the signal, and the dogs bounded forward. Her earlier high spirits dampened by what Marcel had just told her about Brett or, rather, Ingrid. The thought also crossed her mind perhaps it was not a good plan to venture into the wilderness alone with Marcel. Patrick had assured her she could trust him, but... Her confidence returned, but she promised herself to be extra careful in the future not to send out signals which could be interpreted as encouragement. Only one man had ever possessed her body and soul. His memory brought a dull ache to her heart. There would be no one else.

Daylight had vanished by mid-afternoon. They halted before the end of the day at a spot overlooking a lake fringed with spruce and denuded larch.

"That must be Oval Lake."

"That's right. I can see you've memorized the map well."

"It does have an oval shape." A smile floated on her lips. "I can just imagine pioneers or gold prospectors trying to name landmarks."

"That's probably why we have so many beaver names, Beaver Lake, Beaver Creek, Beaver Landing and the likes."

Although Vanessa was getting used to the low temperatures, erecting the tents and feeding the dogs drained most of her remaining energy.

"You were right. The cold slows down the job. Much colder than New Brunswick."

"What takes you one hour in temperate conditions takes two here. I'll light a fire to thaw snow for water."

"Thanks."

They got worked without undue haste and fed the dogs. While they were cooking their meal over the open fire, they heard the distant drone of a snowmobile.

Vanessa pulled a face. "Why can't we get away from those damned things?"

"That's odd. Snowmobiles are forbidden in the wildlife reserve."

"Perhaps they're on a designated trail."

"Not anywhere near here, they're not. Anyway, it sounds like only one machine. It's coming from the lake."

"Then maybe it's a park ranger."

"We'll find out. He's headed in this direction. Whoever it is seems to know where to find us."

Vanessa watched the flickering light of the snowmobile cross Oval Lake and start up the slope toward their camp. Even in the gathering darkness, there was something familiar about the helmeted figure hunched low out of the biting wind. Before the machine roared into the clearing, she knew who it was.

The intrusion incensed Marcel. "Lancaster! What the hell are you doing here?"

"Good evening!" His easy-going smile was disarming. "I saw your fire and figured you must have picked a cozy place to camp."

"Don't you know snowmobiles are off-limits in these parts?" Marcel's voice was an angry growl.

Brett ignored his objections. "Everything going okay, Vanessa?"

"Just fine, thank you. Only, I don't remember requesting a chaperone." Her tone was enough to freeze a whole lake.

Marcel tossed another log on the fire. "If you leave now, you'll make it past Rock Falls before it's pitch black."

"I wasn't planning on going back. In fact, I was about to ask Vanessa if it's okay to share your campfire."

"Like hell!" Marcel glanced from Brett to Vanessa and back to Brett.

Brett remained unperturbed. "What language, Marcel! Hardly in keeping with back country hospitality."

Vanessa frowned. "This is a dogsledding expedition. You and your damned snowmobile are not welcome."

"I which case, I'll pitch my tent at a respectable distance." The mock hurt in his tone was almost comical.

Marcel shrugged. "Now that you're here, camp wherever you want."

Vanessa made coffee. Out of the corner of her eye, she watched Brett pitch his tent alongside hers. She threw another spruce bough on the fire and added snow to the water, which was now boiling. Adding another spoonful of powdered coffee, she poured the water over it. Brett was setting up his tent, whistling a jolly tune. A somber Marcel took a cup. If she hadn't thought that maybe this was another tactic in Lancaster's ongoing battle for her land, she might have thought he was jealous of her being out with Marcel. His arrival was no coincidence. It amounted to harassment. That was it. He was determined to follow her, to annoy her until she'd give up and sell. He didn't know who he was butting heads with.

Marcel scowled at the intruder. "I hope you brought grub along for your supper."

"Marcel! What's happened to your usual friendliness?" Brett dropped an insulated bag at Vanessa's feet and gave her a knowing look. "A man should never come unprepared. You're more than welcome to share my supplies."

While Brett finished pitching his tent, Vanessa emptied the contents of the bag onto the snow. She then threw back her head and laughed. "What kind of meal had you in mind? Pâté de foie gras, smoked oysters and lobster tails! And a bottle of champagne?"

"It shows the superiority of the snowmobile for carrying provisions."

"Very nice. But they're frozen solid."

Brett had the good grace to look sheepish. "Damn! I must have forgotten to plug in the insulated bag. Oh, well..."

Vanessa made no attempt to curb her amusement. "If you keep them in your sleeping bag overnight, you can have a champagne and oyster breakfast." For a moment, she forgot her anger at his latest trick.

Marcel failed to keep the note of triumph out of his voice. "I guess you'd best share some of our humble stew reconstituted from dehydrated food."

"That's most generous of you." Brett sat down beside Vanessa.

"Were you following us?" The suspicion in her tone was close to an accusation.

"Me? No." He had all the conviction of a kid caught with his hand in the cookie jar. "I was scouting out a pleasant route for my guests."

"Don't give me that guff, Lancaster. There's a sign at the trailhead: Snowmobiles are prohibited in the reserve."

"I wasn't following the trail."

"Come on, you know what areas are off limits better than most of us."

"Okay. I'll 'fess up. I was crossing Donek lake below Rock Falls when I saw Vanessa and her team disappear into the forest. Later, I was on a circuit out of Rock Falls lake with some clients. I didn't see her tracks returning and didn't know she was following you, so I decided to make sure she wasn't lost or something. Sub-zero temperatures aren't for amateurs. She's not used to our temperatures or this region."

Vanessa and Marcel stared at him, neither believing a word he said.

"And now I don't even know whether it is wise to stay with Marcel. Women can't resist him."

He spoke with a light, teasing tone.

If he had been within reach, Vanessa knew she'd have slapped him. Marcel raised an eyebrow. "Do you want me to punch your pretty face?"

"It was a compliment." Brett gave an exaggerated sigh.

"There's no need to worry about my safety." To settle her mounting anger, she busied herself with the cooking. Mixing a thick sauce from cornstarch and a cube of bouillon was good therapy for the nerves.

Vanessa left the dishes for the men to clean up and went to spread her sleeping bag in her tent. She debated with herself whether to turn in right away or confront Brett over the petition. This was as good a time as any, because she wouldn't be able to sleep until she did so. She found him sitting across from Marcel by the fire. "Tell me why you allowed your employee to put out that petition concerning my dogs? Yet another one of your tacky moves to force me to sell?"

The stupefied look on the rugged planes of his face highlighted by the fire convinced her of the sincerity of his surprise. Her stomach clenched. He was so handsome in the firelight.

"Petition? What are you talking about?"

She stared back at him across the leaping flames. Did he genuinely not know? Then again, Brett had all qualities of an actor, good looks, mobile features and the ability to play dumb when it suited him. "Don't try to deny it. News travel fast around here and the rumor has reached me. For your info, I'm not selling, and you're not driving any trail across Tapiskoot."

Her words struck home like arrows, without pause. She held his dark eyes, which became even darker, if that was possible. Marcel's mouth twitched.

"I have twenty-four employees. Which one are you referring to?"

"An ill-informed and equally ill-mannered woman by the name of Ingrid Lancaster whom I had the misfortune to meet in the store."

Behind his cup, Marcel snickered.

A quickly repressed smile crossed Brett's lips. "Ingrid been bothering you?"

"*Bothering* would be an understatement. She reinforced your message that I should sell."

"If that's what Ingrid's up to, I wasn't aware of it," Brett said. "But I'll check into the matter."

"Do you really want me to believe you have nothing to do with this expulsion campaign?"

"Let's not exaggerate. Expulsion is not an appropriate word."

"Tell me why I have a hard time believing you." Her unusually severe tone captured his attention.

"You have to, that's all. I'm above such sneaky tactics. Trust a woman to stoop to that."

Anger quickly extinguished the small thrill that coursed through her as she watched the light dance on his features. "I'm a woman, too. I would never lower myself to that type of stratagem."

"What I meant was, I'm damned irritated if what you say about Ingrid is correct."

Marcel sat closer to her by the campfire. He followed the debate, ready to intervene if necessary. Vanessa noticed his clenched fists and hoped he'd contain his anger. She didn't want to become an umpire if they came to blows.

"I suggest you go back right now and talk to her to find out." Vanessa didn't give him time to reply. She strode to her tent. The hiss of the closing door zipper hung in the still air with a note of finality.

Her flashlight projected her shadow against the tent walls. She switched it off before undressing. Snuggled into the welcoming softness of her sleeping bag, and about to drift into sleep, she heard the lilting notes of a harmonica. A voice quietly sang the melody, catching her attention, but unable to determine who was singing. A few moments into the refrain, her point dog, Cousteau, surely the most romantic of the pack, joined in with a plaintive howl. Within a minute, a whole chorus of dogs was serenading the moon. Vanessa closed her eyes with a smile at the craziness of the whole affair of two men, long-time friends and temporarily hating each other, but not enough to prevent them playing and singing together, and her dogs adding their voices. Soon, she was fast asleep.

It was still dark when she awoke from a troubled dream of Brett playing with pups and kissing her. From outside the tent came the men's voices. She lifted the window flap and peered out. Brett and Marcel were hunched around the campfire. The dogs strained on their short lines, nose up in the air at the smell from the steaming pot where a piece of liver boiled in water. Vanessa prided herself on being a morning person, yet these men had beaten her to it. She stretched and pulled on her clothes. With a bit of luck, her companions would have prepared breakfast. Without haste and with an economy of movements learned during long treks in the wilderness, she distributed the broth to the team.

Ilak, a pretty black female with an all white belly, tugged at her chain, impatient to run. Vanessa scratched her behind the ears while murmuring to her. The dog sat alert and ears wiggling.

Marcel's voice rang out in the morning stillness. "Come and get breakfast!"

Vanessa had no desire to continue the previous evening's acrimonious discussion and was thankful that no one was in a talkative mood.

They ate in silence and packed up the camp. Brett stood, coffee mug in hand, with a look on his face that left her in no doubt how he felt. He obviously wanted to draw her attention to talk. She ignored it. He probably wished he could send Marcel off and take her in his arms. Her imagination was galloping out of control. Her dream came back to her. No, she didn't want him to kiss her. She lowered her gaze to avoid making eye contact with him. The night was over, so were the dreams. Brett cleared his throat. "I could break trail for you, if you'd like."

Vanessa and Marcel looked at him in surprise. A horrified scream burst out of their mouths. "Do what?"

For a second, Brett looked sheepish. "It's a peace offering. We use snowmobiles all the time to make a trail for dog races."

"We're not racing." Vanessa's tone was dry.

"I know, but you'll find it easier going on a flattened trail."

"My dogs have no problem making their way, no matter what the conditions. It's good for them."

"Okay, okay. It was only a friendly gesture. No need to bite my head off."

Brett shifted his gaze, reminding Vanessa of a scolded kid trying to make up for his misbehavior. A sudden desire to caress his cheek with its twenty-four-hour shadow washed through her. She imagined it to be soft and raspy at the same time. The end of her fingers tingled, running like a current through the rest of her. Marcel's voice brought her back to reality.

"You know very well you're not permitted on these trails with your snowmobile."

"Who's to know?"

Vanessa and Marcel exchanged glances. "Us."

Brett hastily changed the topic. "Are you staying out long?"

"That's strictly none of your business. But since it's always prudent to tell people about one's plans for backcountry travel, we're swinging round to the north from here, then heading back home. Don't bother waiting for us. We know the way." Her tone was chilly. She had guessed his intentions.

Brett grinned. "Oh, well..." His voice trailed off, and he began loading his snowmobile. He waved a gloved hand, climbed aboard his machine and sped off. The roar of the motor startled the dogs. He turned back toward the lake and disappeared.

"Shall we leave, Marcel?"

"Sure. It won't take long to load everything on the sleds."

Once she was standing on the runners, she quickly put the encounter with Brett behind her. Only the dogs' panting and the swish of the sled runners over the snow broke the silence.

By late afternoon, the party came to a halt in front of her cabin.

Lulik howled her delight from the end of the leash Alden was holding. At a sign from Vanessa, he untied the happy dog to let her greet her team mates by licking their muzzles, though she did growl at Kissimi, who wasn't among her favorites. Vanessa squashed that show of animosity with a stern voice. Lulik promptly ran over to welcome Marcel's team.

Alden raised an inquisitive eyebrow.

"Lulik and Kissimi are sisters, yet I notice they're always jealous of each other. If one of them is harnessed, the free one tries to boss her around."

"Good observation, Alden. They might even have a bit of a fight, but when they are hitched up to the sled, they'll work all day without trouble."

Once the dogs were cared for, Vanessa invited Marcel and Alden to stay for supper. They were about to enter the cabin when Patrick arrived on his snowmobile.

"Hi Patrick! Just in time. Are you staying for supper?"

"Not really. I just came to show you something. Do you have a minute?"

"Sure. Come inside. You can talk while I cook."

While Marcel and Vanessa prepared dinner, Alden played with the pups.

In the kitchen, Patrick took a notebook from his pocket. "Here, take a peek at the in-store bookings and the website bookings. I printed everything as well."

Vanessa gave a low whistle. "All those?"

"Don't be surprised. The winter season really gets under way about now."

"It looks like I have one tour booked every day until the New Year."

"I have a note on the website to book early." Patrick pointed to a couple of lines. "There are even three short ones a day during Christmas week's holiday from locals."

"You said my business would take off, and you weren't kidding. How I'm going to manage that number of outings?"

"How many dogs do you need to take one person?"

"Four is enough with survival equipment."

"But only three if the clients wants to learn to drive the team, right?"

"That's right."

"How do you plan your organization?" Marcel asked.

"Short ride, about two hours, half a day with pause for refreshments, and a whole day with picnic. If all goes well and I have staff, two-day trips with an overnight camp."

"Excellent. In the meantime, you need another ten dogs. Down the road, you might also offer camping trips with several days of exploration."

"I'm here to help!" Alden said in an eager voice.

"Don't worry, you'll be the first one, I'll ask."

"How about the dogs you were planning to acquire?" Patrick asked.

"I better phone and confirm right away."

They spent an hour making plans, and Vanessa had the impression she was being swept up in a maelstrom of madness.

"And there is a message from Skyabove, the internet provider for the area. You are connected now, but with the warning that it can be spotty if there are too many clients on it at the same time."

"At least, it's a start."

"I'll keep taking bookings for you since I'm your agent and bring the printed copies to you. That way, you won't lose any business."

CHAPTER NINE

Next day, Vanessa was humming while she fed her dogs. Patrick's voice startled her from behind.

"I brought you the cartons of meat you ordered. They just arrived at the store."

She brushed the hair from her face. "I didn't know the price included delivery."

"You've got plenty to do. Tomorrow, there's a woman coming for an excursion."

"I didn't know there was anyone booked. Who's she?"

"She phoned this morning. A Mrs. McCourt. In her sixties. She told me she'd always wanted to travel by dogsled. It's her birthday and a gift from her husband. He's bringing her, but he refuses to get into a sled."

"That's no problem. He can sit in the cabin and stay warm."

Patrick unloaded the truck and placed the cases in the storage shed. The low temperatures would ensure the food would remain frozen until needed.

"Do you fancy coffee?"

"Love to. I've got to check on those pups of yours."

Lulik came to sniff Patrick's leg. Satisfied, she moved aside to let him pass. While Vanessa made the coffee, he took delight in examining the pups.

They drank in silence. Unexpectedly, he put down his cup and looked at her.

"Forgive me for saying so, but I can't get you out of my mind."

Vanessa froze. Her lips clamped tightly together. How was she supposed to respond to such an admission... from a married family man? "Patrick, I'd prefer you didn't say things like that. Otherwise, I'll have to ask you not to come here again."

"I know. It's wrong of me. Don't worry. You've got nothing to fear. I have a wife and have no intention of being unfaithful to, even though..." His voice trailed off. His face took on a pensive look.

"We're business associates. That's all, Patrick."

She didn't have to elaborate. A truck was pulling into the yard and running steps announced Alden's arrival.

The teenager stuck his head through the door. "Hi everyone!" He entered the cabin, bringing with him a gust of frigid air.

Lulik greeted him like a long-lost friend. Vanessa was grateful for the distraction. It seemed she was incapable of forming a simple friendship with any of the Donek males, with the exception of young Alden.

Alden's presence helped relax the atmosphere, and she and Patrick resumed their business discussion.

***

The McCourts arrived for the tour. Mrs. McCourt was a tall, slender woman with silver hair. Her lively eyes sparkled with good-humor behind gold-rimmed lenses. Her husband gave the impression of a man who was happiest reading a book in front of a roaring fire. His wife was making the sled outing alone didn't surprise Vanessa.

"As you can see, I'm well prepared for the ride," Mrs. McCourt said. "I bought myself this parka at the Pathfinder Outfitter store in town. The fur is fake, naturally. I'm against killing poor creatures for their coats. Do you think these boots will keep my feet warm?"

Vanessa examined the footwear and gave her approval. "I've put a comforter in the sled for you to sit on it. If you get cold, wrap yourself in it."

"I see there's also a cushion in the sled to rest my old bones on."

"We always place a thick one in the sled, Mrs. McCourt. The trails can be quite bumpy sometimes."

"Please call me Marjy. The snow looks so smooth, I imagined it would be like riding on air."

"Unfortunately, the ground underneath is far from level. The snow faithfully follows the contours of pine needles, roots, stones and all sorts of other irregularities on the trail. It blurs them to our eyes."

Marjy sighed. "Ah, nature is so wonderful." She turned to her husband. "George, aren't you tempted to join us?"

"Thanks, no. I think I'll accept Ms. Riley's offer and toast my feet in front of the wood stove. Have a good time, dear." To Vanessa he asked. "How long will you be gone?"

"We'll be back in about three hours, as long as Marjy isn't cold."

Marjy McCourt insisted on helping hitch the dogs. Under Vanessa's direction, she managed well enough and was as delighted as a five-year-old girl opening presents at her birthday party.

Now that the dogs had got back into the routine, Vanessa planned to give a thrill to her client by using the direct, but steeper, path down to the lake. The energetic team bounded forward with enthusiasm.

With one foot poised on the brake, ready to lean her weight onto it, she enjoyed Marjy's shrieks of delight.

"Fantastic! I'm young and living again."

In the lead, Vercors and Cousteau instinctively swung toward the forest trail. Inuit sled dogs only needed to run over a trail once. They never forget it.

After a half hour of travel, Marjy twisted herself to ask a question. "Is it difficult to drive a team?"

"Not too much. Did you want to try?"

"I do."

"Whoa!" Vanessa applied the brake lightly.

Once the sled came to a stop, she buried the anchor in the snow. Her lead dogs were looking at her, ready to go. They hesitated to sit when she gave them the command, but did obey, reluctantly followed by the rest of the team. With surprising agility, Marjy jumped from her seat and stood on the runners.

"Keep your knees bent and supple."

"And I say *Ghee* to turn right and *Haw* to turn left, correct?"

"Yes, and you have to anticipate the turn. To slow down depress the brake, yes, this bar in front of your feet. You depress it gradually."

"It seems simple enough."

"It is, but I insist on the gradual pressing of the brake. Otherwise you'd bring the sled to an abrupt stop and go flying head first over the handlebar."

Vanessa gave further instructions to Marjy about looking ahead of the lead dogs before finally seating herself in the sled. The dogs didn't wait for the command to go, but she didn't correct them. A little way farther on, the lead dogs slowed down and turned their heads as one to look at their new musher. Vanessa clicked her tongue, and the team resumed their cruising speed. From some way behind, she heard the unmistakable drone of a snowmobile. That was what her dogs had detected and wanted her instructions for. She sighed. *Not again!*

"Start slowing down, Marjy. And tell the dogs *whoa*!"

At the command, the dogs slowed and came to a halt. Vanessa had already jumped out, leading the team off the trail. Her client pushed the anchor down and stood on the brake. Already snowmobiles roared past, one after the other. The unsettled dogs threw themselves farther into the woods, knocking Vanessa off her feet in the process. She shook her fist at the uncouth drivers, long gone now, while Marjy let fly a string of expletives that would have made a hardened gold miner blush.

They resumed their journey, sharing the runners. Vanessa was looking for an opening into the woods. "Let's turn into uncharted territory. This trail's far too busy."

"That sounds thrilling!" Marjy said.

On their return, Vanessa pushed open the door of the cabin to find Mr. McCourt speaking on the phone. He thanked the person on the other end of the line and hung up.

"You'll be happy to hear, Ms. Riley, that I've been acting as your loyal personal assistant. That was a gentleman in Iglulik, which I have just discovered is way up in the Arctic. They want to sell you a team of sled dogs."

"Really! A full team?"

"The man is called Pauloosie." He picked up a notepad. "Here, I wrote it all down, just as the fellow spelled it to me. Apparently, he's retiring and doesn't have kids to take over his dogs. He didn't say how he knew you were after dogs, but he's willing to sell you his for a reasonable price."

"That's incredible! I met him a few years ago and wrote to him the other day asking him to sell me a few dogs."

"He's selling the whole team or nothing. I talked him into including all the harness and lines and he accepted."

Vanessa laughed. "Mr. McCourt, you really are a first rate assistant."

"That's what comes from being in commerce for over forty years."

"Let me bake the muffins I prepared this morning, and you and your wife can sample them before you leave."

Bubbling with happiness, Marjy recounted the ride. After much laughter, Mr. McCourt declared that his wife could come and sled anytime but drew the line at keeping sled dogs back home.

The McCourts had just left when Brett's truck pulled into the yard. He nimbly jumped out, his sport outfit impeccable. He held a thick envelope in his hand.

Vanessa had no time to change and still wore an attractive burgundy padded outfit which did nothing to hide her form.

"Good evening, Vanessa."

His eyes raked her figure with undisguised pleasure. Lulik rubbed herself against his leg. He petted her and smiled. "Her pups are simply adorable."

"I agree. So, what brings you here?"

He sighed and tossed the packet on the table. "The postmaster must have been asleep on the job. He stuck this in my mailbox by mistake. It's addressed to you."

"Couldn't you have simply handed it back to him over the counter?"

He shrugged. "I noticed it's from Harold Glover. What's that old fox up to?"

Vanessa drew a sharp breath, shocked that Brett was bold enough to comment on who she received mail from.

"Mr. Glover is certainly *not* old, as you so crudely put it. I've no doubt he is as clever as a fox. What he's sending me is none of your business."

"Open it then."

She ought to have been annoyed at his brashness, but his easy-going manner charmed her into smiling when she ought to have been angry. "I will, in my own time."

"What's that delicious smell?"

"Butter tarts."

"Mmm, my favorites! And you've made coffee too?"

Despite herself, Vanessa laughed at the way he simply invited himself. This man, whose mere presence made the room shrink, disconcerted her like no other.

Without a word, she placed the plate of golden butter tarts and the coffee pot on the table. While Brett went into ecstasy about her talents as a cook, she threw a brief glance over the materials that Harold, faithful to his promise, had sent her.

Brett glanced up at her. "So?"

"If you must know, Harold has been helping me put Tapiskoot Tours on a better footing."

"Has he, now?"

"This is the business plan he has prepared for me." She tapped a thick, spiral bound document. "He's helping me expand."

"Expand?"

"I learned just a short while ago that my new team will be arriving next week."

"I was hoping you'd tell me you had agreed to sell."

"You must be dreaming."

"Seriously, if you're aiming to expand your business, you'll need a larger place."

"I reckon my eighteen-hundred acres are adequate to accommodate the necessary dog pens and trails I'll need."

"Your cabin is too small."

"None of my guests have complained so far. If any of them want to remain for an extended stay, I'll send them down to your lodge."

"You know, when you get angry, you're even prettier."

"As if I cared about that." That was not entirely true. His words had sent a pleasurable shiver down her back.

"How about coming out for that ride tomorrow? You've been procrastinating long enough."

"I don't know if I can spare the time."

"Chalk it up to research and development. I'll show you trails you never knew existed. And a whole chunk of new territory to explore with your dogs. More than you could hope to cover on your own in a month. How about it?"

"There's magic in discovering the beauty of nature slowly."

She sat with barely a foot or two separating her from him. His nearness made her feel utterly feminine, warm and yielding. With an effort, she snapped out of her trance. "All right, I'll come. But remember, it's strictly a business outing."

Brett scraped back his chair. "You have my word on it." He snatched up his coat. "I'll pick you up at eight. Wear something pretty."

"You weren't listening to a single word I said, were you?"

"Women always tell me that. But I sure did this time. I distinctly heard you accept my invitation. That's excellent."

"You're impossible. You know that?" Vanessa found she couldn't stay angry with him for long. His penetrating eyes electrified every nerve ending in her body. They laughed like a couple of co-conspirators. "Make it closer to nine. I have to care for my dogs first."

"Nine o'clock it will be. I'll bring food and everything else we'll need. But you can bring some of those butter tarts. They're a gourmet's delight."

With a sigh, Brett picked up his coat. His eyes met hers. A moment of hesitation, and he let his coat drop to the floor to envelop her in his arms. His hand slid through her hair. In a daze, she followed his lips until they touched hers. The contact burned her. A strange sensation as though floating in outer space invaded her. She let herself go against his muscular body while a kaleidoscope of colors exploded under her closed eyelids.

When he relinquished his hold, the room seemed strangely empty as she struggled to control her emotions and push him away from her. Her muscles limp and ragged. Such unbridled passion left her breathless. She surprised herself by how much had welled up in her. No man had ever touched to her senses like this man, not even Walter.

Then again, never before had she met anyone quite like Brett Lancaster. No man had been permitted to kiss her, either.

A hoarse whisper was all she could manage. "Until tomorrow, then."

"I'll have a hard time getting to sleep on account of you."

For one insane moment, Vanessa was tempted to reach out and beg him to stay. Instead, she murmured, "Go, now. Goodnight."

Brett stood his ground. His eyes never left her face. Vanessa was overcome with a pang of regret. Then she thought of Ingrid waiting for him back at the lodge. Men! Married or not, they only had one idea in mind. But Brett was different. He had only one goal, and that was to acquire her land. And that was something she had almost forgotten as she felt herself succumbing to his charm.

Why, oh, why did her beloved husband have to die? She didn't want to feel anything for someone else. Vanessa straightened and took a step backward.

He reached for her again. "I'm not in the mood to leave."

"In which case, I'm not in the mood for trail riding tomorrow."

"A goodnight kiss, then?"

"Go!"

He again took her in his arms and kissed her.

"What about Ingrid?"

"Who wants to talk about her?"

"Call for me at nine. Now, goodnight."

Brett turned away and left. Emptiness suddenly invaded the cabin.

Vanessa folded her arms, scarcely able to believe what she had just done. This was all part of his scheme to break down her resistance! She had to remember that. It was her land he was interested in, not her. Of course, he might enjoy the physical conquest, but she couldn't imagine he had any intention of loving her. Sex, yes, love no. And she mustn't ever let her guard down again.

Chapter Ten

I ngrid threw a final glance over the dining-room. She nodded at
Karl. The trainee, always looking over his shoulder, was far too curious, in her opinion. The email she had to hide from him had thrown
her into a vortex of anguish. Stress marred her smooth features. She
was going to take a few minutes' rest and recompose herself. She
switched off the main lights in the dining-room leaving the ambient
light. The guests were all in the lounge or at the bar.

Her peace was shattered the next second, as Dan slipped in through
the side door. He exuded violence. Without a word, he grabbed her
arm and pushed her into her office.

She threw a panicked glance at the stupefied Karl. "Let me go. The
trainee is watching."

"I don't give a damn."

Although she felt like slamming the door, she curbed her irritation
and closed it quietly.

"Right, don't wake everybody up."

"He's going to come to find out what's going on."

"Rob can take care of him."

"So, you come with your gorillas now?"

"One never knows what to expect. Get rid of that woman and her
dogs."

"You don't know who we're dealing with."

"It's an order. Invite her for coffee and slip a pinch of heaven in it."

"I'm not going to be associated with murder."

"You want to take her place?"

"Idiot! Who will pass the goods?"

"I'll find someone else."

Scared beyond words, Ingrid's eyes fixed on him. Thoughts tumbled in her head, one dominating all others. *He's capable of doing just that.* "You'll be caught. I wrote everything down."

"Bitch! It's your responsibility. Get rid of the woman."

"I can't go on the lake. The cops are sniffing around, too close for comfort."

"Manage it whatever way you want, but bring that delivery. Okay?"

"How do you think I can do that with nobody noticing?"

"You do that pronto and then make the trip across the border, as usual. The boss is getting antsy. An' I don't want to lose the business."

"I can't leave in the middle of our busiest time without arising suspicions. Besides, I think we've got a narc staying at the lodge."

"How would you know?"

"Carrying firearms is forbidden in Canada. You know that, and if you didn't, you do now. This one carries, and it looks perfectly legal."

"Get into his room. Find out."

Ingrid's fear ratcheted up a notch. "The housekeeping staff didn't report anything."

"Can't trust them."

"I can trust Toni. She isn't too bright and does everything I tell her."

"Find a good reason for a trip. Say your mother's ill."

"My parents live in Arizona. Leave them out of your schemes."

"Do I have to spell everything out for you?"

Lips bitten raw, Ingrid clenched her teeth. *Won't this ever end?* "I can't leave like that, They'll get me. And if I am, I'll spill the beans."

"Then, you won't live to enjoy your retirement."

She wanted to slap him, claw his eyes out, cut him into small pieces and throw him to the wolves. A deep breath helped calm her nerves. "I've got some ideas to get the neighbor out before the next shipment. That's a lot more sensible than your stupid schemes."

"You've got one last chance." On those menacing words, Dan left the room before Ingrid could do more than stare at his retreating figure.

Scared that he'd bump into Brett returning, she hurried after him, but the snake had already disappeared.

An insidious fear crept into her heart. She hoped Karl wouldn't ask questions. There was no way she could ignore Dan. And death wasn't appealing. She hurried to her room to get dressed for the outdoors and succeeded in getting to the snowmobile garage without being seen. Depression had set in. How could she get out of this mess? She had to protect her parents. They were no longer young, and she had already given them plenty of grief in the past. They believed she now had a stable situation working for her step-brother. To learn that she had caused one man's death and was involved in drug trafficking and God knows what else would kill them.

There was no time to go around the lake and through town. Sergeant Ron Larsen of the RCMP detachment had come several times to speak to Brett. She didn't like the idea of a chance meeting with one of the Royal Canadian Mounted Police officers, either on the lake or in town. There used to be three of them in the detachment, but now three more had been added. Not that she had given them any reason to suspect her. At least she hoped so.

Ingrid debated whether she could take a chance to cut through the Riley woman's property toward the park limit. Surely, the woman's land was big enough that she couldn't have yet explored close to the wildlife reserve. It was worth the gamble. She took the trail leading behind the lodge. When it veered in a different direction, she continued by cutting through the pines. Resentment roiled in her. Driving through the dense forest at night wasn't her idea of fun, not when she was in a hurry. When she estimated she had gone far enough, she turned north and found herself on a trail which appeared to go toward her destination. She swore out loud. In the center of the trail were tracks of sled runners and paw prints. So she was on Riley's property. Too late, she couldn't go back. The trail had to go all the way to Brett's land. It didn't. Enveloped by fear, she bit her already bitten lip and tasted blood. In desperation, she headed straight on. So the Riley woman would see a snowmobile had crossed her precious land, so what? Her machine whined all the way to the top of the ridge and finally she saw a post marking the boundary of the two properties. Now back on Brett's land, she relaxed a little and gunned the engine. Farther along she came across snowmobiles tracks. The shack wasn't far now. She turned east, then later, south. The trail became familiar. She was relieved to see a property marker. Minutes later, she was back on her nemesis' land. Finally, the trail led to the shack. Inside were two packets in the usual hiding place. With trembling hands, she pushed them into the small baggage compartment. It barely closed.

She began retracing her steps. Her fear became so intense, she briefly lost control of the machine. There was no way she'd go back on the Riley woman's trail. She could be out there with her dogs. There was nothing to do but get to the lake and cross it.

Back at the lodge, she hid the packets in the toolshed.

Chapter Eleven

V anessa's headlamp swept the ground in front of her. Brett was already parked in her yard.

"You're early. I've not finished with my dogs."

"Then I'll give you a hand."

After the initial surprise of finding him on her doorstep sooner than expected, Vanessa rebelled. Did he honestly expect her to fall into his arms simply because he offered help with the dogs? *You're dealing with the enemy,* she reminded herself. *This is one small step in his plan to get your land. Nothing more.* Yet the remembrance of their shared kiss still lingered on her lips. The hungry look in his dark eyes threatened to melt her resolve.

"You can give me a hand so long as you don't mind risking dirtying that fancy snowmobile suit outfit you have on. Here is a spare pooper-scooper." Her tone was just a little mocking.

The suit in question was a one-piece outfit in an expensive high-tech black and silver material, a garment Brett had clearly not picked off the rack at the local store, and that she recognized from her first encounter with him.

He shrugged. "Here, give me that pail."

As it turned out, Brett's presence proved more of a hindrance than a help. Vanessa took more time to complete her chores than if she'd been alone. She had to explain everything. Granted, he appeared to take a genuine interest in her kennel setup. One strike in his favor was that Lulik adored him and was never happier than when he fussed over her pups.

Once the chores were finished, Vanessa went into the cabin to change. Brett followed her in. "I brought you a snowmobile suit. It matches mine."

"You didn't need to. I have my parka."

"Parkas are useless on snowmobiles. With the air rushing by, you need something windproof."

"It's windproof."

"Not in the way this specially designed garment is."

Brett helped her into the suit, which, much to her surprise, fitted her perfectly. Briefly, she wondered if it was Ingrid's, but dismissed the idea. The mistress of the lodge was a whole head taller.

"This is brand new. How did you know my size?"

"We stock spare equipment for guests. As for the size, let's just say I'm a good judge of women."

The desire to slam him down for this arrogant, sexist comment overwhelmed her. For the sake of peace, she spoke with restraint. "Experience, no doubt."

Keenly aware of his closeness, Vanessa couldn't help the quiver of her senses. The subtlety of his cologne tickled her nose. It, like everything else about Brett, spoke of money and refinement. It was regretful that she should be locked in conflict with him over a piece of real estate. Otherwise... She checked herself from speculating on what might have been. Assailed by guilt she feared she was sullying Walter's memory.

Brett didn't seem to notice her withdrawal. "Having extra clothing on hand is something you need to consider if you're serious about your business. Tourists never come properly equipped for the outdoors."

"I'll see what I can do about it."

He ran his fingers through her hair on the pretext of lifting it over her collar. "Okay. We're about ready to roll. Put the helmet on."

Tearing herself away from his mesmerizing attraction, she stepped outside into air that crackled with cold. Her breath hung as steam about her face.

It was Vanessa's first experience on the machine she despised, and so it was with trepidation that she climbed onto the passenger seat, taking great care to appear nonchalant. Brett mounted in front and told her to grip his waist. Unaccustomed to such speed, she tightened her hold until a feeling of intoxication engulfed her, brought on by the closeness of the man, the speed or both.

As they tore down the trail, Vanessa tried to take stock of where they were going despite the lingering darkness. An almost impossible task. The machine took seconds to traverse distances her dog team took hours to cover. Soon she was hopelessly disoriented and contented herself by being lulled by the rush of the wind, the blur of trees and the solid support of Brett's broad back.

After an hour or more of hurtling through the snowy landscape, Vanessa frankly began to grow bored. Compared to traveling by dogsled, the snowmobile offered none of the joy of being drawn along by living, breathing animals, each one an individual in its own right. All attentive to her voice and always ready to bolt after a snowshoe hare or a mule deer should they cross their path. On the machine, there was no time for the quiet contemplation of the glories of nature. And although she was physically close to a wonderfully sexy man, there wasn't even a sense of companionship, so focused was he on his driving. From the runners of a dogsled, a musher could always talk to a companion musher or to the dogs.

A bump caught her by surprise and she rocked and almost lost her balance. She tightened her grip on the driver.

Sometime after midday, Brett swung the machine off the trail and pulled up in front of a log building.

Vanessa climbed stiffly down from her seat. The cold had penetrated the insulated suit and bit into the marrow of her bones. Yet she forgot the discomfort when she looked around and saw they were on a wooded ridge, with a breathless view of a lake below.

"This is where we eat lunch. There are a few of these backcountry lodges in the area. You'll need to be familiar with them. You could stop there with your guests."

"That's indeed a good idea. I'll keep it in mind for future excursions."

Vanessa shielded her eyes from the glare of sun on snow. Her keen eyes spotted a raccoon perched on the lower branch of a tall pine. The masked bandit stared at her, his hand-like paws almost at the bird feeder he intended to rob.

Brett saw the smile on Vanessa's lips.

"So you enjoyed the ride?"

"I was watching the raccoon."

"A raccoon? Where?"

Speed, that's all he was interested in. "He's waiting until we go to commit his crime."

Brett looked at the feeder, then up at the animal.

"Ah!"

Vanessa hadn't answered his question, and he hadn't even noticed. The man had no sense of humor. He stood still while she waited for the agile critter, whose eyes sparkled in the middle of his black furry mask, to make his move. Swift and light, the raccoon jumped on the feeder, lifted the lid and extracted a large piece of fat studded with seeds, before retreating to his perch in the tree.

The lodge dining room, with its natural log walls and beamed ceiling, was an attractive setting for the wholesome food that was served. Brett showed no desire to linger over the meal. Vanessa had scarcely warmed up when he gave the signal to depart. Resigned, she shrugged into the suit and took her place onto the passenger seat.

"Would you care to drive?"

She shook her head. "No, I'm too scared."

"It's easy. It drives itself."

Reluctantly, she listened to the instructions. "It's not the sort of challenge I like to take up."

Brett sat behind her and circled her waist. For a second, Vanessa closed her eyes. *How can I drive when his arms make me forget everything?*

She drove slowly and carefully for a few minutes that felt like two hours, then stopped.

"It was great, but my shoulders are beginning to ache." That was a lie. Handling a loaded sled on difficult terrain had given her a strong upper body, but she had enough and wanted to go home as fast as possible.

"I'll massage your sore muscles, if you like."

"No, thank you."

They switched places. An hour later, Brett stopped by a frozen waterfall. Vanessa considered it an appropriate setting for her feelings. The blood in her veins was as solid as the water hanging over the cliff.

She managed to speak. "Right now I could do with a cup of hot chocolate."

"And this is the break I've been waiting for to break out those tempting butter tarts." He flashed her a bright smile. "And this time I didn't forget to plug in the insulated bag."

A smile formed on her frozen lips.

Although only mid-afternoon, it was already dark when they returned to the cabin. Alden greeted them, eager to help.

Brett switched on his helmet headlamp. "I imagine you have to take care of your dogs."

"That's right."

"I'll stay and give you a hand."

Too surprised and too numb with cold to speak, Vanessa simply nodded. She imagined he'd want to head back to his lodge, to Ingrid. What was their relationship if they weren't blood relatives? She wondered. With Alden there to help, the three of them soon finished the dog chores. Alden waved goodbye. When she finally stumbled indoors, she set about boiling water for coffee and saw Brett sprawled on the floor next to the pups. The mother came and licked his face, while the eager young dogs crawled all over him.

"Want to stay for supper?" She didn't know what demon pushed her to invite him. The words tumbled out of her mouth before she could think. Anyhow, it was a way to thank him for the ride.

A flicker of regret crossed her face. He'd only exploit the intimacy to soften her up to make her accept his crazy land deal. Despite his underhand maneuvers, she couldn't deny his appeal as a man.

"I'd love to. Tell me what can I do to help." Brett's eyes were brimming with undisguised pleasure.

"Set the table, please."

Vanessa placed the hastily prepared meal on the table. They ate in companionable silence, their hunger whetted by the frigid journey they'd made together through woods and over lakes.

"Do you have any idea how much country you covered today?"

Vanessa hesitated while she refilled their cups. Was he trying to impress her with the speed and power of his beloved machines? "Judging from the way I ended up a solid block of ice from the neck down, I reckon it was lots."

Deflated, he swallowed hard. "Yes it was. Four hundred miles."

"All that in seven hours."

"Well, it was more than your dogs could cover in a week."

"Am I supposed to be impressed?"

Brett took a gulp from his cup and scalded his mouth. Vanessa almost felt sorry for him, seeing the hurt on his face. To mollify him, she fetched the map and unrolled it on the table. "Perhaps you could show me exactly where we've been."

He produced a pencil and traced a winding line on the map. "Too bad you can't do that with your dogs."

"Not in one day, but I'd love to explore the area further. I can see camping and staying at the lodge. It would be interesting for tourists. We didn't meet another snowmobile all the time we were out, and the trails looked little used. I found that appealing." There, she had said something nice about the trip.

"As a matter of fact, I didn't take you over the official trails. We cut across country most of the time."

"I had that impression." Although she was interested in returning later with her dogs, she had some doubts she could find the route again. All the landmarks had vanished in a blur of speed. Leaning over the map brought her dangerously close to him. She couldn't avoid the contact. As if touch by lightning, her nerve endings tingled. He must have had similar emotions, for when he again spoke, his voice caught in his throat.

"How many days' travel by dogsled do you estimate that to be?"

"I reckon six to eight days. That would give me plenty of opportunity to admire the scenery."

The barb in her last sentence was lost in space. He turned his head to look at her, his face inches from hers, his eyes on her rosy lips. Slowly, he placed his arm around her waist.

Vanessa shivered under his touch. Her heart pounded against her ribs as she struggled to find words to stop him. Her mind, dazed by sensations, no longer cooperated. As soon as his lips touched hers, she lost the will to resist.

She could no more push him away than hold back the falling snow. Two large paws placed against each of their shoulders abruptly broke the intimacy. Lulik, ever curious, wanted to know what the humans were up to. She stood tall on hind legs, her damp muzzle wedged itself between their two bodies.

Brett scowled at the intruder. Vanessa, her head still swimming with exquisite sensations, chuckled. "My dog's jealous."

"She'd better get used to it, because I have every intention of taking up where we left off."

"It's perhaps better if we didn't."

"We have plenty of time."

"The day was enjoyable. Let's not spoil it." She wasn't meaning the speedy journey.

She struggled to master her senses and lay a finger on his lips to stay the words of protest. Playfully, he tried to nibble her hand, but she snatched it away.

Without another word, he left. Vanessa rested her head against the door jamb, letting the invading cold steady the turbulent emotions still raging within, sending her into a drunken stupor. She watched him cross the yard to his snowmobile. Although she'd never lacked male admirers, none had ever troubled her the way Brett did. But she needed all her strength to resist his advances. They were only made to soften her, to persuade her to let him through her land or sell it to him.

It left her ashamed that when he was around, she forgot Walter.

Stern warning tumbled from her lips. "Watch out! It's all part of his grand plan. Don't start getting soft over him. His goal is to get you to sell, or at the very least, let him cut through your land." In the night air, her voice rang out with crystalline clarity. A couple of her dogs raised their heads, in the hope they were going out.

Finally, cool enough, Vanessa rebuked herself for her idle chatter. Back inside, she returned to the table for one last look at the map.

Chapter Twelve

B rett sped over trails of iridescent silver toward the lodge. Moonlight glittered on the frost-encrusted pine needles and bounced off the snow to make long, mysterious shadows. The imprint of Vanessa's slim and toned body, that had made his blood sing, stayed with him. He almost turned round, but the wait would be deliciously tantalizing. No doubt he'd find a pretext tomorrow to go and see her again.

He parked his snowmobile and, with a spring in his step, walked to the front door of the lodge.

A blast of warm air hit his face. Raucous laughter flowed from the main room. Brett shook his head. He'd never fully come to terms with that, the commercial aspect of the lodge operation. Finding strangers occupying what was his home always grated on his nerves. It was sometimes difficult to smile to order. And he considered it a daily chore to attend to the thousand details that required his attention. The only reason he was willing to put up with it was that it earned him the right to escape, as he had done today, into the wilds of the north country.

***

Ingrid recognized the frustrated look on Brett's face. So, little Miss Riley didn't sleep with him. A plan formed in her head. If she could get him into her own bed, he'd forget Vanessa, and she could find some way to make her leave. Memories of her teenage years came back to her. There was one point when she believed he may even have shed the brotherly attitude. He hadn't, though, choosing to go off snowmobile racing and being the expert driver for some brand's promotional videos. Of course, he was still mad at her for leaving without a word and upsetting their parents, but she'd been able to worm her way back into his life. After all, he had hired her, hadn't he? That meant she must mean something to him. Sleeping with him wouldn't be a hardship.

"Well, well, where have you blown in from?" Ingrid's voice carried a hint of intimacy.

"I told you I'd planned to go and scout out a few fresh trails. Our guests are always asking for new areas to explore."

"Yes, I know. What you didn't tell me was you intended on doing your exploring with our new neighbor... the one with the dogs. Did she carry you in her dogsled, or was it a cozy twosome on your machine?" Ingrid lambasted herself. She had meant to attract him and there she was just being a jealous harpy.

He shut the lobby door behind him. "Since when do I have to report to you? If you really want to know, I invited her along so that she could get an idea of the country."

"Aren't we trying to persuade her to leave?"

"You're so right. In the meantime, it's better if she knows her way around. If she takes clients out and has an accident, it reflects badly on the whole of Donek's tourist industry."

That silenced Ingrid. She realized that playing the jealous woman wouldn't work on Brett. She could see that he was repressing anger.

She had to play it carefully. Her life was at stake. A small smile stretched his lips. Maybe she had a chance.

"Looking after the interests of the tourist industry? What a load of nonsense! If it's sex you're after, you don't have to go that far. Besides, she's not your type, darling. Too scrawny. Concentrate on running her off the property. What you need is a real woman. Someone who knows you, knows what you want." She stepped toward him, her eyes laden with thinly veiled lust.

Brett deftly moved aside. "I'm dealing with the question of the land. Trust me."

Ingrid gasped in despair. That was the wrong thing for her to have said, but she hadn't been able to control her words. Obviously, he didn't want to hurt her feelings. She was too good a manager for him to lose her. However, she didn't miss the impatience in his voice. She'd have to try another tack.

"Oh, I get it! I'm sorry I misjudged you. The mutts'owner didn't want to sell, so now you're obliged to seduce her. Poor you! Making love to her would be like climbing into bed with an ironing board." Why on earth was she so baleful? It wasn't going to help her.

Stunned, Brett held his tongue. In school, Ingrid had been pretty, but none too smart, and she'd been the object of countless practical jokes. But he didn't recall her being catty. Not that they had had many school years together since he was six years older. He sighed and closed his eyes. His mind vividly replaying the day, brought back the image of Vanessa's svelte figure. His blood still tingled in his veins. Lowering his eyelids, he saw her open-necked wool shirt molding the intriguing outline of her firm body. Hers was the toned body of an athlete. And it tempted the devil within him. A guest called Ingrid away. Brett watched her sashay into the dining room, her hips undulating provocatively. A bad taste flowed in his mouth.

He went upstairs to change before going in to greet the lodge guests. His hands still prickled with the feel of Vanessa's graceful body and the remembered weight of her shiny hair. Scrawny? Like an ironing board? What rubbish! Vanessa was an uncomplicated beauty that Ingrid was incapable of seeing. And unlike her, Vanessa possessed a deep love for the outdoors. Ingrid became hysterical if the wind threatened to derange her hair, or the blowing snow spoil her too perfect makeup. Poor Ingrid, blinded by bitterness and envy, deserved his pity, not his scorn.

He paused before going downstairs to chat with his guests. Did he really want to talk yet again about his racing exploits or his former expeditions along the Labrador coast? Or his three wins in a row of the Grand Prix Ski-Doo de Valcourt? Snowmobile enthusiasts couldn't stop talking about this one and only event, pitting against one another the world's top snowmobile drivers. Even the World Snowmobile race paled in comparison.

Chapter Thirteen

Early in the morning, Vanessa watered the team she was taking out and checked the map one last time. She was set to explore the park reserve toward the south, where it was more mountainous and bordered Alaska. Despite Marcel's logic about knowing the land was more important than relying on a piece of technology, she was taking her GPS. For ultimate safety, it was vital she knew how to use it in the mountainous terrain if need be.

With only the panting of her dogs and the occasional raucous cry of a raven perched on a pine branch to break the silence, a wholesome feeling of contentment enveloped her. On the way home, she swung through a wide arc back toward the north. It'd make a nice loop for a day's outing, and she was confident she'd remember the way. A clearing appeared at the top of a hill. She stopped to water the dogs and eat a bite herself.

After the pause, she oriented herself and once more gave the team the signal to start. She came upon snowmobile tracks. Another of those machines that didn't respect the rules. There was a good reason why motorized vehicles weren't allowed in the wildlife reserve. The constant weight and speed packed the snow into ice, which stayed until summer and prevented the underlying vegetation from growing again in the spring. That, plus disturbing wildlife.

Less than half an hour later, she heard noises, not only the strident sound of engines but voices raised in anger. She halted the dogs and signaled to them to lie down and hoped they'd remain quiet as she gave each a treat of fat. Below her, down the slope, she saw through the sparse trees three snowmobiles, three people in a clearing, and beyond it a lake. They appeared to be having a heated discussion. Two of them jumped on their snowmobiles and departed across the lake in a cloud of snow. One person remained standing in the middle of the clearing. Vanessa crouched low. She knew that silhouette. Her platinum blond hair in disarray was unmistakable. The woman climbed on the remaining canary yellow snowmobile. Vanessa stifled an exclamation. Ingrid! It had to be. How was that possible? Ingrid was at the lodge. Vanessa had been told by Patrick and Marcel that the elegant manager didn't know how to drive a snowmobile and hated the outdoors.

Yet, the woman skillfully gunned her machine and she soon disappeared from view, in the opposite direction to the other two snowmobilers. Fearful of having made a mistake and strayed off course, Vanessa checked her GPS. Her eyes popped out of her head when she read the GPS again. To her relief, the Alaska border was still a long way to her left. That meant she was still in the nature reserve on the Canadian side. Those people had driven off toward the steeper part of the park on their way to the American border. Since the area was devoid of towns or settlements, it puzzled her, then worried her. What were they doing and why had they been meeting Ingrid? What was going on?

Without a noise, she turned the team to abort her planned loop route and made her way home. Once there, she took the map and discovered she had followed the wrong valley from her planned itinerary. That in itself wasn't a great deal, but that minor error in navigation had brought her upon something suspicious. That wilderness meeting she had witnessed had not looked like an innocent encounter between wilderness travelers. Without delay, she amended her planned circuit. Marcel was right about being aware of the GPS's limitations.

American Thanksgiving Day had arrived. Because there was a sizable number of ex-pat American residents in Donek, the whole town celebrated, too. A whirlwind of activities and phone calls left Vanessa gasping for breath, but finally everything was organized with Marcel's help. They worked well together.

Chapter Fourteen

Her new dogs were set to arrive in Whitehorse, at the airport of the territorial capital. She had planned to pick them up with Patrick's help. They were to stay with a relative of his near Whitehorse. She didn't feel altogether comfortable in accepting his help, but there wasn't much else she could do. Her dog transporter held only eight dogs, and she was getting sixteen. Patrick was renting her a brand new transporter, which he had installed on his truck.

Vanessa arrived half an hour early for her meeting with Patrick. Dawn had yet to streak the sky when she parked her truck alongside his in the yard behind the Pathfinder store. He was busy checking the attachments of the new dog transporter.

"Your canine travelers from the Arctic will finish their journey in style."

"Thank you for renting it to me until I can purchase it, Patrick."

"I had the transporter built to fit onto a trailer as well as a truck, should you need to. All you need now is a trailer."

"A trailer would only be if I had to transport all the dogs at once."

"You never know, you might be invited on some expedition."

She laughed. "Not a chance, but I'm so grateful to you for driving to Whitehorse with me. How can I repay you?"

"How about a kiss on account?"

Vanessa recoiled. Desperately, she searched for a way to put him back in his place without hurting his feelings or damaging their business relationship. "I guess Alden is delighted to have the dogs all to himself for the weekend."

"You're scared?"

"Patrick, you are a married man."

"I got married young. Too young. I had to. Alden was on the way. I thought I was in love, but it was only infatuation. You changed my life when you arrived in Donek."

"What a touching story!" Harsh and contemptuous, a man's voice resonated in the chill morning air.

Vanessa spun on her heel. "Brett! What are you doing here?"

"Interrupting an early morning tryst, by the look of it. And I make no apology." Brett glowered at Patrick. "Someone is conveniently forgetting their wedding vows along the way."

Patrick's face flushed with anger. "It's not what you think."

"Oh, but it is. You were about to leave on a cozy two-day trip with Vanessa. Married men just don't do that kind of thing."

Patrick stumbled over his words. "If you must know, I'm helping her to collect her dogs. Someone's got to drive the second truck. It's obvious."

"Is it? Why not your wife? Two women together."

"Frances knows that Vanessa and I are business partners. She has absolutely no interest in dogs."

"Does she know about your romantic leanings?"

"What the hell are you on about? I don't need this."

Vanessa stepped between the two men. "Brett, what I do is no concern of yours."

"An affair with a married man? I don't agree with you."

Brett's intrusion and his angry snarl reminded her of one of her more pushy male dogs correcting a youngster over some misdemeanor. "How dare you accuse me of having an affair! For the record, there's nothing going on."

"Nothing at the moment, maybe. Let's just wait and see."

"You've no right to make such insinuations!" Vanessa was beginning to lose her temper. "What kind of woman do you take me for?"

"Exactly what you are. Sexy and single."

Her slap caught him full across the cheek. Slowly, he raised his hand to finger the livid imprint of her hand.

Vanessa bit her lip. "I've never been goaded into doing anything like that before."

"You'd better apologize," Patrick growled at Brett.

"Apologize? For having told the truth?"

The blood drained from Vanessa's face. "You rat! Because your mind is in the gutter, you put everybody in the same filth."

Patrick took a step forward, but she held up her hand. "Enough! It's already six o'clock. We have to leave to get to the airport in time to meet the plane."

"In which case, tell Patrick to go back home to his wife. I'll come with you."

She looked at him in shocked surprise. "I don't need you. You must have things to do at the lodge."

"The lodge runs itself."

Patrick's shoulders slumped. A dejected look clouded his face. "He's right, damn him! I'm sorry I got carried away. I didn't really mean it. I'm just excited at having to work with the huskies again. Tongues will wag if I go with you. I ought to have thought about that before." He jerked his head toward Brett. "He can drive my truck and go with you."

"Maybe, I don't want him along."

Patrick sighed deeply. "Perhaps it would be best if neither of us went with you. I'll get some kennel crates and tie-downs from the store. We can lash the travel crates on top of your transporter."

"No, that wouldn't be safe," Brett said.

Vanessa sighed. "He's right. I'm leaving on my own. I will find a way to board the dogs in Whitehorse and will make a second trip."

She had never imagined the simple task of driving to an airport to collect dogs would lead to such complication. Vanessa moved a few steps away and reached for her cell phone while the two men still argued. As she hoped, there was a musher who offered boarding facilities. She walked toward her truck only to hear Patrick.

"Do you want to take my truck?" Patrick offered the keys to Brett.

"No, let's put the transporter on mine."

"I'll get the tools to make the switch." He went into the storeroom.

Brett gripped her by the shoulders. His warm lips taking hers stifled her cry of protest. Thrown off guard, she struggled for breath. The sharp predawn cold was instantly forgotten. *Exactly what you are. Sexy and single.* Through the sensual mist that enveloped her, his words came flooding back, dousing the all-consuming flames. With renewed strength, she broke free.

"I don't know what you hoped to gain by your nasty little game. If it wasn't for the fact my dogs have already spent twenty traumatic hours in transit, I'd tell you to go —"

"I'd go anywhere, so long as it's with you."

"That's a tired cliché. You know that. What about Ingrid? Did you tell her you intended coming with me?"

Patrick's return cut short the exchange.

Brett brought his truck up to do the transfer. Vanessa still seethed. Of course, he had to have a three-quarter ton just sitting around! But her half-ton served her well enough.

Vanessa scrambled into her truck. Brett turned to face her, his arms waving madly.

"Wait for me. We must plan our route."

"You crept up on me like the great detective you are. Well, I've got news for you. I don't need anyone. Especially not you. I'm leaving." Her window wound up.

She choked back tears of rage and put the truck in gear. As she swung out of the yard, the glare of her lights caught Brett, his face a study in abject misery.

While she drove through darkness, toward the town limits and the main road beyond, an idea formed crystalized in her mind. She would manage on her own. No need for those bellicose males. At the Whitehorse airport, she would take possession of her new dogs and place them two to a compartment in the transporter and maybe a couple in the cab. They'd be cramped, but they were tough and would survive the discomfort. A break every two hours would enable them to stretch their legs. Closer to Whitehorse, she intended to phone the musher with the boarding kennel. If that didn't work she'd camp somewhere. And if Brett decided to follow her, she'd have the pleasure of telling him to go to hell. His kind of help came at too high a price.

"What possessed me to let that man kiss me? And when he did, why did I respond?" Her voice rang hollow in the cab. She still rankled over his behavior in the parking lot. *It's the land, stupid! That's all he's after. Your body would be the icing on the cake. And you're behaving like a moonstruck adolescent. He kisses you and you fall right into his lap!* She resolved never again to give him the opportunity to get that close.

A tear rolled down her cheek. *Walter...* How could she have forgotten? No, not forgotten, but put him in the back recesses of her mind.

If Brett thought he'd conquered and subdued her, he was sorely mistaken. Her new resolution soothed her jangled nerves. Now that she could put the incident behind her, she concentrated on driving. A Yukon winter highway posed a challenge to even the most composed and seasoned driver.

Once she was on the Alaska Highway, she noticed several sets of headlights behind her. There was no way of knowing whether one of them was Brett's. Not that she cared, but he wasn't a man to give up easily. Even if he wasn't directly behind, he knew the way to White-horse airport better than she did. Whatever happened, she'd ignore him and proceed with her plan.

Chapter Fifteen

By late morning, the eastern sky was aflame with one of those spectacular north country dawns. Straight from a painter's palette, luminous pinks and greens erased the night from the horizon. Vanessa marveled at how nature's beauty spread over the land and hills and helped ease the anguish she felt.

On the outskirts of Whitehorse, she stopped to place a call to the Northern Lights boarding kennel, and was relieved by the warm reception from the musher's wife. She cut through the bustle of traffic to reach the air cargo terminal. To her acute annoyance, the first thing she saw on entering the parking lot was Brett's truck, conspicuous by its new dog transporter. Her earlier rancor came surging back with a vengeance. She parked near it.

The customer service area was empty save for the last man in the world she wanted to meet. Brett was leaning nonchalantly against the counter, talking to the agent.

Vanessa groaned. The employee raised an eyebrow when she approached. Brett grinned at her and moved aside.

"Hi, I'm Vanessa Riley and I'm here to collect a shipment of sled dogs coming down from Iglulik. The flight number is——"

"Yes, Ms. Riley. I have all the papers ready for you. I should inform you that your dogs didn't get on the First Air flight."

"What?"

"They're arriving by a private carrier. It was an arrangement the company had to make. You see, they were not able to board sixteen dogs on the scheduled flight."

"Not able..?" A leaden feeling weighed heavy in the pit of her stomach. The picture was abundantly clear. Unable to accommodate such a large shipment of animals, the airline must have handed them over to a charter company. But at what additional expense?

She looked away to regain her composure. Brett had gone outside and was watching her through the glass door. He waved to her. The jerk! He was enjoying her discomfort! Vanessa turned back to the clerk and was about to explain that she had no way of paying for the additional costs when she saw a wide smile on the man's face.

"Don't worry about a thing, ma'am. Your dogs were boarded on an Air North Hawker-Siddeley cargo plane at Iglulik. Apart from a refueling stop, the flight was direct. They didn't need to be transshipped, which was much better for the animals."

"I'm sure they've been well taken care of. Tell me how much I'll have to pay?"

The man cocked an eye in Brett's direction. "There's no surcharge, ma'am."

Vanessa's jaw sagged. "Nothing to pay? How come?" Suspicion sprang to her mind. "Has someone covered the extra expense?"

Fire darted from her eyes. The agent nervously adjusted his glasses. "There's nothing to be concerned about. Everything is right on schedule. The flight is due in at sixteen hundred hours. As soon as it reaches the terminal, you'll be able to collect them straight off the plane. Air North is used to transporting expedition dogs. If I'm not mistaken, the animals won't be crated but just attached in the cargo bay. They probably didn't even have enough crates up in Iglulik. Anyway, even if they did, crates take up too much space. Now, if you'll excuse me, I've got things to attend to in the back."

The man disappeared through the swing doors. Vanessa spun around on hearing a sound behind her. "What do you think you're doing, paying for the transport of my dogs?" Her angry voice echoed in the cavernous terminal.

"Me?"

"Don't play the dumb idiot with me!"

"Okay. Since the switch of aircraft was done without your consent, I took the liberty of doing a spot of old-fashioned horse trading with them. The difference was a paltry sum. I settled it."

"Do you mind telling me the exact amount of the bill?" She produced her checkbook from her purse. "I'd hate you to think that by settling up my bills, you were somehow making a down payment on my land. That would be a very grave mistake on your part."

Brett threw up his hands in mock indignation. "You are always accusing me of false motives. It's quite unjust."

"Well, tell me. How much?"

Since he made no reply, she leaned over the counter and grabbed the copy of the bill of lading and invoice. Vanessa hastily scribbled a check. She fought a rising panic. This, coupled with the business expenses she had already incurred, left her account dry. The savings she meant to keep on Harold Glover's advice were now wiped out. The extra fare on the charter had not been part of her business plan.

"Don't get all het up. Let me assure you that I was only trying to cut through the red tape. You should thank me, because if my watch is correct, the plane has already landed."

Vanessa looked up at the wall clock above the counter. He was right. It was six minutes after four. A smiling crew member in a flying suit came toward her.

"Ms. Riley?"

"Yes. That's me."

"Our four-legged passengers are waiting for you."

"I'll be right there."

"You'll find the dogs as docile as lambs."

Her adrenalin pumping, Vanessa ran back to her truck. She picked up a handful of tether chains, turned to go back into the terminal, and collided with Brett.

"Vanessa, dear, we're going to have to change our way of meeting. Let me help. Why the chains?"

She breathed deeply to control her wayward body and its excited reaction at the brief contact. Anger took over at his flippant tone.

"To bring the dogs to be picketed to the truck. I have strung this cable between the two bumpers. Like that the dogs can stretch their legs."

She returned to the cargo terminal, impatient to meet her new team. The baggage handlers had already rolled a ramp up to the plane's open cargo door. Vanessa saw a group of the finest Canadian Inuit sled dogs she had ever seen clustered at the entrance, looking out at the unaccustomed landscape. The dogs nosed the air in an effort to identify the alien smells.

The pilot pointed to a big gray dog. "Apparently, that guy is the boss of the pack."

"That must be Neviartok. It means *the one who is noble*." Vanessa had memorized the list of names and the corresponding coat markings. "I'll unload him last."

"There's no doubt he's the top dog. The others were a bit agitated after we took off. One growl from him and they all lay down. They hardly made a peep all the time we were airborne. Beats carrying human passengers, any day." He chuckled. "Well, of course they didn't use the bathroom, but we had paper towels and bags on hand. That, coupled with the seal meat aroma, made for a memorable flight."

They all laughed. A strong marine odor indeed emanated from the dogs' fur.

"The smell will soon disappear. I'm so grateful to you for getting them to me safely."

The pilot handed Vanessa a package. "Pauloosie sent you his whip. It's a beaut. Twenty-five feet of braided walrus hide. If you ever have a mind to sell it, I'll be your first taker."

Moved by Pauloosie's gesture of confidence, Vanessa shook her head. "Sorry to disappoint you. No way would I ever sell it."

"Too bad. It's not often a traditional Inuit hunter parts with his dogs. Rarer still with his whip."

"I'm mighty proud Pauloosie sent it to me."

Brett frowned. "You don't whip the dogs, do you?"

"Of course not. It is only for signals. Snap it to the right and they turn left. I'll use it when I'm on lakes or in wide open spaces."

Vanessa and Brett, helped by the flight crew, unloaded the dogs and walked them across the tarmac to the truck. The intelligent animals responded to Vanessa's soft words and rubbed themselves against her legs.

Under her direction, the men picketed the dogs on the line. Vanessa then brought several large thermoses of a meaty broth and poured a bowlful for each animal. Suspicious at first, the dogs soon lapped up the welcome liquid. Two bowls later, they licked their chops with their pink tongues.

Vanessa familiarized herself with her new team, patiently checking each dog against her list. She stopped in front of a handsome black and white female. "Tupiq?" The animal made no response. "You must be Sukka, right?" At that, the dog raised her head and wagged her plumed tail. With infinite gentleness, she raised herself on back legs and rested her front paws on Vanessa's shoulders.

"I see you're an old softie." She scratched her behind the ears.

Brett watched her. She ignored him.

The dogs milled about to the limit of their chains, sniffed the truck, anointed the wheels and stood up against the unfamiliar transporter to investigate the smells.

"I notice they touch each other's muzzles from time to time," Brett said.

"It's a way of assuring themselves that everything's okay in the pack."

"You make them sound like a bunch of wolves."

"Despite what some people believe, they're not part wolf, but they're a very primitive animal, with a pack mentality and hierarchy. That's a wolf-like behavior, though."

"They sure don't act savage. Not with you, anyway."

"These are true working dogs and well-used to people. I must load them up now and go the kennel to board half of them."

"Haven't you organized anything?" His tone carried a hint of sarcasm.

"Patrick and I were going to stay with a cousin of his in town."

"With Ernie?"

"Yes. That what he's called, but now it's out of the question. I have booked a space at a boarding kennel."

"He'll gladly open his door to us."

Vanessa was not sure if he was simply joking. "How on earth would you know?"

"Ernie is the owner of Northern Lights Racing & Boarding Kennel. I know Ernie well. He races his dogs in the Donek Challenge. I've met him several times. If he's expecting you, it won't bother him if I turn up instead of Patrick. One time when the Donek Challenge racers were pulled off the lake because of a storm, I put him and the others up at the Lodge. So, he owes me. Not that we count."

"You know where he lives?"

"Sure, I do. He's got a place on the edge of town. You'll like Ernie. He's another dog nut."

"Thank you... I think." His confidence swayed her. The short Yukon day was already over. Dusk had fallen. She briefly thought about camping it out. Even if she found her way to a campground, it was likely closed at this time of year. To camp beside the highway was not a good idea, either. A solution was creeping in her mind. She would go to the Northern Lights kennel, board half the dogs and immediately set off for home. It was only six or seven hours' drive. The road was good. Then she'd catch a few hours' sleep and come back for the other dogs.

They loaded the dogs onto the two transporters. He produced a pair of walkie-talkies and handed her one.

"What's this for?"

"Communication."

She rolled her eyes. "Thanks! I've just arrived from Mars."

"You follow me because I know the way. But when you need to stop, you press this button and tell me. I'll find a suitable spot to pull off. Easy."

She had to agree it was practical. They were soon on their way. There were no incidents, and they found the cousin's house in the Stone Creek subdivision, right on the margins of the city. The howl of sled dogs greeted their arrival.

Any fear of imposing on strangers, even though they ran a commercial kennel, evaporated the moment she met Ernie. The jovial, bearded giant of a man welcomed them warmly. "As you can tell from the unholy racket, I have a bunch of dogs. I'm just dying to see these dogs of yours. I'll give you a hand to unload. The missus has a hot supper ready on the stove."

Vanessa let out a deep sigh of relief. In no time, they had her dogs spanned out on two long picket chains. She spent some time with each dog to ensure they settled down. Not that they needed it. They appeared to take everything in their stride.

Ernie removed his cap and ran his fingers through his hair. "Amazing! This is the first time they've seen trees and they're not even fazed out."

"Did you see the big gray one, Neviartok?" said Vanessa. "He lifted his leg against a tree as if he had always done it."

"I imagine they lift their legs against everything that's remotely vertical," Brett said.

"Still, this is so different," Ernie said. "Do you need more food? They wolfed that meat down pretty darned quick."

Vanessa laughed. "Those dogs can eat till they burst, puke it up in a corner and come back for more. Then they'll go back to the regurgitate and eat it."

"Gross!" A kid about ten sprung behind the group. "Mom says dinner's ready."

"Okay, Spark, we're coming." Ernie turned to Vanessa. "You sure about more food?"

"I gave them a generous portion. We've got to travel in the morning. It's better if they don't have too full a stomach, not after their long flight."

"Come this way."

They trooped into the house and washed up before they and the family sat down at the long table. The boy Ernie affectionately called Spark stood up to say grace. Ernie's wife, Madeleine served a hearty vegetable soup in wooden bowls. Moments later, she brought in a steaming dish.

"Here is a *tourtière*, a meat pie. Can you cut, Ernie? I'll get the second one."

A savory aroma escaped the pie when cut.

Vanessa smiled at their hostess. "Not only does it smell heavenly, but it's delicious."

Madeleine blushed. "Thank you. It's a dish from home." At Vanessa inquiring look, she added. "I come from Quebec."

"It's a beautiful province. I used to attend the sled dog races there." She took a forkful of the tourtière to stop herself from talking, fearful of the memories dog races evoked.

Ernie turned to Brett. "Have you given up snowmobile racing?"

"Entirely. Comes a time when a fellow has to choose."

"I don't know. I've got a wife and a family, but I still race every winter."

"That's because we help, dad," Spark said.

Laughter greeted the young boy's words.

"Not only you all help, but Spark has already won a one-dog race for the under ten mushers."

"Congratulations," Vanesa said.

An eight-year-old girl piped up, "I help too,"

"And you're very good, Rose," her father said.

"Me too! Me too!"

Everyone smiled to the six-year-old eager twin boys.

Brett shook his head. "I don't have a family to help. Racing lost its appeal." His eyes strayed across the room as if seeing a ghost.

"Seriously?" An incredulous expression spread over Ernie's face.

"One day I looked at all the trophies and asked myself why I was doing it. I loved seeing new places and meeting people, but after thirteen years, there were no more new places to go to."

Vanessa frowned. "When did you start racing?"

"In high school, in the junior category. It was fun, but I needed a change."

"Was that after your friend's accident?" Ernie asked.

A haunted look passed over Brett's face. "We were out for a ride. I had stupidly challenged him. He overtook me and was winning. He turned to laugh at me in triumph. In that moment of distraction, he wavered and lost control of his machine and shot over a cliff."

A respectful silence threatened to lengthen. Ernie pushed his chair back. "I always wanted to ask you why you bought that derelict resort instead of the snowmobile dealership that was up for grabs here in town."

Brett laughed. "I guess I needed something different. The lodge was a ruin. I rebuilt it. Essentially, it's the kind of operation that allows me to get away when I want to. A store has fixed opening hours. Too constricting for me."

Madeleine interrupted them. "The kids are hanging on every word but it's past bedtime. You two guys put them to bed. I'll do the dishes."

"I'll help," Vanessa said.

With tales of mushing, snowmobiles and racing the rest of the evening passed quickly.

It didn't take long in the morning to load the dogs back into the transporters. After the warm hospitality, and learning so much about Brett, Vanessa didn't want to be petty and refuse his help. They got home in good time. Alden bounded out to help. Brett lent a hand to picket the new arrivals in a second temporary pen.

"You'll have to build some proper pens in the spring."

"That's the plan." What she didn't say was that with her savings gone, and it'd have to wait. Unless the business made a lot of money before spring. Suddenly, she realized he had said building pens in the spring. Did that mean he no longer thought about trying to get her to move?

"I'm not going to cash your check until your business is flourishing."

Did he guess her predicament? She pulled a face while bending down to check a collar. "If you don't cash it, I'll go to the bank to make a direct deposit in your name."

He gathered a line and rolled it. "And I could do the same. Let's not play games. You need to keep some cash on hand. You can repay me a little bit every month as the business develops if you insist. Don't be stubborn about it."

It pained her to have to accept, but he was right. She'd be in a tight spot if he cashed her check right now. "Thank you. Come in and have coffee." The least she could do was to be hospitable and serve him coffee, but it irritated her deeply that she was in his debt.

Brett followed her. Lulik literally jumped into his arms. Alden came in.

"I've prepared a bit of supper. Nothing fancy."

"Hey, lentils stew is just great for a hungry man," Brett said. Hi gave a smile to the teenager who was known for not eating any animal products.

"Thanks for your help, Alden."

The young man beamed with pride. After supper, Vanessa sent them both on their way. Brett tried to linger, to no avail.

Chapter Sixteen

The first outing Vanessa made with the sixteen dogs of her new team created considerable excitement among the Donek dogsledding fraternity. As a precaution, she started with a run on the lake. The large lake enabled the dogs to run long enough to exhaust some of their energy. In no time, a crowd had gathered off the Donek marina.

She approached and gave the command to slow down. There was a flutter in the team, but the dogs continued. She repeated the voice command without success. The dogs were not used to her voice giving commands. Not being very experienced in handling the long whip, Vanessa hesitated. It was now or never. Her hand reached for the short handle and with a flick of the wrist, she sent the rawhide tip flying in front of the dogs. They stopped instantly. She only had time to jump on the brake to prevent the sled from hurtling into the center of the dogs.

Mentally thanking her mother for the rhythmic gymnastic classes of her youth, and the hours of practice with the ribbon, she brought back the whip with another flick of the wrist and twirled it over the team once before moving the twirl behind her and letting it drop to the ice. The dogs lay down without a murmur and stayed put. "Not so bad." Vanessa rolled up the thong. She wouldn't tell anyone she had spent several hours practicing in the open space behind her cabin. It was just a little harder to handle the whip from the moving sled.

A man detached himself from the spectators. "Wow! That was a fantastic show! I'm Jimmy Redhead."

"Right, I heard about you. Champion racer."

He smiled. "I love the way you handled those dogs. But why are they spread out like that?"

"Its called a fan hitch. It's the traditional way in the Arctic. It lets them pick the best footing over ice ridges."

"I suppose there's plenty of space up there."

Vanessa eyed the people coming closer. "The dogs are friendly, but it's all very new for them."

Jimmy turned back and shouted. "Don't come too close for the moment. Give'm plenty of room."

She saw Brett's head above the crowd. He took on the task of traffic director with a couple of other mushers she recognized. The spectators lined up on the side at a respectable distance.

The mushers came closer. "Can they run in tandem? You'll need that here in the trees."

"I'll train them to run in tandem, but at the moment, I have to learn their behavior and let them get accustomed to this strange environment. I intend to do that on the lake, where I can use the whip commands, as that's what they are used to. They also have to associate my voice with the whip commands. When I understand how they work together, then I'll start trail training." Still standing on the brake, Vanessa took a deep breath. The dogs and the people behaved well. "I'll be training them four at the time in the woods."

Marcel made his way to the front of the team and talked to each dog, giving them a friendly pat. Jimmy walked back from petting each dog. "I wouldn't mind driving a couple of them with you."

"That'd be great." She smiled and pointed her chin toward Alden. "You might have to fight my young helper, though."

They laughed. When she turned, Brett was standing at her elbow.

"Would you like me to add some ballast for the next round?" He didn't wait for her answer, but settled himself in the sled.

She shrugged. "Looks like you already have."

"Okay, then. Let's go."

"Pauloosie said the team can respond to voice command. If they don't and pitch you off, don't blame me. Jimmy, want to share the runners?"

He jumped on her left runner. The dogs pricked up their ears, hesitated and then stood and took off, the brake useless against their power. "I'll have to teach them to stay put until I say go."

"It must be they're used to go when they feel the weight in the sled. I have some dogs that do that," Jimmy said.

Some way down the lake, she flicked the whip to the side. The team turned as faultlessly as if they'd always been under her command. She skirted the shore under the critical gaze of the spectators. Above the scrape of the runners and the panting of the dogs, she heard a murmur of admiration come from the throng. On the return run, several youngsters ran out, begging to be given a ride. Brett vacated the sled to the laughing kids.

Vanessa waved to him. "Climb on the runners with me." She instantly regretted her imprudent invitation. His closeness rekindled the fire in her, hot enough to melt a hole in the ice. It made no difference that she strove to concentrate on handling the team. More spectators arrived. Her giving rides to the eager children was the best promotion she could have wished for.

She was oblivious to the keen wind whipping her unprotected face. Brett turned his head and leaned closer. The intense look in his eyes drowned out the tiny voice of reason clamoring inside her head. The spell lasted a few memorable seconds until the shrieks of delight from the cargo of laughing kids brought her back to reality.

Soon after darkness descended, she waved to the spectators and drove the team back to her cabin. Brett followed on an Indy 600.

The next few days flew by. Between training her new team on the trails and the paid excursions, Vanessa had no time to think about Brett. Jimmy Redhead was a frequent visitor and was the happiest of men when he took a team by himself.

"My grandfather used to tell me about his childhood. He had dogs. Native dogs. Big like these guys."

"That's why you love them so much, eh, Jimmy?" Marcel ribbed his friend but showed he had a lot of respect for him.

"In my culture, we identify with the wolf and the dog."

"The wolf represents strength and the dog work, is that it?" Vanessa said.

Jimmy nodded. "Yeah. I am Dog Brother. I was given the name because dogs always come to me. I can never hurt a dog. If I do, I'll be cursed. I heal them."

"I heard you take such good care of your team," Vanessa said.

A small smile came to his lips. His eyes bored into hers. "You do too. Now, I'd better get back home to feed my team."

"Racing this weekend?" Marcel asked.

"Just a little conditioning race."

"I'd like to see them in action." Vanessa said.

"Come to the race."

After Jimmy's departure, Marcel and Vanessa organized the next day's bookings.

"I can do the two short runs with half of Neviartok's pack for one and the other half for the second run," Marcel said.

"Okay, I'll take Vercors' team. You really want me to picnic at Twin Lakes?"

He laughed. "It's very pretty and deep in the park. You won't meet any snowmobiles there."

"I hope I'll find it."

"You will. You haven't got lost yet." He put on his parka. "I'm off. See you tomorrow."

In the morning, Marcel arrived with a bison hide.

"What's that for?"

"For your sled. Your tourists are from California. They're going to be cold."

"I have extra parkas and sweaters."

"Trust me. You put the hide in the sled, they sit on it and you tuck the flaps around them. They'll never complain of the cold."

"Thanks."

The middle-aged couple arrived and exclaimed in delight about everything. When it became too much of an effort to talk in the moving sled, they just sat back and enjoyed the scenery.

Through the trees, Vanessa spotted a lake. "We're coming to Twin Lakes. That's where we stop and picnic."

"Wonderful! I'm famished."

Vanessa and her team emerged on the edge of the lake, and she almost let out an expletive. Two snowmobiles were sitting on the ice near a beaver lodge. The drivers stood talking. Vanessa commanded the dogs to slow down.

At her voice, the startled snowmobilers looked toward her. In a fraction second, they jumped on their sleds and roared away.

Vanessa directed the team beneath an overhang bank, which offered a shelter from the wind. Her mind reeled. One of the two drivers she could have sworn was Ingrid. That canary yellow snowmobile was the one she had seen at the other lake she had identified on the map as Mercy Lake. She brushed away any thoughts of why these people were there and took care of her charges.

No further incident occurred to mar the rest of the day. Her clients left enchanted.

When the chores were done, Marcel and Vanessa sat sipping coffee.

"You're sure it was Ingrid?"

"Pretty sure. It was definitely a woman, and her platinum blond hair and slim body are quite distinctive."

Marcel frowned. "What machine did she have?"

"A yellow thing."

He smiled. "Don't let Brett hear you call his snowmobiles a *thing*. He's got so many, there could well be a yellow one. You wouldn't know the brand, of course."

"I can tell if a dogsled is made of hickory or ash a mile away, but snowmobiles, I haven't got a clue."

They shared a chuckle. "They weren't supposed to be there. No surprise they fled when they saw you."

"Just as well, they'd have spoiled our picnic. But the other day, I was exploring the reserve toward the south, not far from the border where there's a lake. There were three snowmobiles stopped in a clearing, and I distinctly saw the same woman. I feel pretty sure it was Ingrid. There are not many people with platinum blond hair around here. She mounted a yellow machine. If I'm correct from the map, it's close to Mercy Lake."

"South, you say, so, yes, it's probably Mercy Lake. Show me on the map."

She switched on the GPS and showed him the coordinates. They checked the map. Marcel confirmed her findings.

"What was she doing out there?"

"Having an argument with a couple of snowmobilers, or so it seems. They rode off toward the States. She went west. Toward home, I suppose."

"And word has it she can't operate a snowmobile."

"Not the woman I saw. She knew how to handle the thing. I realized afterwards I went down the wrong valley. I mean, it wasn't the one I was planning to explore, but I was still in the reserve."

Marcel laughed. "Using your famous technology."

"Laugh if you want, but until I know every single tree and rock, I will keep my *technology* at hand. Even though it led me astray."

"Of course, it could be the navigator's fault."

Vanessa laughed with him. "Yeah! That's most likely. Does that mean I should avoid Mercy Lake?"

"No. Snowmobiles aren't supposed to be there, but we know some of them don't give a damn about the regulations. It's a pretty place to take clients for a picnic. There're a couple of ways to get to it. From what you said, the encounter doesn't sound like people out to enjoy a ride. So it may never happen again."

After planning the next few days, Marcel took his leave.

Chapter Seventeen

For days on end, during the few short hours of daylight, the sun shone benevolently over the land. Brett frequently found an excuse to drop by. One afternoon, she greeted him as he was helping a woman out of his truck.

"This lady was looking for Tapiskoot, but came to Wolf Hollow by mistake."

"Thanks for driving her here."

"I'm happy to act as chauffeur."

"You're a perfect gentleman." Vanessa's tone was lightly mocking. "Thanks, anyway. I'll take over now."

He gave a deep sigh and climbed back behind the wheel. He'd hardly gone a minute when a black Escalade pulled up into her yard.

"Hi, I'm Dexter Weiman. I didn't phone for an appointment." The potency of his smile alone could have thawed the Ice Maiden. "I'm just wondering if I could take a ride. I'm staying at Wolf Hollow, but I saw your dogs the other day, and I fell in love with them."

His easy going manner would have charmed anyone with a less level head than Vanessa. "Hi Dexter. I'm on my own today. If you don't mind waiting a little while, I'll take you out after I come back with Mrs. Berg."

"I don't mind waiting."

"Make yourself at home. You can go into the cabin if you need to warm up. Say hi to Lulik and the pups as you go in. They live on the porch in that dog playpen for the time being."

He cocked his head. "I can see them. Very cute."

Vanessa settled Mrs. Berg in the sled and the team took off.

Dexter smiled to himself. His job was being made easier by a trusting Vanessa. His agent, Mrs. Berg, played her role to perfection. He went inside and took care to remove his snow boots at the door. The simple furnishing, framed paintings and photographs on the log wall all spoke of openness, just like the layout of the cabin itself. Only, there weren't many places where a ten kilo packet of a certain white powder could be hidden. He continued to the bedroom. The sensation of intruding into a woman's domain hit him, but he brushed it off.

If he followed his gut instinct, he'd rule out Vanessa as a possible suspect involved in trafficking. In his job, however, gut feelings weren't allowed to overrule strategy and evidence. Yet it was that very instinct that often made the difference between a case successfully prosecuted and an utter fiasco. With a sigh, he searched the closet, looked under the bed, and glanced at the picture of Walter on the bedside table. Now, no one could accuse him of not turning over every stone.

The woman he was looking for clearly wasn't Vanessa Riley. Still, he had to check out the outbuildings. He put his boots back on and hurried outside. The barn revealed nothing of interest, only flattened packing boxes systematically stacked along a wall, a few bales of straw and a couple of dog sleds. The first shed contained packs of frozen dog meat. Logs of dry wood occupied the second shed.

He breathed a sigh of relief. In fifteen years in the Mounted Police, with the Covert Operations of the Drug Branch, he had never been wrong. Now he looked forward to Vanessa's return. His duty done, he was going to enjoy a sled ride for himself.

***

A couple of nights later, a ruckus from the dog pens awoke Vanessa. This wasn't the howling at some wild animal going past. With automatic reflexes, she shrugged into her outdoor clothes, grabbed her headlamp, and rushed out. The night cold slapped her in the face. The dogs calmed down as soon as she spoke to them, while checking each picket. Only Neviartok continued howling. Vanessa hurried to the temporary pen housing her new dogs and immediately saw that the white male, Pidgajok, was missing. His collar lay on the snow, still attached to the chain. A gaping hole in the wire fence showed where he had escaped.

Vanessa rubbed Neviartok's ears and took her silent whistle from her pocket. She wasn't sure whether Pidgajok would remember the recall whistle, as she had only practiced it twice with her new dogs. The dog would hear it within a radius of two miles. She had no doubt he'd hear it and would know where it came from. However, she wasn't sure he had learned and could apply the command to return.

The long wait began.

Now that she was up, Vanessa fed and watered the dogs, then went inside to cook herself breakfast. Every ten minutes, she went out and whistled. Worry etched lines in her forehead. She never thought a gentle male like Pidgajok would slip his collar and enlarge an already existing gap in the fence. Females were the ones most likely to take an unauthorized hike.

Solitude weighed heavily on her. It was at times like this she wished she had someone to share her anguish. A wave of regret flooded her heart. How she missed Walter! Then Brett's image flitted across her mind, and she promptly shook it off. That arrogant man was not her idea of the perfect companion.

The shrill ring of the phone startled her. There was only one excursion booked for that day, Marcel could take it. She had no intention of going anywhere until Pidgajok came back. If this was another client, she would turn him down. A glance at the clock told her it was too early for business.

A sharp voice on the other end startled her. "Can't you control your dogs?"

"Sorry, who is speaking?"

"Ingrid Lancaster. Your dogs are making the racket of the century and waking everybody up!"

Vanessa groaned. Ingrid was the last person she wanted to deal with this morning. Moonlight was filtering through the spruce branches. The clear sky promised a lovely day.

"My dogs are quiet. They have been for the last four hours."

"What about the one howling outside the lodge? Or maybe it's a wolf and we should shoot it!"

"Don't you dare! If it's a white dog, he belongs to me, my Pidgajok. It's one of my new dogs. I'll be right over." She put down the phone.

A mixture of anger and relief washed over her. Ingrid might be obnoxious, but at least she cared enough to call. Pidgajok had been found. Vanessa ran to her truck and turned on the ignition. The engine coughed and died. Again and again. The battery spluttered in the intense cold. She slapped her hand to her forehead. She had forgotten to plug in the block heater. Frustrated, she went to the cabin for her snowshoes. No. There was a better way. She ran to the small basket sled. In record time, she had Neviartok and two females hitched up.

"Hike!"

Her three-dog team bounded forward to the accompaniment of vociferous protests from the other dogs missing out on the fun. The packed snow surface of the road provided a firm footing for the dogs to run flat out. Occasionally, the runners scraped on bits of gravel, but Vanessa didn't hold the team in check. In a matter of minutes, they made a grand entrance into the forecourt of the lodge.

The dogs ran straight to the wooded area behind the lodge. Vanessa heard a plaintive howl and saw a group of people trying to entice Pidgajok to come out from the security of the trees. His response was to raise his head and howl.

Vanessa secured her team well away from the crowd. As she advanced, she blew her silent whistle. Pidgajok, unused to life in the south, eyed with suspicion the ring of humans and prepared to bolt. It was then that Vanessa saw a silhouette edging up behind the dog, who turned his head to see this new threat.

Unsure of the dog's reaction, she pretended to run toward the sled, hoping his chasing instinct would make him follow. "Pidgajok! Pidgajok! Come here, boy!" She was relieved to see him prick up his ears. At that moment, Neviartok vented a howl of authority. The runaway hesitated, then leaped forward and ran over to the boss dog, throwing himself on the ground in an abject display of submission, on his back, urinating on his exposed belly. Neviartok corrected him nevertheless with a few bites to the neck.

While Vanessa talked gently to him in that undignified posture, she slipped the collar she had brought over his head and got him back on his feet, then put on his harness. Once the dog was secured to the sled, she relaxed. All four dogs looked at Vanessa, and when they saw she wasn't about to step on the runners, they lay down.

She turned to Brett. "Thanks for bringing up the rear."

Before he could answer, the spectators swarmed around.

"Sled dogs! We thought that one was a tame wolf!"

"Can we pet them?"

"They're so beautiful!"

"Look at that magnificent bushy tail."

"How often do you have to brush them?"

"Why did he run away?"

"Did you hug him so he'll come back to you if he runs off again?"

Without much success, Brett tried to herd his guests back inside the lodge. They complied only after they had found out where Vanessa lived, so they could visit and book a ride.

"Stealing my clients again?"

"Be reasonable. I'm doing no such a thing. Anyway, thanks for helping me catch Piggy."

He burst out laughing. "Piggy! Poor Pidgajok, you've lost your grand name. Do you realize all the trouble you caused, you naughty dog? Disturbing my guests, too, and bringing them running outside in the cold air in their light clothes."

"I hope you're not serious. They're not kids! Let them do what they want. I'll go now, so you'll have no further disturbance from me or my dogs."

He stood so close that she felt the heat of his body through his open coat. A shock of dark hair fell across his forehead to give him a dashing appearance. Whether he intended it or not, he swayed against her and kissed her.

Blood suffused Vanessa's cheeks. A brief instant of lucidity brought her back to the reality of the present. She moved a few paces away, chest heaving, breathing labored. As if lost for words, she gazed into his dark eyes.

Then she remembered his motives.

Without another word, she climbed onto the sled and swiftly pulled up the snow anchor and released the brake. The dogs poised themselves, eager for the signal to be off down the road.

Brett watched her until she disappeared beyond the screen of spruce trees. He shook his head, then trudged through the snow to the lodge where his enthusiastic guests awaited him.

Ingrid met him in the doorway. "What took you so long?"

"Ingrid, you're asking too many questions these days."

"Some of our guests want to speak to you."

"Okay, I'll go into the lounge."

Her parting comment burst from taut lips. "They want to ask you about those damn dogs and that woman!"

CHAPTER EIGHTEEN

B rett picked up his gloves. "I'm off!"

"Again?" The tone was resentful.

Brett tipped his chin. "My dear Ingrid, this is my day off. Yours was yesterday, and I coped with how many guests?"

"Don't deny you enjoyed doing it."

Briefly, he contemplated the pouting ruby lips, pouting for his benefit. Once, a long time ago, he had almost made a fool of himself on account of those sensual lips. He didn't really know why he had given her this job. Desperation for a capable manager or, most likely, to reassure his father and his step-mother, who worried about her wayward daughter. "Of course, I did. Took them all out for the weekend. Great time."

"I suppose you're heading precisely two miles north-west!"

There was venom beneath the sweetness, but Brett didn't heed it.

"As a matter of fact, I'm going to town."

"Why can't we spend the day together? Jon is perfectly capable of running Wolf Hollow on his own for a day."

Her pleading tone grated on his nerves.

"Grow up, Ingrid." He zipped up his parka and pulled on his woolen cap. "It's been a long time since you took off on your great adventure."

"What if my mistake has haunted me ever since?"

"Then I suggest you see a shrink. Ciao!"

In the bright sunshine, his irritation melted away. He climbed in his truck and sent it roaring down the road. His positive frame of mind helped him conduct his business in record time.

He called in at the municipal office to talk to the administrator. "I've a question for you, Don. How come there is no land access to my lot B-North on the land registry?"

"Ah, you too."

"What do you mean?"

"I've already had that enquiry. These lots weren't drawn up by the Council. The Crown sold them piecemeal. The rule on that side of the lake was that each parcel of land had to have lake frontage. Edmund Noles didn't bother to buy the lot on the north side of his property since he already had a large lake frontage. It remained empty until you came along."

"How about pushing the road through?"

Don shook his head. "It stopped at Edmund's land because of the rocky outcrop."

"Could be blasted off." Brett put his finger on the map.

Don chuckled. "Too expensive just for letting you ride to that piece of land. Besides, it'd block access to the lake for Ed, er, sorry, Ms. Riley. Can't do that. It's in the bylaw that the all lots have to have lake frontage."

Brett scratched his head. "Couldn't we amend the by-law?"

"You're kidding! We'd be deluged with requests from land-bound cottagers who came after all the lake lots were gone. And besides, blasting the rocky promontory wouldn't pass the environmental assessment. So, no go."

"Okay, I had to try."

"Surely it's not a big thing?"

"My manager seems to think it is. It's a bit inconvenient, to say the least."

Brett took his leave and strode toward the marina. Acquaintances seemed to materialize from nowhere to delay him. He dealt graciously with everyone until he could bolt to his vehicle parked near the ice-bound dock.

He drove back to Eagle Point, passing the lodge without a sideways glance. Brett slowed down to a crawl when Vanessa's cabin came in sight. The dogs gave him a welcoming howl. He parked in the yard and walked toward the door.

His euphoria faded when no one answered his knock. An uneasy feeling gnawed at his nerves. After a couple of minutes, it was plain that Vanessa wasn't home. Disappointment hit like a punch in the stomach. Lulik, on the porch with her pups in her makeshift enclosure, jumped into his arms. He cuddled her, then crouched to pet each squealing pup. The dogs in the pens called to him. A row of empty pickets on one side confirmed she was out sledding. Absently, he patted a dog's head. The others strained forward on their chains, begging for attention.

After reacquainting himself with Vanessa's eager canine friends, he extricated himself and went to the edge of the slope. He let his eyes roam the lake, hoping to see a familiar silhouette. Numbing cold penetrated his parka. He shivered. For all he knew, she could be gone for hours. Dejected, he leaned against a lofty pine and contemplated the line of trees that fringed the yard site. For the first time, he understood why she loved this place so much. All around lay unsullied nature. Tiny noises, the rattle of a dog chain, a boreal chickadee chirping on a nearby twig or a branch springing back up after letting go of its load of snow tampered the silence. Away in the distance, the high-pitched whine of an engine was the only reminder of human activity. There was something enchanting, almost mystical, at being at the end of the road, literally and figuratively.

He was about to move from his lookout spot when something caught his attention. He listened to a panting sound like an old-fashioned steam locomotive toiling up a gradient. Intrigued, he walked to the edge of the ridge and looked down the trail. Before his eyes adjusted to the sharp glare of the sunlight, peals of laughter filled the air. Then, below, he saw a team making its way up the steep slope. Two young girls seated in the sled were laughing.

All of a sudden, he too was laughing.

The girls waved at him. "Hi Brett!"

From her position behind the handlebar, Vanessa gave him a friendly wave. A familiar heat enveloped him.

"I'll settle the dogs first and be right with you."

"I'll help."

In a decisive voice, she directed what he should do. Once the dogs attended to, the teenagers departed, with a promise to be back.

"Don't they pay before they leave, or do they pay at the start?"

"Do you want a job as my manager?" Vanessa gave him a teasing smile.

His eyebrows lifted. "Are you telling me they had a free ride?"

"That's correct. They did."

"That's no way to run a business. You'd better sell before you go bankrupt." His banter failed to bring another smile to her lips.

"They're only high school kids. Classes are canceled on account of some teacher's meeting. Janine and Taylor wanted to come and learn about the dogs that Alden is always bragging about. I didn't expect them to pay."

"Soon you'll have the whole of Donek dropping by for a free ride."

"I'll deal with that problem when it happens." Her dry tone indicated the end of the matter. Besides, she was suspicious of his reason for being there. He looked relaxed enough, but he still must have the same fixed idea in mind, that of wanting to buy her land.

He stood smiling at her, handsome and unsettling. The memory of that stolen kiss outside the lodge warmed her frosty cheeks. An invisible magnetic force drew her close to him.

Vanessa shook off the image. "It's nice seeing you, but I have no time to talk. The other dogs are waiting to be taken out."

"Do you have to run them even when you don't have clients?"

"I'm acquainting myself with the personalities of my new dogs to make sure I don't separate two buddies."

He his first instinct was to scoff, but immediately checked himself. "Buddies?"

"Just like people, dogs have preferences. They work their hearts out as long as they are next to their favorite friends."

"Well, I'll be darned! How long will that take you?"

"I'll go half-way around the lake. Maybe an hour and a half."

"It'll be dark by the time you come back."

"I know, and don't like it much, but I need to work with the dogs. I wear a reflective jacket and a headlamp. Right now, you're delaying me."

"I've never driven a sled, but..."

He stopped and looked at her expectantly.

"But?"

"Would the dogs throw me off and run away?"

Vanessa laughed. "Probably, but we can try. We'll take two sleds." Her heart sang. The chill of the day dissipated. She quickly showed him how to harness and hitch the team to the center gang line. Her instructions were clear and precise. When she looked at Brett, his eyes showed respect.

Once on the lake, he carefully followed until she slowed down so that the two sleds traveled side by side. Vanessa was all business, observing the dogs' behavior, calling a name here, giving an encouragement there. When she ordered a halt, and the sleds were secured with ice anchors, she shifted two dogs from their places on the line. After some enthusiastic licking of muzzles, the teams moved on.

Brett looked stunned. "Those two look a lot happier now in their new places. How did you know to do that?"

"Those four really get along well together, but a number of times, I saw Pikkatik dragging behind to be near Toopak. Now next to him, he'll pull all the way to the North Pole."

It was dark by the time they returned and finished feeding the dogs. Vanessa was actually grateful for his help. With the new dogs, it took twice as long to care for her canine charges. And having company made the task more agreeable.

Brett caught her by the elbow. "Now that we've done all the chores, would you care to go out for dinner?"

Startled, Vanessa made no answer. Her defensive instincts bristled, thinking of the motives behind the invitation.

He turned on his devastating smile. "Believe or not, thanks to it being a tourist destination. There's a choice of restaurants in Donek. I know a place where you'll have the finest French cuisine possible. Chef François is a culinary artist at the hotel. Without him, Donek wouldn't be the same. Tourists fly in just to have a meal by François."

"If you tempt me like that, how could I refuse?" It was only another of his tactics. A small voice warned her, but a warm feeling, induced by Brett's dark, persuasive gaze, drowned out that voice.

He threw himself casually onto the sofa. "Get changed. I'll wait."

Vanessa disappeared into the bedroom and opened her closet. Practical outdoor clothes filled the rack. Surely, she remembered bringing at least one dress?

After she had rummaged in the depths of the closet for some anxious moments, she triumphantly withdrew a dress of emerald silk that she'd worn to her cousin's wedding. She held it against herself and studied the effect in the mirror. A little too dressed up for Donek, or more accurately, a Donek restaurant in Brett's company. It would have to do, for it was the only one she had. The delicate folds of the soft fabric molded her figure and flared about her thighs with every movement. Her black thermal leggings hugged her shapely legs. The low scooped neckline exposed too much of her shoulders and chest. Awful! My face is outdoors tanned and the rest of me is as white as chalk. There's a bolero jacket somewhere that goes with this dress. Where did I put it?

She found it. Her hands fastened the false diamond clip. The deep emerald color enhanced her eyes. Now that she was in business, she resolved to write home for the rest of her clothes. With a smooth movement, she twisted her long hair into a coil at her nape. An application of pale-viridian eye shadow and a touch of mascara completed her toilette.

Back in the bedroom for her purse, her eyes strayed to Walter's photo on the bedside table. A weight fell on her shoulders. Yes, I'm being unfaithful. The thought twirled in her mind. She picked up the frame. Laughing blue eyes looked back at her. I still love you, Walter, but I'm only twenty-eight. You'd want me to have some fun. It's only dinner, you know. With a sigh, she put the framed photograph back on the chest of drawers while she transferred her wallet, a comb and lipstick to a small embroidered purse. The bag strap snagged the edge of the frame and whirled it to face away. Vanessa lifted the strap but didn't straighten the picture.

She returned to the living room. Brett gasped audibly at the vision framed in the doorway.

"What a transformation!"

Vanessa blushed at the compliment. Her cheeks burned. "Do you want to freshen up in the bathroom, or go back to the lodge?"

"I'll wash up here, that is, if you think I look decent enough in this attire."

Vanessa didn't want to examine him too closely. It did disturbing things to her sanity. "You'd look suave enough in work clothes, which those definitely are not. All you need is a necktie."

"I have one in the glove compartment."

"Now, that's a coincidence! Why should I be surprised?"

By way of a reply, he gave her an enigmatic smile and disappeared into the bathroom. At his reappearance, Vanessa's nostrils twitched and her lips curled into a smile. "Oil of Roses soap certainly suits you."

Brett grinned. "All the guys around here use it."

She gave a slow shake of the head. He was so confident in his masculinity. "And you shaved."

"I found a neat pink razor in your bathroom cabinet."

They shared a laugh and, shaking off the spell, she pulled on her elegant, but as yet unworn, heeled-boots she had bought at Pathfinder. Brett went out to warm up the truck. He came back carrying the necktie.

"You planned this dinner outing, didn't you?" There was trepidation in Vanessa's voice.

"I always carry a tie and jacket in the truck. Just in case I have to go and meet some important guest or attend a meeting."

Truth or not, Vanessa didn't care. Underneath his padded overall, he was wearing a good suit, but had had no hesitation jumping on the runners and afterward helping with the dogs. The man had too many facets to his personality for comfort. Yet, a thrill of expectation settled over her. It was eons since she last had gone out and was looking forward to the evening.

Although the restaurant was busy when they arrived, the maître d' hurried over to meet them.

"This way, Monsieur Lancaster, Mademoiselle."

He led them to a secluded table decorated with a single red rose in a fluted vase and two lit candles. Brett held her chair for her. A faint scent emanating from the candles floating in a crystal dish caressed Vanessa's nostrils.

"Who's the artist?" She pointed at half a dozen paintings of city scenes she recognized as being Paris.

"François brought them over from France. We should ask him."

"How come he ended up in this remote corner of the globe? With his talent, I'd expect him to want to be in Montreal or Toronto."

"I'm not entirely sure, but I suspect a love affair gone wrong gave him the need to get away as far as he could."

"I can relate to that."

A sconce light above their table discreetly supplemented the candle light. "It doesn't feel like we're in Donek. Such style and refinement seems out of place."

"We like to think we attract all manner of tourists, those who seek the upscale as well as those who like to rough it."

His appreciative gaze brought a flush to her skin. For once, she couldn't find words to carry on even the simplest conversation. She picked up the menu the waiter had left. Most of it was in French.

In a whisper, she said, "I don't have a clue what to order."

"Don't worry. Here's Chef François coming now. He'll give us his expert opinion."

Resplendent in chef whites, Chef François extended his hand to Brett.

"Brett, mon ami. It is a big pleasure to see you."

"Same here, François. Let me introduce Ms. Vanessa Riley."

François bent over her hand. For a second, she thought he was about to kiss it.

"The most belle femme in the world. You make François very happy to meet you, mademoiselle."

He turned to Brett. "Tell me what you desire, and I shall make it personally."

"What would you recommend for Mademoiselle and me?"

"Oh, for you and the most beautiful femme, I shall make a Crème de volaille princesse, a Truite muguette, and la Gigue de chevreuil aux marrons."

Brett smiled. "That's sounds perfectly delicious."

"I will let you choose your wine. But I have a new shipment of red Bourgogne dry. You will find it just right for le chevreuil. And, of course, I have always the finest Pouilly and Monbazillac in the white wines for the fish."

"Perfect, we'll try the new Bourgogne."

"Excellent! À tout à l'heure, mes amis." François made a low bow and returned to the kitchen.

"Forgive my ignorance, but what was all that about?"

"He said, see you later, my friends."

"No, I got that, before, about the food."

"We're starting with chicken soup smothered in cream."

"That's about the princess bit?"

"You're the princess, sweetheart, but it also happens to be the name of the dish. See, you understood. After that, we're having jellied trout filets. You'll be amazed at how artistic he can be."

"Okay. And the gigue?"

"That's venison."

She frowned. "You mean deer?"

"That's right." Vanessa pulled a face. "That's what I thought. Not for me, thanks. The thought of that graceful animal on a platter just cut my appetite."

Her sudden change of attitude surprised Brett, but she didn't care.

"You have no problem eating beef or fish. I don't see the difference."

"But there is. I don't meet them on my outings, looking at me with those deep, innocent eyes. And Alden has convinced me that eating animals isn't fair when there is so many alternatives."

Brett signaled the waiter and spoke rapidly in French. The man bowed, then hastened toward the kitchen door.

"What was that you said about à la regency?"

He countered her look with a disarming smile. "So you do understand some French."

"My high school days are some distance in the past. One word here and there doesn't help much."

"You realize François is going to be very hurt? He's very proud of that dish."

Her eyes flashed. "I'm sorry about his feelings, but I won't——"

Brett held up his hand. "It's all right. I asked the waiter to tell François to prepare Tournedos à la Regency instead. François claims he created those special meatless tournedos and will be flattered that you asked for them. He'll make the other dishes without animal products."

"Tournedos?"

"It's an imitation of beef rump. I hope that's okay."

A smile lightened up her face. "Yes, in fact, I'm looking forward to try that special dish."

The wine waiter came with a bottle in a wicker carrier and poured a finger of wine in Brett's glass. He dutifully sniffed and tasted it. He nodded his approval to the waiter.

"I must tell you I don't drink wine, sorry."

"With French food, you have to."

"I never do, and I'm not about to begin now." Her stubbornness set her eyes ablaze.

"You should try a little. Wine opens up a whole new world of pleasure. It's good for the soul, too."

Heat added color to her cheeks. She began to wonder if this outing wasn't becoming a bad mistake. His gaze lingering on the smooth swell of her breasts beneath the short jacket made her uncomfortable.

Fortunately, the Crème de lentils princesse arrived to break the spell. They ate in silence, though Vanessa was unable to resist commenting on the delicacy of the soup. The trial sip of sweet Monbazillac, titillated her palate. She enjoyed it, much to her chagrin, but she didn't finish the glass. The waiter placed the dish of special tournedos with its crown of creamed potato on the table. Vanessa accepted a taste of the red wine that Brett and the waiter treated with such respect. Again, she took one sip and left the rest in the glass. She reached for the water.

The padded back of the chair was comfortably soft. Vanessa leaned against it. The subdued light of the candles, the muted murmur of voices and the soft music conspired to lull her into a feeling of well-being. A smile of contentment spread over her lips.

François came to their table. "Everything alright?"

"Wonderful," said Vanessa.

"You outdid yourself, mon ami." He pointed to the paintings on the wall. "By the way, who's the artist?" Brett smiled at Vanessa.

"Édouard Vuillard. As you can see, he was an impressionist. My great-grandfather had a restaurant where Vuillard used to eat. But most often he couldn't pay. So he gave a painting to my ar-rière-grand-père, and then another, and another."

"How interesting," Vanessa said. "Such history."

After Chef François moved on to other diners, Brett leaned forward. "Would you care to dance?"

A quick glance showed her that another couple was already dancing. "I haven't danced since my senior prom." Her husband didn't like to dance. A fleeting pain played across her features. This evening, she decided she wasn't going to think about Walter. This was the beginning of a new life, her own life.

"Then it's high time we rectify that." He stood tall and debonair, his hand outstretched.

Less sure of herself than she had been at that distant senior prom, Vanessa tentatively placed her hand in his. A sensation shot up her arm, almost as though she were on fire. It consumed her body and quickened her heart rate. Brett drew her to him and led her onto the minuscule dance floor, where they swayed to the muted, languorous music. When it was over, Vanessa stifled a sigh, regretting that the magic had come to an end.

"Let's have dessert."

"I think I've already eaten my fill."

"How about a Yukon Zero? It's an ice cream, very light, with a swirl of cream on top. You'll be pleased to know it is made with fava beans juice and flavored with vanilla. It's great."

"I trust you." She realized the implication of her words. Trust? Did she really trust him, more than over a choice of dessert, that is? She was no longer sure. In that instant, she preferred not to have to think. For a few enchanted hours, all she wanted was to relax in the company of her good-looking date, a man who made her senses reel. She was also vaguely conscious that she was having an effect on him.

Brett slipped his keys to the waiter with a request to have his vehicle brought to the door. A renewed feeling of excitement coursed through her veins when Brett took her hand. His heavy-lidded eyes threatened to probe her very soul.

In the vestibule, he helped her with her coat. His warm hands settled a moment on her shoulders. An aura of expectancy hovered in the air.

He drove with one hand on the wheel, the other holding hers. At the cabin, he put his arm around her shoulders and pointed a finger skyward. "Can you see Polaris?"

"You mean the North Pole Star? It's right at the end of the Little Dipper. The other star I recognize is Sirius."

"The Dog Star. That figures."

They laughed and gazed up at the velvety sky, strewn with a million sparkling treasures, until suddenly the green veils of celestial fairies dancing in the sky hid the stars. They twirled skirts streaked with white, rolled and saluted before exiting the vast stage of the firmament.

She didn't ask if he wanted coffee. They both went inside as though it were the most natural thing to do. Brett sat on the sofa and casually stretched out his long legs. Vanessa put water on to boil. She set the cups on the low table. As she brushed past him, he reached for her hand and drew her down to him.

The feel of iron-hard muscles, deceptively masked by his soft shirt, sent quivers down back. Strong arms wrapped her in a nest of warmth from which there was no escape, not that she wanted to. She rested her head against his chest and counted the disorderly beats of his heart.

The kettle whistled long enough for the automatic switch to click off, and the hiss to peter out.

His hand found her hair clasp and removed it, letting the glorious locks cascade over her shoulders. Vanessa's world swirled drunkenly around her.

The inevitability of the moment was so powerful she voiced no protest when he carried her to the bedroom. "I must warn you. If we go any further, I won't be responsible for my actions."

She sighed. "I'm the one being irresponsible."

"There'll be no turning back."

An exhilaration overwhelmed her. This man she could love. A swell of tender feelings swirled around her. She arched against him to savor all of him and to drown herself in his caresses.

***

Later, Brett was first to break the silence in a voice shaking with spent emotion. "I love you, Vanessa."

She stared at him, unable to discern his expression as the shaft of moonlight from the open drapes played tricks on her hazy vision. Her brain struggled to encompass the transformation. In the space of one short evening, she had cast aside her self-imposed principles. Yet, it felt as though Brett was the one she had been waiting for. Everything had happened so swiftly. His embrace overwhelmed her with a flood of tender feelings and made her feel fulfilled. His words touched the deepest fibers of her being.

Brett raised himself on one elbow to look at her. "I know now that what I feel for you is love."

Vanessa sat up, in spite of his restraining hand. Her mind was suddenly swimming with ominous thoughts. Nobody, not even a man like Brett, could fall in love that fast. Her heart began to beat faster. The only man who had loved her was dead and gone. She had betrayed him.

"No. Please don't say that."

"Why not? It's true."

A chilled blast of reality exploded in her brain. "It's not true. You only want me to sell my land to you."

"Your land? Damn your land! It's you I want. I've been dragging myself around like a zombie ever since you came to Donek. Now I know the cause. I'm in love with you."

"I guess it's normal for men to say that when they have sex."

"Vanessa! We didn't have sex. We made love. Love! Don't you understand the difference?"

She got off the bed and gathered up her robe. Her assurance volatilized, she teetered on weak legs to the bathroom. Love? No, Walter had made love to her. But that was such a long time ago. She didn't want to analyze what she had felt with Brett. Yes, it had been exciting and fulfilling.

Brett's voice filled the room. "Vanessa! I love you! I've never loved anyone before. Please listen."

Vanessa spoke through the narrow gap left by the half-closed door. "Please go now. Neither my land nor my body is for sale. Consider that this evening was an aberration. A horrible mistake!"

In one bound he was at the door. Too late. She slammed it shut in his face. He rested his forehead against the wood panel. His voice quivered with emotion. "Vanessa! Listen to me. Vanessa…"

She drowned out his voice by turning on the shower. Her brain tried to encompass what had happened over the past few hours. The food, the wine, the dancing, it had been merely the prelude to the carefully planned seduction. And she had fallen for it! Brett was single-minded and ruthless. His objective was and had always been to reduce her to a limp mass of putty in his hands so that he could buy her out. Love! What a joke! He was incapable of knowing the meaning of the word. The man would stop at nothing.

The hissing water soothed away the tears that flowed freely. She had to admire his skill at dropping all mentions of the land. It had lulled her into believing that his affection was genuine, that there could be something between them. The joy she experienced in his company, the sound of his voice, the way he looked at her, came rushing back. She had been close to falling in love with him. It culminated in her reckless abandon. The discovery shattered her self-confidence. Believe him? Trust him? She was certain she never could. For a moment, she lived in cloud-cuckoo land. It had to stop. Her sanity returned slowly.

To add insult to injury, she knew that a triumphal Ingrid would be at the lodge to welcome him back. Mission accomplished.

The shower ran cold. She stepped out, dripping water on the tiled floor. Beyond the closed bathroom door, a cold and hostile silence gripped the cabin.

Brett had gone.

CHAPTER NINETEEN

Laughter, the howl of dogs, and above all, Vanessa's melodious voice reached Brett's ears. He got out of the truck and waited. Unaware of his presence, Vanessa, her back turned to him, was talking to a group of clients. His incessant need for her was aggravated by her refusal to answer his calls. A fresh fall of snow had kept him busy with the rush of eager clients at the lodge. He knew that Vanessa, too, had been occupied with demands for sled tours.

Only when she waved to her departing visitors, did she see him standing beside his vehicle. She seemed to recoil.

"We must talk."

She straightened her shoulders and appeared indifferent. "There's nothing to talk about. I'm not selling."

"Listen to me, damn it! I don't care about your land. It's about you and me."

"Don't come here and tell me you don't care about the land. I despise your method of operating, and your offer is far too generous. No matter what you'd pay me, I still refuse."

"What offer are you talking about?"

She shrugged her shoulders. "As if you didn't know. Your oh-so-official offer to purchase that came in my mail, when I didn't reply to the messages you left on my answering machine."

"What are you talking about? What offer to purchase?"

"Don't tell me you forgot."

Brett had temporarily forgotten. Before he had met her, he had drafted one more offer to purchase intended for Edmund, but that was long before Vanessa arrived. That offer was still in his desk drawer at the lodge.

Vanessa burst into laughter. "If that's all you wanted to say to me, Mr. Lancaster, you may leave. I have other business to attend to."

"Just a minute, I never sent an offer to buy your land."

"This time, the postmaster made no mistake. It was properly addressed to me, in my mailbox at the town's post office."

He remained transfixed, his eyes unwavering, not missing a single shift in her expression. She abruptly left him and, and taking care not to look at him, went into the cabin.

Brett considered how he was going to handle the delicate situation. Without thinking, he walked into the dog pen called by an outburst of howling. Lulik tugged at the end of her chain, pink tongue lolling from her mouth, surrounded by her pups. Absently, he reached down to pet her. On the other side of the yard, the cabin door remained resolutely shut. In that instant, the truth came to him. Ingrid! The woman must have taken the document from his desk, entered Vanessa's name and mailed it, presumably following his dinner date with her. The sheer audacity of the action left him gasping.

Anger sprung from deep inside. Vanessa was on the other side of that closed door. His immediate problem was to get her to listen long enough for him to explain how the woman he had taken pity on had betrayed him. Even then, would Vanessa believe him? He had to try, but first, he had to deal with Ingrid. He smacked a fist into his palm and rushed back to his truck. The moment he arrived back at the lodge, he called Ingrid into his office.

On seeing the stormy look on Brett's face, she ignored his invitation to sit. Instead, she drew herself to her full height.

"Ingrid, explain yourself."

"Explain what?"

Brett choked back his anger. Confrontation was not something he was good at. It brought a sour taste to his mouth. "You sent Vanessa that offer to purchase, didn't you?"

"Ah, it's *Vanessa* now."

"That's none of your business. Answer my question."

"Of course, I did. That's what you wanted. We had discussed the offer. I found it buried in your desk and figured you were so busy you forgot to send it. I saw no reason to delay."

"Who gave you permission to rifle through my desk and act on my behalf?"

"I'm the manager of the lodge. I was only looking out for the lodge's best interests."

"That offer to purchase was written up long before Vanessa arrived on the scene."

"It's my job to make the resort as prosperous as possible, with the minimum of inconvenience, not only for us but for the clients as well."

"That doesn't give you the right to search my desk or my office, nor does it give you the right to act without consulting me. In case you forgot, I'm the boss. Pack your bags, you're fired."

Ingrid's jaw sagged. "Fired? You can't. This land deal is too important for us. I felt you had delayed long enough. We had to send the offer." A seething malice burned in her eyes.

Brett clenched his jaw. His voice was level, devoid of emotion. "Ingrid, you're through here. Once more, pack your bags and go."

"Be reasonable. We're talking business, big business. What does it matter if Ms. Riley was a trifle offended? She'll get over it."

"Do I have to spell it out? I said you are dismissed as from this minute."

"This is our busiest season. You can't manage on your own."

"I said, now!" The shout must have been heard across the lake.

She trembled. "You can't fire me on the spot. I've got a contract!"

"I'll pay your salary for the balance of the damned contract. Now, go!"

She flinched. "Brett, for old times' sake———"

"Don't old times me. Those days are long past. My compassion has dried up. You've outstayed your welcome under my roof."

"Look, Brett, I'm sorry. I made an honest mistake. How was I to know she'd get upset? If you want me to leave, give me time to find a job first. I'll train Jon to take over until———"

"Now!"

"But I've nowhere to go. I can't afford to stay in a hotel in town, especially not so close to Christmas."

Brett ran a hand over his face. "Okay. You've got a point. Keep your room for one month. Jon doesn't require any training. He knows everything he needs to. Do not involve yourself in the lodge business. Understand? Use the time to find something. One month."

Ingrid murmured a few words. Whether of thanks or a curse, they were unintelligible. Her tortured face showed the strain and her shoulders slumped. "Forgive me. I didn't mean to cause problems."

"Go and do what you have to do, Ingrid. Leave me alone, I have to think."

CHAPTER TWENTY

Ingrid closed her office door and moved to the window. Her fingers tapped her mobile's keys in quick succession. To her relief, she got an immediate connection.

"Dan. I've got bad news."

"What?"

"I've been fired."

"You're the bad news!"

"One month and I've got to be gone. You must find somebody else for your business."

"Crap! Find some way to stay on and solve that little neighbor problem."

"That's exactly what I was trying to do. Brett doesn't want to buy the land anymore or cross the property."

"You're a fool. You've got to go through. It was quick and easy, far away from prying eyes. We can't run into town. The cops are watching."

"Dan, I'm out of it as of this minute."

"You'll find a way or you know what I'll do."

Tears sprung under her eyelids. How had she once loved this man? Panic set in.

"I think I've a plan."

"It'd better be a good one."

The blank screen shocked her. Angrily, she wiped her eyes. Sometimes, she thought that prison would be a better place than living under Dan's blackmail.

Chapter Twenty-One

A tear ran down Vanessa's cheek while she sat on the ground to play with the pups, oblivious to the cold. After making love with Brett, she had spent the rest of the night thinking about his admission that he loved her. It left an ache in her heart. And to think that when she sent him away, she had almost immediately called him back! For one glorious moment, she believed she could fall in love with him. Perhaps it would be easier if she did sell up and move away. To start afresh in a new place, far from him. The idea became attractive.

If it hadn't been for the absurd dispute over land, she and Brett could have enjoyed each other's company. She was convinced that the candlelight dinner and the subsequent seduction were but a ploy in his grand scheme, and she had fallen for it. Once he had breached her defenses, he cynically mailed the outrageous purchase offer, thinking she couldn't refuse, that she'd be so humiliated she'd leave.

The cold finally got to her. She led Lulik and her pups back into the pen on the porch and went indoors, only to slump on the couch. Moments later, the racket of the dogs signaled someone entering the yard. Wearily, she forced herself out of her melancholic state, assuming Patrick was bringing her order of meat. It was Alden's cheerful voice she heard greeting the dogs. Vanessa wiped the dampness from her

eyes, and, putting on a brave face, stood up to meet him. To her surprise, both father and son were there.

"Hello Alden, and Patrick. Nice of you to come."

Patrick hoisted a large carton off his shoulder. "You're so busy these days, we hardly see you anymore."

She forced a chuckle. "You're the one who books all my tours." She stood by while father and son stacked the cartons of frozen dog chow in the shed. Afterward, Alden disappeared into the pen to play with his pup.

Patrick lowered his voice. "There's a big shindig in town on Saturday night. It's a pre-Christmas tradition. Will you come?"

Under Patrick's imploring gaze, Vanessa became acutely self-conscious.

"You'll be going with your wife. I don't want to intrude."

"But you won't be intruding!"

"If I go, I'll say hi to everyone, but won't sit with you." Her voice was firm.

"Who will escort you?"

"Who needs an escort? I haven't said I'm going for sure. I'm happy with my own company." She realized she was being a shade too forceful.

"Has someone hurt you? You seem on the defensive."

She weighed her answer carefully. "A woman who chooses to live on her own often has to justify what she does or doesn't do. It's funny how nobody asks a man such questions."

"A point well made."

Alden came back. "Vanessa, when can the pups run along with the sled?"

"Not for another three or four weeks. But there's only a couple of short rides booked for Saturday. I'll tell you what we can do. We'll have time before or after the rides if you want to come over we'll put them in a box in the sled. We'll go for a couple hundred yards on Tapiskoot's trail, turn round and on the way back, we'll let them run behind the sled."

"That sounds like fun. Count on me. I'll be here early."

Patrick hid a smile. "That means you expect me to give you the day off?"

Alden looked crestfallen. "Oh, bother! I'm supposed to work at the store."

"We're going to be very busy, but probably not until ten o'clock. How about you run the dogs and be back at the store by eleven?"

"Dad, you're a pal."

Vanessa smiled her thanks at Patrick. "See you at eight, Alden."

***

Dexter Weiman returned to Wolf Hollow and made a show of booking in for the weekend. He nodded to a fit young man in a snowmobile suit on his way out, and watched Ingrid come back in. His colleague had told him she had spent the day in town and made a lot of phone calls.

"Good afternoon, Ms. Lancaster. How come you never come out on a snowmobile outing?"

Ingrid smiled with genuine warmth. "I don't care too much, or rather, I'm not that good at riding. I much prefer to stay warm here."

"Too bad, I was hoping we could go out together."

Her smile was professional. "I made sure Jon gave you your regular room. I think we should name it after you."

"I'm flattered." He picked up his keycard and walked upstairs.

So Ingrid Lancaster wasn't good at riding a snowmobile. She could have fooled him. It had taken her precisely ninety-five minutes to do what is normally a two-hour run the other day. *I wonder if we're barking at the wrong tree. I'm beginning to have the same gut feeling that served me well in the past. Beautiful Ingrid, who professes not to like snowmobiles, could be the intermediary he was looking for. And now we know all about the shack, but it's on Ms. Riley's property.*

CHAPTER TWENTY-TWO

The morning was still dark when Marcel arrived to make a start. "Before I load the sled, I wouldn't mind a cup of coffee."

"I knew you would. The pot's on the stove. How I'd love to go camping with you and those guests!"

"Do you want to swap?"

"Nice of you to offer, but I promised to deliver a lecture on life in the Arctic to Miss Docherty's fifth-grade class before the Christmas break."

"How about coming to the dance with me on Saturday?"

"I wasn't sure about going. You'd save me from the dismal prospect of sitting on my own."

"I bet you've already had a hundred offers and turned them down for me."

"Is conceit your middle name, Marcel?" Their laughter made Vanessa feel better.

"Too bad you have those short rides today."

She smiled. "And tomorrow, too, with the kids."

"You sound a bit out of sorts. Something happened lately?"

"No, nothing much."

"Anything to do with Brett?"

She stood up to put wood on the stove and to hide her face from Marcel's shrewd eyes.

"I thought he would be taking you to the dance."

"Even if he asked, I'd refuse." Her tone was more abrupt than she intended. "Have a chocolate chip cookie with your coffee. I just baked them. Let's not talk about Brett."

"Suits me."

Instead of reaching for the cookie, Marcel covered her hand with his. In her hurt condition, she welcomed his touch. If only she could see Marcel as more than a friend and colleague, life would be simpler.

Vanessa drew back her hand. "The dogs are agitating. The clients must be on their way." She made for the door. Duty called.

***

Saturday arrived, and Vanessa once more reviewed her modest wardrobe, now augmented by the box containing her dresses and other more formal wear her mother had sent. The dark blue pantsuit tempted her. At least with that, she could wear her long underwear to ensure she stayed warm all evening.

Next, her hand caressed a long, brushed velvet dress in striking magnolia color. She liked the sensuous feel of the material. Simple, yet so classy! The image of Brett came drifting into her mind. He'd be the man to appreciate her in that. She banished the thought. It mattered little whether or not he liked it. Brett Lancaster was out of her life for good.

In a stubborn gesture of defiance as much as anything else, she tried on the dress over her long thermal underwear. The neckline, trimmed with a burgundy satin braid, was high in the front, plunged steeply in the back and appeared laced together by a shimmering ribbon of the same rich burgundy color. The material molded her figure and accented the sensuous flare of her hips, before falling in gracious folds about her legs. To her relief, her woolen leggings, fitting like a second skin, didn't show. Long close-fitting sleeves, edged with the same burgundy ribbon as the neck, lent her a decidedly alluring appearance. She pinned her hair high on her head and allowed one dainty tress, with gold reflects, to escape the coil.

No sooner had she put the final touch to her makeup than there was a knock on the door.

"Come in! I'll be ready in a moment. Make yourself at home."

Marcel caught his breath when she entered the living room. "Wow, you look like a million bucks!"

Vanessa, who could never get used to compliments, hoped she wasn't blushing. "Thank you."

An awkward silence stretched between them. His eyes appraised her from head to foot, and his bold expression conveyed his approval.

"I should wrap you in furs and carry you off in my arms."

Vanessa waved her hand in the air. "That wouldn't be practical. I intend to put on my insulated boots and don my big parka, so I don't freeze between here and the community hall."

"Here in Yukon, we call them dance halls, like they did back in the Gold Rush era. At least let me carry your pumps."

Vanessa smiled at him. It was strange seeing him decked out in a dark suit and tie, his beard neatly trimmed. "You look good dressed like that."

"It sure is a change from padded overalls, but it beats me why we have to sacrifice comfort for elegance."

"Don't complain, it's only once a year."

"Alas, it's not. There's Christmas, the New Year, St. Valentine's, weddings and funerals."

He zipped up his parka and turned to Vanessa who was struggling with hers.

"Allow me."

His agile fingers soon got the fastener working. He pulled the tab up under her chin and looked into her eyes, holding her close for a few seconds.

Vanessa stiffened. For one moment, she thought he was about to kiss her. "We should leave."

The dance hall was just as Vanessa had imagined it would be. Colored balloons, streamers and spruce boughs, ornaments hid the otherwise austere decor. In the corner, strings of tiny lights and strands of tinsel decorated a tall spruce. Under the tree, beribboned fake gift boxes lay in artful disorder. People sang along with the music provided by a small orchestra of two fiddles, a guitar and an accordion.

A crowd was already gathered around tables, groaning under a bounty of tempting food. Vanessa had sent in her tray of butter tarts the evening before. Most people were locals, but there were a number of vacationers and visiting cottage owners. Once she and Marcel had deposited their outerwear at the coat check, he guided her toward the buffet. From all sides came greetings and appreciative comments from his male friends.

Instinctively, Vanessa's eyes searched for the tall silhouette of the only man who could make her heart beat a different tune. But Brett was nowhere to be seen. A mixture of relief, or was it disappointment, rose in her throat. To dismiss him from her mind, she switched her attention to Marcel and the animated conversation around her.

The band struck up a tune to the cheers of the audience. Marcel dragged her onto the dance floor. The pressure of his hand and his burning gaze unsettled her. She tried in vain to feel some emotion for him. Maybe, if she made an effort to respond, she could obliterate Brett from her mind.

The pace became too frantic, even for Marcel. He led her back to their table. The next number was more sedate, and Marcel offered his hand again. Vanessa rose, only to bump into the hard body of a man who had just stepped between her and Marcel.

"I believe this is my dance," Brett said.

Marcel glared at him. "Get the hell out of here, Lancaster!"

The two men eyed each other so fiercely that Vanessa feared they'd come to blows.

Brett's reply was equally stern. "I'm talking to Vanessa, not you."

"She's with me, and we were about to dance. Excuse us. Move aside."

"Nobody tells me to move aside." His voice was threatening yet so quiet.

Vanessa had never seen Brett look so angry, or so belligerent. In the tense atmosphere, she remembered what his real motives were. She held out her hand to her escort. "Let's dance, Marcel. The music's already started."

Brett's frustration was palpable, but he drew back.

"What's bugging him?"

"Brett's being his usual arrogant, possessive self. Let's not talk about it."

"That guy thinks money can buy anything or anyone he wants."

"You said it."

After a few steps, they slowed down and stopped.

"Brett doesn't take rejections easily." Her own flippancy surprised her.

"We were having fun till he arrived."

Vanessa looked into his eyes. "I'm having fun with you. Now, are we dancing or not?"

Marcel held her tightly. Out of the corner of her eye, Vanessa saw Brett dancing with Ingrid. If it could be called dancing. She draped herself over him, her short, strapless dress practically falling off her body.

Vanessa convinced herself it didn't matter. That she had no interest in Brett or who he chose to dance with. Yet, the more she thought about it, the more her heart ached. Now, he was partnering another woman. Why did that make her light-headed?

At the end of the dance, she excused herself to go to the ladies' room and splash cold water over her face. She stared at her reflection in the mirror and wondered why she should feel miserable simply because he had danced with Ingrid, *his sister*, for heaven's sake! He could dance with anyone he chose to, if you could call dancing the way he held her. She repeated to herself it didn't concern her, but it still rankled. This was stupid. Reason told her to put Brett out of her mind, but reason could do nothing to quell her racing heart. It simply wasn't listening. *It's only physical. Get over it.*

A malevolent woman's voice behind her intruded into her thoughts. "That's a nice little number you've got on!"

"Ingrid! Thanks. You look great yourself. That mini looks almost sprayed on." Cattiness wasn't something Vanessa ever indulged in, but the opportunity was too good to pass up. Anyhow, it was too late. The words were out. Ingrid scowled and examined her dress in the mirror. Either she failed to understand Vanessa's barb or else she was playing a clever game.

A honeyed smile came on the face of her nemesis. "It isn't everyone who can wear a dress like this. Some women need to hide their legs and... chest."

"I find long dresses give one more freedom to sit down. But I do like the way yours is cut. It's quite becoming, if you like that sort of thing."

Ingrid tugged her dress upward a fraction of an inch. "Have you thought more about Brett's offer?"

"That's none of your concern."

"On the contrary, Brett and I work very closely together on everything."

"No doubt!" Sheer willpower kept Vanessa from reacting further. She knew perfectly well what was implied. The memory of her night of love in Brett's arms made it worse. Though she admitted to herself that maybe she was reading more into Ingrid's loaded words than was really there. The woman was trying to get a reaction from her. "If you'll excuse me, my escort is waiting."

The dance hall was a torrent of noise and heat when she returned. A feeling of alienation swept over her. It was as if she didn't belong here anymore. All around her, happy couples engaged in carefree chatter and the simple pleasures of food and drink. The only place she could feel free and happy was with her faithful dogs out in the wilds of nature.

The sight of Brett with a local beauty in his arms grated on her already frayed nerves. No matter how much she repeated to herself she didn't care, it tore at her insides to see the woman clutching him with scarlet tipped fingers. Anger began mounting. He didn't look like he minded the woman's blatant advances. This was the man who professed to love her? Unbelievable.

For one furtive moment, Vanessa's eyes met Brett's. She abruptly turned away, longing to return to the quiet of her cabin. Marcel, with two glasses in his hands, stood on the opposite side of the floor, in conversation with Patrick and Stefan Browne, a guide at Wolf Hollow.

No sooner had she resumed her seat than a plump, bustling woman strode toward her and dropped into a nearby chair.

"Hi there! I'm Frances Carrigan. I understand my husband Patrick has fallen in love with you."

In total disbelief, Vanessa stared at the woman.

Mrs. Carrigan's lips formed into a lopsided smile. "Don't pretend you don't know."

Vanessa's face went blank. Ingrid and now this woman! What had she done to deserve all this?

"Patrick?"

"Drop the innocent, girly stuff. You're welcome to the jerk. I'm filing for divorce. I'll cite you as the other woman."

"No way!" Vanessa fired her two words into the woman's face. "I have nothing to do with Patrick except business."

The violent reaction appeared to take Frances aback. "It's the only solution."

"No, it isn't. It's up to you to work on your marriage. Your husband is my business partner. Nothing more. The relationship between the two of you is none of my concern."

"Patrick doesn't love me, probably never did. I was seventeen and four months pregnant when we married. Talk about a sorry mistake."

"Your son Alden is a fine young man. He loves you both and isn't responsible for your mess. He needs a mother and a father."

"Since you arrived, Patrick has been, well, different. He's impatient with me."

"If you have any love for him, you'll find a way to recapture the romance you shared when you were young."

"Not as long as you're around."

Vanessa gave a bitter laugh. "Everybody wants me gone from this place."

"You're young and single." She sighed with unveiled envy.

"Nobody told me when I wanted to make my home in Donek that so many people would be hostile."

"Do you have someone?"

"Does that concern you?"

"Marcel doesn't limit himself to one woman, you know. Next, Brett is the most eligible bachelor in town. He's another guy who's left a trail of broken hearts in his wake."

Why did this last comment hurt? Vanessa blinked back the tears. Brett meant nothing to her. She didn't want him in her life. "What has all this got to do with me? Who needs a man? I'm content on my own."

"You should get yourself a steady man to help with your business. If you did, my husband would stop acting like a stupid goat. But I've got to thank you. Your suggestion about romance has given me an idea. And business too. I have always resisted being involved in the store, even when Patrick really needed someone. I suppose from the start I've always unconsciously wanted to punish him." She stood up, paused as though wanting to say something more, then melted back into the crowd.

Dismayed, Vanessa cupped her face in her hands. Stubbornness had brought her to this north untamed country. That same quality, she decided, was going to help her overcome her present problems. Nobody would drive her away against her wishes.

She straightened up, a renewed determination in her eyes, just as Marcel leaned to place the glasses on the table beside her. His hand faltered.

"I'm terribly sorry. Did I spill some on your dress?"

"A mere splash. My own fault, I shouldn't have moved so brusquely."

"I saw you with your head in your hands. Do you have a headache?"

"No, I've just had Frances."

"I'm sorry, I don't follow you." Then his eyes lit up with mirth. "Oh! No! I get it. You should know Patrick can't look at a girl without Frances screaming adultery and filing for divorce. She's quite somebody!"

"That, she is! But I think deep down she's a very unhappy woman."

"It doesn't help that Patrick's the biggest flirt in town. But he's decent enough, he doesn't play the field."

"Glad to know that. I was worried for a while."

"Would you like me to take you home?"

"That's the best offer I've had all evening."

"That bad is it?" He helped her up and, with a hand at the small of her back, guided her toward the exit and the lobby.

"Actually I had a good time with you."

"Thanks, I appreciate your saying so."

"I'm being honest."

"I know. Uh, oh! Look who's coming."

She deliberately averted her eyes. "The enemy who wants to buy me out."

"I'm not sure how you define Mr. Brett Lancaster. I'll be the perfect gentleman. Have five minutes talk with him while I warm up the truck."

Vanessa stood still, pretending to examine the blank wall and resolutely refusing to look round. The fine hair on the nape of her neck bristled and the sense of his presence brought goose bumps to her skin. "Leave me alone."

"Not until you turn round and look at me."

"Then will you go?"

"Not until I speak to you."

Still with her back to him, she kept her tone as bland as possible. "I'm on my way home."

"I'll drive you home."

"No thanks. Marcel is taking me."

"You can't avoid me forever. We're meant to be together." There was a persuasive edge to his sexy voice.

"Never!" She spun round to face him. "You and I have nothing in common. Nothing!"

His somber eyes widened at the flash of fire in her gaze. She strode off toward the coat check. Before she reached the counter, he seized both her hands in his and drew her close.

With her hands pinned to her sides, she was powerless to move away. Deliberately slowly, and with complete disregard for anyone watching, he lowered his head until his mouth touched hers. As light as a snowflake, yet as hot as a burning ember, his lips possessed hers. She endeavored to remain impassive. Her eyes closed despite herself. She attempted to move away. He brushed her lips with his in one final kiss.

"This, sweetheart, is what we have in common."

Her chest heaved as she struggled to regain control of her embattled senses. "It's all a question of chemistry. Any woman would react in the same way." Her voice sounded as though someone else was speaking.

"That's a lie, and you know it. We've proved it. Let me take you home."

"No!" Her tremulous voice lacked strength. She sheepishly accepted her parka and boots from the teenage attendant who had pretended to be reading a book.

Unable to trust herself, Vanessa avoided his dark eyes while she pulled on her snow boots.

Marcel's voice cut into the charged atmosphere. "Are you ready to leave, Vanessa? The truck is nice and warm."

"Coming." She stumbled past Brett without giving him a second glance. Marcel placed a defensive arm around her shoulders and led her toward the exit. The cold night air helped to appease her ravaged senses.

They drove to the cabin in silence.

***

Ingrid joined Brett in the dance hall foyer. "Surely, there must be an easier way to get her to sell."

Startled, he looked at her as if discovering a stranger. "I wouldn't expect you to understand."

"Oh, but I do. I know we've had a tiff, but come and dance with me and I'll make you forget your worries." She linked arms and brushed her hips against his.

He pushed her away. "Thanks, no. I've had enough."

Ingrid pouted. "You've only danced once with me the whole evening."

Her alluring pose and seductive tone were lost on him. His mind was filled with the image of Vanessa being taken home by Marcel.

"Sorry, Ingrid. I'm not in the mood. Goodnight." He strode off, leaving her staring after him with wide eyes.

"Hey, wait! Who's going to take me home?" Her voice rose to a shriek.

Brett ignored her plea. A man pushed himself off the wall and encircled her waist. "Don't fret, baby. I will!"

Ingrid's blood left her face. "Dan!"

Chapter Twenty-Three

The symphony of howls that greeted their arrival lifted Vanessa's spirits the way nothing else could. The truck pulled into the yard, its headlights sweeping the pens.

"Uh-oh, a dog's loose!"

They both shouted at the same time. Marcel came to a stop by the gate. Vanessa, holding the skirt of her dress in one hand, tumbled out. Her free hand unhooked the two latches and braced herself for the dog barreling toward her. Lulik planted her paws on Vanessa's chest as she encircled her arms around the red dog's neck.

"Here, I have her collar. You need new collars. These are a bit worn."

"I know."

"Stefan's wife makes good collars and harnesses. And if you want any bead work, she's a master."

"I'll get in touch with her. In the meantime, I'll take Lulik and her pups into the cabin. She was nosing all the dogs." Vanessa rounded up the pups and Marcel lifted them in the back of the cab. "I can't wait for spring to bury those pen panels into the ground and have the pack socializing again."

Lulik didn't wait for an invitation to jump into the front of the cab and up on the seat.

"They really love you, those dogs. Get in. You're quivering like a leaf in the fall." His breath hung as a plume in the frigid air. Vanessa squeezed in.

With a chuckle, Marcel put the truck in gear and circled the now quiet pens. He stopped on the side of the cabin by the kitchen door. Vanessa vacillated. Courtesy dictated she ask him in for a nightcap, but she didn't want to encourage him. Lulik and the pups cascaded out of the truck and made a beeline for the cabin door.

"Would you...?"

"... Come in for coffee? Yes, please, but I shouldn't. I have a feeling this is the wrong time to tell you I'd like to know you better."

"There'll never be a right time, Marcel. Come on in, anyway. No, don't say anything."

"I promise."

Inside, Marcel added logs to the stove and looked at his blackened hands.

"That lot of firewood was recuperated from a burn. Go and wash."

Vanessa kicked off her boots at the door and padded about in stockinged feet. Her hair, disarrayed by Brett's passionate embrace, fell to her shoulders. She removed the last pins and shook out the tangled mass. Marcel was watching her. "Just beautiful. You could do a hair commercial!" His whimsical tone was in keeping with his promise to her.

"I said go wash your hands." She was beginning to relax and even chuckled while she corralled the pups into the indoor pen. They were now rather big for it, but they settled down to sleep. Lulik stretched out in front of the wood stove. Marcel headed to the bathroom.

A commotion in the kennel outside interrupted the coffee making. A diesel powered truck screeched to a halt in front of the porch. She sighed. Brett!

Vanessa looked toward the bathroom hoping Marcel would come out right away. She wanted him there, in the living room, when Brett came in. The knock sounded again as her hand hovered over the latch. *Pretend there's no one here. He might go away. Marcel's truck is in the back. There's no one here.* She opened the latch.

"I came" His words came in a cloud of frozen breath.

For a while, neither of them moved. Vanessa shivered in stockinged feet on the plank floor, her voice a raw whisper. "You had better go."

Brett's eyes remained fixed on her slender form. "You avoided me all evening. Give me a chance."

Deep turmoil etched into her face. He walked past her into the cabin before she could reply. And with him in rushed the cold air. Vanessa realized the futility of arguing with him and closed the door. Lulik jumped on him.

"I wasn't expecting you."

He winced. "Why not? Is Marcel still...?" All the while, his hands smoothed out the dog's thick fur, a gesture which had her almost purring.

Of course, all females succumb to his charm. The instant awareness that she had the upper hand gave her back confidence. "What's it to you?"

"You can't!" Not a spoken word but a growl.

Vanessa scowled. "You're too full of your own importance."

He held out his arms. The tips of his fingers rested lightly on her shoulders. A sigh, which was more of a strangled sob, escaped her throat. Heat emanated from him, inviting her. Inevitably, her body leaned forward as if drawn by some primal instinct toward his broad chest.

"I needed to see you." His tone was pleading.

"Now that you've seen me, you can go back to your lodge." Her flippant remark cost her all her energy.

He narrowed the distance between them. "You're beautiful in that dress."

"Thanks. I've already been told that this evening." Vanessa tried to put a hard edge to her voice but did not succeed. A volcano had awoken inside her. She pushed away and stepped back.

A flicker in Brett's eyes alerted her to a movement behind her. She swung around. Marcel, in shirt sleeves, his tie over his shoulder and with several shirt buttons undone, padded barefoot from the bathroom. "Oh, hi Brett! Did you come to join us for coffee?"

Brett dropped his hands to his side and glowered at Marcel. "No thanks. I was just leaving." His face hardened into a tight mask. Jaw clenched, he looked straight into Vanessa's eyes, the subdued light hiding her brimming tears. Vanessa read something akin to contempt in his. Without another word, he stalked off into the night.

Vanessa turned to face Marcel. "I'm sorry..."

"You didn't tell me to play the part of the lover. I did it all by myself."

"It's not fair on you. It's like I'm using you."

"I enjoyed that little episode. I'm glad to help. Right now, I think I, too, had better go or I'll have trouble maintaining my good behavior."

"Marcel, I think you're the kindest man in Donek."

"I'd be happier if you could think of me as more than just a kind man." He held up his hand. "I know. I'll see you tomorrow. We've got a tour business to run." His grin helped restore her fragile composure.

Marcel replaced his jacket and stuffed his necktie into his pocket. He retrieved his boots. At the door, he gave her a bear hug.

"Thanks, Marcel. For everything."

For a while, she braved the numbing chill on the open porch, listening to the sound of his truck fade away. It wouldn't be difficult to fall in love with a caring man like that. Then why didn't she? It was always Brett's dark eyes that drifted into her mind when she least expected it. She reminded herself she hadn't come to Donek to find love. This was where she had planned to turn her dream into reality. And she still intended doing just that. Why should she move? The conflict with her neighbor had a resolution; she only had to complain of harassment to the Mounties and they would warn him to leave her alone. It left a bitter taste in her mouth, but if it came to that, she'd do it. Hopefully, it would be enough without having to resort to legal means and court orders.

Lulik's wet nose nuzzled her hand. Vanessa bent to stroke her head and saw the look of concern in the animal's wise brown eyes. "You feel my anguish, don't you, Lulik? You know when I'm upset or happy and you're always there to share my joys and sorrows. You never fail me. You're not complicated like humans are. Your love is absolute and unconditional for those who love you."

Lulik's answer was a velvet soft tongue across Vanessa's cheek. "Let's get back inside. Unlike you, I'm not wearing a fur coat."

CHAPTER TWENTY-FOUR

As soon as he returned to the lodge, Brett killed the engine and strode to the snowmobile garage. Minutes later, he was venting his frustration by speeding through the night, across the windswept lake and up through the trees. The beam from his snowmobile headlights pierced the forest darkness.

Oblivious to the pitching of the machine over the bumpy trail, he tried to erase the image of the long-haired goddess from his mind. She was his. They belonged together. No wonder men were driven crazy if this was what it meant to be in love. He wanted her to be there beside him when he awoke in the morning. He needed her in his life, the way the earth needs the sun. Yet he couldn't hold her. She was a free spirit, and she had shut him out, cruelly wounding him by inviting another man into her life. That other man, though his long-time friend, was not worthy of her. The gritting of his teeth resonated in his head.

The thought of Marcel caressing her incensed him. Maybe he had been wrong to tell her he loved her. He should have courted her slowly and proved his love before he spoke. Maybe she was still grieving for her husband, dead five years ago. Instead, his out of the blue declaration had scared her off. To complicate an already complicated picture, there was the stupid matter of the land. She hadn't believed him, and she wouldn't now, not after all that had happened.

And she had turned to his friend. Knowing Marcel, it wouldn't take him long to make love to her. Marcel had a way with females. Vanessa was a passionate woman. Brett choked with rage. The laid-back Marcel would give her all the comfort she needed, all the support. Marcel wasn't after her land. He hadn't complained about her dogs because some manager told him to do so. Brett gave himself a mental slap across the head. He hadn't seen to what extent Ingrid had manipulated him. He had just not seen it coming or more likely, had ignored the warning signs. Why was he incapable of seeing hidden motives in people's words or deeds? He himself was not a complicated individual. When he said something, he meant it.

So intent he was on his thoughts that he didn't hear the engine falter. A moment later, the motor died so abruptly he was pitched forward into darkness. For one uncomprehending instant, he stared at the dead machine before reality flooded his brain. In his eagerness to obliterate the hateful scene of Marcel, half undressed, emerging from Vanessa's bathroom, he hadn't checked the gas in his machine. He stood up and shook off the snow. Gingerly, he flexed his arms and legs.

Brett jammed his wool toque low over his ears. Dance shoes and a city suit were no protection in the frigid outdoors. Despite his parka, he shivered from the cold. So absorbed by his thoughts while driving, he hadn't felt the keen edge of winter.

The small baggage compartment contained only a spare fleece jacket and a flashlight. He switched it on and cursed when he saw the feeble yellow flicker it produced. The cold had drained the battery. He should have put it inside his pocket or switched on the heated bag. Practical matters had not even crossed his mind. Although he knew what to expect, he checked the reserve fuel tank. It, too, was empty. Grimly, he unzipped his parka and put on the jacket underneath. In the hope his body warmth would revive the battery, he tucked the flashlight into his inner pocket.

His eyes now accustomed to the dark, he looked around in an effort to determine his surroundings. Clouds filled the sky and the lack of any light from the moon and stars rendered it difficult to orientate himself.

He spent five minutes chastising himself for leaving without his survival equipment. Love really had made a fool of him.

He shuddered and turned his attention to the urgent matter of survival and seeing about extricating himself from the predicament he had foolishly got himself into. His watch indicated the time elapsed since setting out. From that, he calculated his approximate distance of travel. Although his route had meandered through forest and lakes, he knew he was too far from Donek to walk back in the cold, through deep snow, even following the trail in the packed snow left by his snowmobile. In dismay, he glanced down at his shoes. When leaving the dance, his mind was so roiled up, he hadn't even put on his winter boots. His best chance was the Evergreen Lodge. He reckoned it should be some way in the north-west. He thought, hoped, he had remained on the right trails. It had to be, if not, he doubted he would survive very long. Ellis and Rebecca would help him, no matter it was the middle of the night. He worked out his direction with the compass in his watch, praying he had instinctively taken the right trail, and forged ahead.

No one had traveled the trail recently. This he knew from the pristine condition of the snow. He reached a clearing after an hour's hard slogging through unbroken snow and recognized an outcrop. He was on the right track. Numbed with cold, relief renewed his failing strength despite the weather closing in. A few large flakes of snow struck his face, harbingers of what was to follow. He calculated it wouldn't be more than another hour before he reached the lodge. The cold numbed his feet and rose up his legs. A suit, even over long underwear, was not the accouterment needed for backcountry trekking.

Like an automaton, he trudged on through the snow and focused his attention on making sure he didn't go astray in the dark. Despite the cold gnawing at his face, perspiration beaded his skin under his clothes. Aware of the danger of sweating in extreme conditions, he slowed down. Hypothermia was gaining. Just as his pace began to drag, he stumbled on a hard-packed snowmobile trail. His spirits lifted as he painfully pushed himself upright. The trail would lead him directly to the lodge, of that he was sure. Now that the walking was easier, his mind began to relax a little. He had already lost feeling in his legs. Instinct and his mind made them move on, one step... another...

When he staggered into the yard of the darkened lodge, two enormous shapes bounded toward him. "Bingo! Princess!" He slurred the dogs' names. The pair of Tervuerens barked briefly and whined, rubbing themselves against his legs. Bingo pulled back and barked a signal toward the lodge.

A man's voice called from a window. "Who's there?" Light flooded the area in front of the log building. Ellis opened the front door. "Damn me, Brett!"

Brett crumpled into the lobby. He grabbed the wall to stand again, swaying from fatigue and hypothermia. Ellis rushed to hold him.

"Sorry to wake you up, Ellis."

"No problem. But you're covered in frost and snow. Trouble?"

"Ran out of gas." His words slurred.

While dragging him to an armchair in front of the dying fire, Ellis pointed a finger and laughed. "You? You ran out of gas? You must either be drunk or in love. Anyway, sit and get thawed out." His voice took a hint of concern. "You're not even wearing a snowmobile suit!"

"Long story." The edge of unconsciousness tugged at his body.

The dogs slipped in and headed straight for the mat beside the stove.

Ellis removed his friend's clothes rigid with ice. Soon, naked and wrapped up in a wool afghan, Brett was lying on the sofa in front of the wood stove, but not too close, sipping warm water. Bingo and Princess came to sniff him. In one bound, they were on the couch leaning against him. Their body heat acting as a furnace. Ellis massaged his limbs, keeping his friend's feet against his chest. He told him how lucky he was not to have frostbite.

Pain shot through Brett's limbs as warmth returned to his body. Ellis went to get an Icelandic wool blanket and a tray of Danish pastries and coffee.

"I'll make you up a bed. You sleep here tonight. In the morning, we'll take a can of gas and go back to your machine. I'll lend you some suitable clothing too."

"Thanks. I appreciate it."

"So, tell me, who's the woman? There's got to be one. Only a woman could make you forget to gas up."

"Don't laugh. I'm in love with her, but she doesn't believe me."

Ellis whistled. "Met your match, did you?"

Brett stared at the flickering firelight without answering.

"Anyone I know?"

"No, she's new to these parts." He propped his chin into his hands.

"The Dog Lady?"

Brett jerked back his head. "The who?"

"That's how she's known around here."

A dreamy look came over Brett's face. "She's... she's unique."

"I have to meet this woman who's been able to unsettle you. In the meantime, I'd better show you to your room, before Becky comes down to find out what all the ruckus is about."

Ellis banked the stove. "Okay, you lazy critters, I guess you can sleep here tonight. You've done your part." He patted the dogs and led the way upstairs.

After a few hours of sleep, Brett, in pain, roused himself. Ellis was already downstairs, brewing a pot of coffee.

"Eat to get enough energy. How do you feel?"

"So painful it was as if I had been it by a train."

"Sleepy?"

"No. My mind never gave up. I did not hallucinate."

Another cup and more pastries, Brett's color returned. In his borrowed snowmobile suit and boots, he climbed onto the snowmobile's passenger seat. Ellis strapped a jerry can of fuel to the carrier and they set off.

"I can hardly believe I walked all this way last night in dance shoes," Brett shouted over the engine roar.

"It'll take more than that to kill you."

After refueling, Brett fired up his machine. Ellis followed him to the outskirts of Donek. They covered the distance to Donek in less than a couple of hours. The two friends parted with a laugh and a handshake. At the lodge, guests drifted into the dining room. In the private quarters, Ingrid, in a stunning white peignoir with dramatic décolleté, hurried to the side door.

"Brett! Goodness me! You look a fright. Where have you been... or ought I not ask?"

"Stay out of my hair."

"Let me help you." She took a step toward him.

"Get on with packing your bags. I don't need help."

"We have to look over the schedule for today. A lot of staff are down with the flu."

"Jon is taking care of scheduling. You're not working here anymore. Now move."

He headed for his apartment, but Ingrid was on her feet and cut him off at the foot of the stairs.

She placed a manicured hand on his sleeve. "Brett, can't we..?"

Brett brushed her aside and took the stairs two at the time.

CHAPTER TWENTY-FIVE

"Lulik, back to the pen! I have to attend to the housework, and your pups can't stay here. They still need you to learn good sled dog manners." Vanessa wondered if other people talked to their dogs the way she did. Most likely because it was the best therapy she knew. Dogs didn't understand the spoken word, but they recognized the stress or the joy in the voice. They never failed to give comfort or share in the excitement.

Later, on her way to town, she passed the drive leading to the lodge and her heart constricted. A spiral of need took root in the pit of her stomach. It was the need to be loved, the need to love a man. Nothing would make her happier than to close her eyes and rest her head on such a man's shoulder. A sigh burst from her. But that could never be Brett's shoulder. If only she could trust him. If only she could end the feelings tearing her heart to pieces. Though, wouldn't he take those feelings and scatter them to the wind? Her emotions swelled and ebbed, leaving her drained. It had never been like that with Walter. They had fallen in love at a race meeting, married quickly and went on to win races. They thought as one. Happiness was having each other.

The parking lot was almost empty when Vanessa arrived at the grocery store. With practiced efficiency, she loaded her shopping cart. Her next clients weren't scheduled until the mid-afternoon, but there was a camping trip to prepare for and Marcel was calling in at noon. She had never been so busy or enjoying her work so much. That was so long as she didn't think about Brett.

List in hand, she pushed her cart along an aisle, oblivious to a woman with her back turned. Moments later, she was startled by the woman's high-pitched voice.

"So we meet again!"

"Ingrid!"

"Shopping, I see."

Vanessa wondered what the obvious remark was leading up to. "Why else would I be doing here, in the grocery store?" Her reply was cool, but polite. There was no point in aggravating the tension that already existed between them.

"For a person on her own, you sure have a full cart. I suppose you don't come here too often."

"I'm pretty busy most days." What was the woman leading to?

"Good for you. Who would have thought that you could make a living from a bunch of dogs?"

The woman was definitely leading up to something. Vanessa ratcheted up her guard. "Someone had to try."

"And you succeeded. I do admire you so. By the way, you do have a commercial kennel license, don't you?"

The question caught Vanessa off guard. "When I talked to the Chamber of Commerce last summer, they said I didn't need one."

"It's not the Chamber of Commerce that's responsible. It's the municipality."

"I paid my property taxes and asked many questions about keeping dogs in the community or rather outside the town limits. I don't recall any talk of a commercial kennel license. I don't sell dogs."

"But you must have one. All the mushers do."

"How would you know, since the clerk told me I didn't need one?"

"Brett is on the council. I guess as long as you let him share your bed, he'll let you get away without a license."

Vanessa flushed bright crimson. A malicious smile played over Ingrid's lips. "Well, you wouldn't be the first one to fall for him. As usual, he'll get what he wants and then, it'll be goodbye, Vanessa, sweetie pie."

Anger flared in Vanessa's eyes. "What makes you so sure I've fallen for him, as you claim?"

"My dear, we were brought up together. We enjoy what you might call an open relationship. We know what the other is doing. If he fancies a girl, he'll even go as far as to offer marriage, if that's the only way to get what he wants. Don't flatter yourself too much. In your case, it's not your body he's after so much as your land."

A wave of nausea rose in Vanessa's throat. "I can assure you that as far as Brett is concerned, there's no question of marriage or sharing of beds, or me giving up my land. I'm here to stay, and stay I will. Thank you for your invaluable information. Excuse me, I've got some important matters to attend to."

"Don't take it like that, honey. I'm really on your side and want to help." Ingrid's voice dropped to a whisper. "You don't realize what I've had to put up from Brett, over the years."

"That's your problem, not mine." Vanessa swung her cart round and left the woman standing.

The checkout clerk looked at Vanessa's hand shake as she swiped her card. "Pretty cold outside, isn't it?"

"Yes, it is."

Vanessa carelessly dumped her carton of groceries in the box of the pickup. On the edge of town, she stopped on the shoulder to retrieve the bags of perishables and bring them into the cab so they wouldn't freeze. No point in spoiling good food on account of her meeting with the venomous woman.

All the way home, Ingrid's words echoed in Vanessa's head and dripped poison into her heart. The woman was lying about Brett, surely? But why was she hurting so badly? *It's love*, murmured an insidious voice in her mind. But love is supposed to make a person happy. At this moment, she felt more wretched than she had ever been in her life. She slowed down past the entrance to Wolf Hollow Lodge and glimpsed a group of people dressed in snowmobile suits milling about in front. Brett was doubtless among them. She looked away and gunned her truck down the road.

The clients who came that afternoon kept her so busy that she had no time to think. When the day was over, she dropped, exhausted, into an armchair. Her respite was short-lived. A truck entered her driveway. *If it's him, I'll pretend I'm not here.*

This time, her fears were unfounded.

"Hello, Vanessa. Merry Christmas!"

The boy's cheeky smile lightened Vanessa's mood.

"Oh, hi Alden!"

"Can I go and see my pup?"

"Do that. I'll get you cookies. I suppose you're hungry?"

"As usual." His awkward grin was full of youthful charm.

"I'm going to spoil your appetite for dinner." Vanessa felt like laughing with him.

"No chance of that. You know I'm leaving right after New Year on my exchange trip?"

"Yes, you told me." Vanessa tried to hide her regret. She valued Alden's help.

"Well, I've decided not to go."

"You can't! It's a wonderful opportunity for you. Too good to miss."

"It was until you came. I've always wanted to work with dogs, and we're now at the busiest time. You're off shortly on a four-day camping trip, so you need me to deal with things here. I'm canceling my exchange."

"No, Alden, no. You made friends with that young man in Alaska. What's his name?"

"Poyuk."

"Right. Poyuk would be very disappointed if you didn't turn up. Though it was considerate of you to think of me."

"But you can't manage on your own."

Vanessa suppressed a smile. "No, you're irreplaceable. But I'll get Janine and Taylor to come and help. They're not as skilled as you, but they're learning fast. It's amazing how enthusiasm makes up for lack of experience."

"I gave them some pointers on handling the dogs."

"In which case, you may leave with your mind at rest. Everything will be fine back here."

Alden gave a loud sigh. "If you're sure."

"I am. Imagine passing up the chance to live six weeks in Alaska, where the sled dog is king! But I do appreciate your willingness to sacrifice such an opportunity. Anyway, did you pick a name for your puppy?"

"Would Kiviok be good?"

"It sure would."

"I read a book on Inuit people. Kiviok was a shaman."

"He was indeed. A tragic shaman. He lead his people out onto the ice and they drowned when the floe broke."

"But my Kiviok won't do that. I'll teach him well."

"I know you will."

"Alright, I've got to get home. Where are you spending Christmas? My dad wanted to invite you, but mom objected. She said it was a special day for us as a family. She told me she and dad are going to renew their marriage vows. She works in the store now."

"That's wonderful! I'm so happy for you. As for Christmas dinner, Marcel and I have been invited over to Jimmy Redhead's place."

"Nice guy. I've heard Stefan is angling to come and guide for you. He'd rather handle dogs than a snowmobile."

"But the lodge pays better than I can."

"I agree. With four kids, Stefan sure needs the money."

"Now, off with you, Alden. And have a good time in Alaska."

When the young man had gone, thoughts of Brett came tumbling into Vanessa's mind. How was he spending Christmas? Would there be a big party up at the lodge? Rumor had it that it was the place to be during the festive season. At least, she knew he'd be too busy to come and see her. Though, the thought of him spending Christmas with Ingrid made her feel sick. She was quite sure that the woman was trying to get under her skin by insinuating she, Ingrid, shared Brett's bed. Even though they were not related by blood, they were still family. So the thought of a shared intimacy came across as tacky at best. All the same, what was it to her? He was welcome to her and she to him.

***

The morning was shaking off the night and Vanessa was already in the pen trying to clean up, hampered in her task by the young dogs, who clamored for her attention. Lulik was excited and jumped up and down in circles. Vanessa patted the dog's head, whose muzzle pointed in the direction of the driveway. A familiar vehicle was working its way along the snow choked road up to the cabin. "All right, calm down, Lulik."

Vanessa put away her tools and picked up the bowls to wait for Brett to arrive.

"Merry Christmas, Vanessa."

"Hello Brett. Merry Christmas to you."

Her heart beat a tattoo against her ribs, but she dominated the impulse to rush into his arms. Lulik howled frantically for attention. She knew she shouldn't jump up on people, but that didn't stop her. Brett tore his gaze from Vanessa to pet his canine admirer. Vanessa followed slowly and watched him hug the furry animal. A howl of jealousy sounded from the pens.

"Amazing how that dog loves you. Now that you've patted Lulik, you're obliged to do the same to the others." Vanessa leaned against the gate and watched him make the rounds.

"I just came to ask if we could call a truce? Seeing it's Christmas Day?"

"Truce it is."

"Do you have plans for today?"

"Marcel and I are going out for a traditional dinner." Shame washed over her as she continued to let Brett believe that she and Marcel were living together.

"I see."

The two words fell from his lips with such misery they plucked at Vanessa's heartstrings. She nonetheless resisted the feelings that drew her toward him.

"In which case, I guess I'd better go." Brett's eyes raked Vanessa's body, only half concealed by the unzipped parka. As if searching for an excuse to stay, he picked up each wriggling pup in turn and stroked the woolly fur. "They're mighty big for twelve weeks. Look at these hefty paws."

"That's the breed. They're already living in the pen getting to know the big dogs."

He finally got behind the wheel of his truck with obvious reluctance.

On her own again, Vanessa was determined to make Christmas Day a happy one. She secured Lulik and the pups and got ready.

Chapter Twenty-Six

With Boxing Day and the parties over at least until New Year's Eve, Ingrid turned her attention to the pressing business of getting rid of Vanessa. So far, nothing had worked. Then she'd have to convince Brett to reconsider and keep her on as manager. Although he had told her not to get involved with the guests, she did so behind his back. Guests tipped well and Jon paid no attention to what she was doing. A plan had formed in her head and now was the time to execute it. She grabbed a pen and wrote furiously.

She tore the paper from the notepad and called her junior employee. "Toni, drive into town and get these items from Pathfinder's, would you?"

The girl's face lit up. "I sure will, ma'am."

"Did I hear you say that your boyfriend Alden is leaving tomorrow?"

"That's right."

"You're going to miss him, I guess. Well, no need to rush back. I can manage here. Oh, by the way. While you're at the store, ask Mr. Carrigan for the list of the bookings for Tapiskoot. Ms. Riley is too busy with her dogs and clients to go to town to fetch it."

"I'll gladly do that for her."

Ingrid watched the girl go. For the next three hours, she busied herself near the foyer to keep an eye on the front door.

Toni had a dreamy look in her eyes when she returned. She handed three bags to Ingrid.

"Thanks." Casually, Ingrid peered into the bags and, to her satisfaction, saw a file folder marked Tapiskoot in a red bag.

"Any other errands you need doing, ma'am?"

"Not immediately. You can go back to your duties until I call you." The silly girl didn't even understand that she had been told to take orders only from Jon.

As soon as Toni disappeared into the kitchen, Ingrid took the folder to her office, closing the door firmly behind her.

In-store bookings for the next two weeks were laid out in Patrick's neat handwriting. She scanned and printed one booking, took some measurements, switched on her computer and found a template with the word 'canceled' written as though made by an ink stamp. When she finished scanning and printing the Tapiskoot bookings with the template, most entries were marked *canceled* with reasons given, such as 'sickness' or 'unexpected emergency' appended next to them. Ingrid gave a grunt of pleasure at the technology at her disposal and hid the booking sheets copies under the desk calendar. Later that day, she intended making a few well-placed phone calls. Now there was the matter of the emails. She didn't have a clue on how to begin hacking into someone's emails or computer, but if she could get access to Patrick's computer, it'd be easy.

She returned to the kitchen, and replaced the folder with the originals, now amended to her liking, in the red shopping bag. She then buzzed Toni on the intercom.

"Yes, ma'am?"

"I was planning to go to Tapiskoot, but something's cropped up. You did get the booking folder from Mr. Carrigan, didn't you?"

"It's in the red bag, ma'am. Actually, Mr. Carrigan wasn't there, so Alden gave it to me."

"Ah, yes, here it is. Would you run down to Tapiskoot for me and deliver the folder?"

"Of course. I'll take care of it."

Hopefully Vanessa would be out sledding somewhere. Ingrid watched through the window until Toni's blue Toyota disappeared beyond the trees. Ingrid then retrieved the copies she had made and reached for the phone. Two hours later, she was on her way to town.

She entered Pathfinder store and went directly to Patrick's office. "Hello Patrick. Did you get that part, Brett ordered?"

"Right this morning. It's still in the crate in the shed. Did you want to take it?"

"If it's not too much trouble."

"I'll get it and put it straight in your car. It's good you came today because I won't be here for a few days. I'm leaving tomorrow."

"Conference?"

"The annual trade fair. Can't miss that. There're so much new stuff coming out."

As soon as he left, Ingrid, barely believing her good luck, sat at his computer. She pushed the office door half closed. Her lucky streak continued. The email on the screen was addressed to Vanessa, with the website bookings attached. Without hesitation, she sent it to herself. She then wrote a brief note about the lack of clients due to the flu outbreak and sent it to Tapiskoot. The message showed the reply arrow. With the spotty internet connection outside town, she hoped it wouldn't arrive until after Patrick had gone. She left the screen on the inbox and snatched the new in-store booking sheet.

Satisfied, she sidled up in the store and absorbed herself in examining the thermal underwear on a nearby shelf, seconds before Patrick came back.

"It's in your car."

"Thanks, you're a dear."

Patrick went back to his office and swiveled the chair in front of his computer. He frowned at the inbox on the screen. "Did I send that email? Ah, yes, the arrow shows."

"Sorry, boss," a clerk poked his head in. "Someone, a Mr. Palle I think, at the front desk asked for you."

"Yeah, he phoned." Patrick pulled down the Tapiskoot page bookings from the website. "Oh, good, that's all done." He made his way to the store counter.

Between customers and preparations for a four-day business trip, Patrick was busy. He called the store manager. "Gary, when I'm gone, don't forget to check the Tapiskoot mailbox for the bookings which come through the website."

"Don't you worry. I'll forward them and will get one of the girls to deliver the print copies to Ms. Riley, if I can't go myself."

Back at the lodge, Ingrid disappeared into her office to make a few more phone calls.

CHAPTER TWENTY-SEVEN

Together, Marcel and Vanessa finished the chores, while their contented clients patted the dogs one last time before leaving. Vanessa mounted the steps to the cabin and unhooked the red shopping bag from the door handle.

Marcel looked up. "Vanessa, while I'm in town, would you like me to check your mailbox? It must be full if people leave messages on the door."

"Someone must have delivered the bag. It's next week bookings, but thanks, I'd appreciate if you got my other mail. In the meantime, I'll get some supper ready."

"I'll run. See you soon."

Marcel came back an hour later with an armful of mail and dropped it on top of the red bag on the side table. "Whatever you're cooking, it smells good."

"It's my secret recipe for cupcakes. The rest of the meal is keeping warm on the stove."

They ate a leisurely supper and sat in front of the stove to drink their coffee.

"Marcel, you're sure you don't want to accept that guiding job in the Sawtooth Mountains?"

"It lasts about three weeks right in the middle of our busiest period."

Vanessa nodded. "I'd keep your position open."

"What I really mean is that you'd have difficulty coping on your own."

"True, but you're giving up a well-paid opportunity."

"I'm making a good enough living at Tapiskoot, and it'll only get better."

"I hope so. The scenery must be fantastic in those mountains. Does the outdoors company have other guides?"

"I spoke to the lodge owner up there a couple of days ago and he still doesn't have a spare guide. That's why he asked me, even though he'll have to pay my flight from Canada. If I don't go, he'll have to go with his clients himself. He's close to retirement and by far prefers to stay home rather than lead a strenuous expedition."

"The clients who came on our last camping trip were really singing your praises."

"You were the one who charmed them. They want to come again. Anyhow, I'd best be on my way."

He put on his boots and parka. With one hand on the door handle, he looked into Vanessa's eyes. "You know, I feel an incredible happiness just being here with you and the dogs."

Vanessa opened her mouth to protest, but he raised his hand.

"Don't say it. I know." He kissed the top of her head and opened the door, blasting her with an icy gust of wind.

From outside, Lulik whined so plaintively that Vanessa relented. "You like it inside, don't you, old girl?" She let the dog in along with the six growing pups. "My! my! Puppies! Your fur is so thick. So you missed me?" For the next hour, she played with them. Finally, she took them back to the pen before they completely wrecked the house.

It wasn't until noon the next day, on her return from giving a sledding clinic to a group of visitors, that Vanessa had time to open her mail. In rapid succession, she made heaps of the letters, magazines and junk mail, the latter to be pitched into the stove. In high spirits, she opened the folder from the red bag, and took out the booking schedule.

At first, she thought she'd made a mistake. Her finger ran down the page. Most of the bookings were canceled. Her eyes opened wide as she stared at the sheets of paper in her hand. Only a bare handful of locals remained for the entire two-week period, and those were short excursions on the lake. She rushed to her computer. There was no more doubt. The email from Patrick confirmed the sad news. The many cancelations left her stunned.

There was no time to get depressed. Her afternoon clients would arrive at any moment. She hastily stuffed the folder and the mail into her desk drawer. A tense smile fixed in place, she went outside to welcome the guests Marcel had picked up from their hotel in town.

Twilight was casting strange shadows among the spruce trees when they returned with the group. Once they reached home, chaos reigned until the dogs were picketed and fed. Vanessa was unable to share the excitement of her clients. Marcel did his share of work, making up for Vanessa's lack of spirit by laughing and joking with the people over the events of the day.

She failed to understand the cause of the merriment. In her distracted state, she missed half of the story. Nor did she mind as long as they were satisfied. Once they had warmed up over steaming mugs of hot chocolate, they coaxed their host and hostess to eat supper with them back at the hotel.

The night was well-advanced when Vanessa was able to take Marcel aside in the hotel parking lot. "Is it too late for you to get hired back on the Sawtooth Mountains expedition?"

"It probably is. They're leaving Monday. But I told you, I'm taking care of your camping tours."

"That's the problem. There are no bookings after the weekend."

"What?"

Vanessa forced a smile at his look of disbelief.

"We've had a few cancelations. The lot, in fact."

"Why on earth would so many people cancel?"

She sighed. "It looks as though the flu is taking its toll. I think those are city folks used to their comfort. If they don't feel too good, they don't fancy spending a day out in the cold."

"Alright, we'll just have to tighten our belts." He placed a reassuring hand on her shoulder.

Vanessa moved out of reach. "I don't know how long I might be without clients. I'd rather you tried to get that job."

"I ought to share the hard times with you. I have savings." His voice was soft, so much so that tears welled up in the corner of her eyes. She was thankful for the darkness. One thought filled her mind. Sharing the hard times, as well as the good, that was what love was all about, wasn't it? But she didn't feel anything for him beyond a profound respect. "Lean times won't pay your mortgage."

"I don't have a family to support and my log cabin is too small to merit a mortgage."

"All the same, it won't impress your banker." She tried a laugh, but it sounded more like a whimper.

Marcel pulled her into his arms and kissed her on the lips.

"I know I shouldn't kiss my boss. That was just a brotherly kiss. Are you okay?"

"Please, promise me you'll phone and get on that expedition."

"I will. The pay is sky high. It'll buy some dog food."

"Oh no, Marcel. You don't need——"

"Quiet, woman! In times of need, backcountry people stick together. Just wait and see." He opened the truck door for her. "Get in before we both freeze in this wind."

Vanessa drove home, comforted by Marcel's tenderness, yet unhappy because she was unable to give him more than friendship.

Next morning, she was rearranging her schedule, when the phone rang. Marcel announced he was hired to guide the Sawtooth expedition and was leaving immediately to catch a plane.

"That's great news!"

"Are you sure you can manage for the next few days?"

"It's only for the weekend. Taylor and Janine will be here to help. I'll double up the picnic party. Taylor's getting good at handling the sled."

"I should have known you'd have it all figured out."

"Have a safe trip to the Sawtooth" She put down the phone and threw herself into the preparations. The next three days promised to be hectic. Then it would be the void, brought on by the spate of cancelations.

CHAPTER TWENTY-EIGHT

On the following Monday, Ingrid returned to Pathfinder's. She noted with relish that Gary was looking harassed in his effort to keep things running smoothly and staff and customers happy. As silently as a cat, she sneaked into the office and reached for the computer. She glanced nervously at the half-closed door. Patrick compiled all the bookings into one document, but Gary didn't. It was taking more time than she wanted to spend in this office. In a matter of minutes, she had forwarded all the emails to herself. Finally, she deleted them all. She grabbed the in-store booking sheet and hurried out.

"Gary, I see you're super busy. I'll take the bookings for Tapiskoot. It's just a stone's throw from the lodge. I'll deliver them, no problem."

"Thanks, that saves me a trip. I hate this January sale period. The boss always manages to get away at this time, lucky guy. But I guess it's good for the business."

"And for the customers who love it." Her parka wide opened, she was undulating her body and batting her eyelids, perfectly aware of the effect she was having on hot-blooded Gary. Her scheme was working nicely.

***

Vanessa pored over her account books for the hundredth time. If she hadn't gone to the expense of three additional sleds and the tents, she could have weathered this bad spell. Up until now, that sizeable outlay had been justified, so too was the extra clothing she'd purchased to lend to clients who, in spite of her recommendations, came unprepared. In addition to these costs, she had paid Brett the cargo surcharge for her new dogs, an ever-present reminder of her confrontation with him in the Whitehorse cargo terminal. Then there were those expensive ads in the outdoor magazines and the banner she took on the web. Two weeks without revenue would wipe out her profits and the meager savings she was rebuilding. Brett hadn't cashed the check, but she was leaving the funds aside in her second account to cover it for when he did. In her mind, this was not her money.

She pulled out the invoice from Pathfinder Outfitters and wrote a check to cover the sleds, the dog food and clothes. Now her balance showed red. Patrick, she had no doubt, would extend her credit, but she had her pride to think of. Business would pick up again. This was the downside of self-employment. One never knew what to expect.

Again, her thoughts drifted back to Brett. He was away somewhere in the north, leading an expedition. Although she daren't admit it, even to herself, she missed him despite their conflict. There would be no more visiting when he returned. Not now that he believed Marcel was her lover.

As she contemplated the bleak days ahead, she wondered how genuine his declaration of love had really been. Not that she imagined anything would bring an end to the bitter wrangling over trails and land. Perhaps he hadn't counted on her being so stubborn.

If she'd let her feelings take over, where would Ingrid fit into the puzzle? She shook her head. Brett's love was an absurd notion.

Ingrid's words came back to haunt her. *He'll even go as far as to offer a girl marriage, if that's the only way he can get what he wants... in your case, your land.* Vanessa raked her hand through her hair. She didn't want to give any credit to the spiteful woman's word but couldn't help remembering them. "*Right! Remember that and stop building stupid dreams!*" She spoke aloud to lift herself out of her somber mood and soothe the hurt. Outside, light snow floated leisurely about the cabin and got hooked on the trees. She watched, with amusement, the pups chase snowflakes drifting into their pen. By afternoon, the sun was shining. Days were getting marginally longer. In the pen, the young dogs frolicked in and out of their straw shelter, and the adult dogs rattled their chains as they shook and stretched. Vanessa decided to take out a team to keep them conditioned.

The muted thump of an occasional pine branch, springing back after discarding its load of snow, was the only sound in the stillness of the forest. Surrounded by such tranquility, Vanessa found it hard to remain melancholic. Only, the calm didn't last long. Like her, snow-mobilers were out enjoying the crisp sunshine, a promise of longer daylight hours ahead.

After a while, she was able to ignore the noise and hear only the panting of her huskies as they plowed through the new snow. Her cheeks glowed with good health. She adjusted her sun goggles to protect her eyes from the dazzling expanse of white. One thought filled her mind as she rode the runners. From the moment she set foot in this idyllic place, a reversal had damped her every joy.

But she'd get over it. She had to.

CHAPTER TWENTY-NINE

When Ingrid went back to Pathfinder Outfitters, the store wasn't as busy. Gary was in the office.

"Hello, Gary."

"Ingrid, how nice to see you. What can I do for you?"

Her voice dropped a shade lower. "Lots of things. How about starting with lunch?"

Gary's eyebrows flicked upward. "That sounds good, but unfortunately I've got to stay here through my lunchtime. We're short staffed today."

"No problem. Why don't you run up to the Pizza Hut? We'll eat here."

He brightened. "I'll be back in a jiffy. Don't go away." He stood and shrugged into his parka.

"I'll stay right here in the office and man the phone."

As soon as he was gone, Ingrid sat in the chair in front of the computer and scanned the emails. In no time, she'd repeated her earlier trick. Triumph, tainted with petty revenge, washed over her. Dan would be happy. It wouldn't be long before Ms. Riley would be out of business and gone. Then Ingrid could quietly disappear, away from the Dans of this world, to rebuild her life.

***

A week went by. Vanessa waved to the departing clients until their car vanished round the bend in the drive. She fingered the slim check in her pocket. Not much for a two-hour excursion and the only one in three days. Inside the cabin, she stared at the phone and willed it to ring. Maybe some of the cancelations would call back to say they were over the flu. With no outside work to do, she was amazed how fast she got through the housework and other chores. No matter how much she tried, there was nothing else to fill her time. Several books lay on the coffee table waiting to be read, but she couldn't summon the concentration.

She rolled dough for plain biscuits. They were inexpensive to make. By scrimping on food, she could make her supplies last longer. Many times, she had been tempted to phone Patrick after his return, but held back. He knew she was temporarily without clients. No doubt he was overwhelmed with work now that Alden had gone. Some of his employees, too, may be down with the flu.

***

Ingrid slunk behind a rack of parkas in the Pathfinder store. Unfortunately, she was unable to avoid Gary. With so much on her mind, the last thing she wanted to do was spend time flirting with that idiot, but it was the only way to get into the office without arousing suspicion. On the other hand, he did kiss well. It made her self-imposed duty a little easier to bear.

"What a beautiful sight on a gloomy day!"

She laughed. "Come on, Gary. The sun's shining."

"But not in the store. Frances is sick in bed, and Patrick's just a bear with a sore throat."

"Why don't you tell him to go and tend to his wife? I'll keep you company."

"That makes the prospect a lot better. Excuse me a moment, I must see to those customers. Stay right here."

A half-smile on her lips, Ingrid rolled the soft edge of a fleece jacket between her fingers. He needn't worry. She wasn't going anywhere.

Moments later, Gary came back. "Patrick's going home. He admitted catching the flu from his wife. Let's go to the office."

Although they couldn't close the door completely, Gary pulled Ingrid in his arms and kissed her soundly until a buzzer sounded.

"Darn, I've got to go on the floor. Keep warm till I come back."

Ingrid feigned a rasping voice. "Darling, it'd take a whole pumper truck to extinguish the fire you lit in me."

His lips curled with a satisfied smile. With a last peck on the cheek, he left the office. Ingrid didn't waste a minute getting to the computer. Luckily, Patrick hadn't yet downloaded the booking emails. She made quick work of them all.

When Gary returned, she was standing in the same spot as she had when he was called away.

"Where were we?" He didn't wait for her answer before claiming her lips. "I told the staff I was taking a coffee break. My apartment's just round the corner. My wife is out visiting her parents."

CHAPTER THIRTY

A strident howl from Lulik attracted Vanessa's attention. There was only one man that Lulik greeted with such enthusiasm. Brett must be on his way, and by snowmobile, judging by the sound.

Vanessa smoothed her hair and secured it at the back of her neck. By the time the knock sounded on the door, she had regained her composure.

For several seconds, they stared at each other. A feathery flutter began in her mid-region and spread in widening circles to the tips of her fingers and toes. Under his pervasive gaze, her lips quivered imperceptibly.

"I'm glad you're home. I have a favor to ask you."

"A favor?" She motioned him to come inside and closed the door.

"I found an injured husky on a trail. It's obviously been abandoned. I brought him along, thinking you'd know what to do."

"Let's take a look at him. He's he in your toboggan?" While she talked, she put on boots and a parka.

The sandy-colored dog, wrapped in a down sleeping bag, lay motionless in the toboggan behind the snowmobile. It barely had the strength to lift its head and let out a low moan.

Vanessa grimaced. "We should call the vet."

"I already have. He's out on a call. His assistant promised he'd come as soon as he gets back. I did say to come here. I hope you don't mind me taking that liberty."

"Of course not. You did the right thing."

Vanessa spoke softly to the dog and extended her hand for him to sniff. She drew back the sleeping bag and touched an unusual lump on the hip. The rigid leg, too, was swollen.

"My guess is he has a dislocated hip and probably a broken bone. It looks like he's been out there for quite some time. The poor guy is dehydrated, and the leg's frozen."

"What does that mean for him?"

"Most likely, it will have to be amputated. Let's carry him inside. I've got a dog carrying board in the shed."

"I've seen it. Stay with him and I'll get it."

Brett ran and was kneeling beside the toboggan in no time.

"Hold the board level."

"I'll lift him."

"No. He could have other injuries. But if I slide him by the skin of the back, it'll minimize the damage."

With gentle hands, she grabbed the skin over the dog's back near the neck and the rump to slide him onto the board.

"I hope I didn't do something wrong when I picked him up off the snow."

"You had no choice."

"I was careful to hold his spine straight. I know as much as that."

She nodded her approval. They carried the board into the cabin. "I'll get some ice to keep that rear leg frozen until the vet gets him to the clinic." Vanessa used a puppy blanket to isolate the frozen leg from the rest of the body and keep the ice, wrapped in a towel, on top.

For the next hour, they took turns using a large syringe to inject tepid water down the dog's throat. He swallowed readily.

"He drinks, so that's good, but he really needs intravenous fluid. I don't have the necessary equipment."

"Isn't that something you ought to have?"

"Normally, it's not necessary. This dog was injured several days ago, beaten up by the look of it. Eating snow didn't provide enough liquid. He's also weak due to lack of food. By the state of his front paws, it looks like he dragged himself some distance."

"I'd like to find the bastard who beat him and abandoned him."

Anger animated Brett's features. Vanessa empathized with him. She, too, felt angry.

"I hear someone coming. It must be the vet."

The dog's eyes had brightened and were just beginning to follow Vanessa's movements.

Dr. Dave Roberts greeted them cheerfully. "What've we got here?"

Expert hands soothed the dog and assessed the injury.

"This is not one of your dogs."

"No, Brett found him abandoned out on a trail."

"I'll have to amputate the poor fellow. Unless you think it'd be better to put him to sleep. Life on three legs for a husky isn't terrific."

Brett shook his head. "He's made it so far. He's a fighter."

Vanessa stroked the dog's head. "He'll adapt."

"I thought you'd say that." He repacked the ice.

"Wouldn't it be better to thaw it?" Brett asked. "Maybe it could be saved?"

"When did you last get your fingers so cold you couldn't feel them?" Dave said.

"Not so long ago."

"Can you remember how painful it was?"

"Oh, yeah, I do. I wasn't thinking." Brett looked sheepish.

"And your fingers weren't frozen solid. Besides the pain, the tissues are mostly dead now. Gangrene would rapidly set in." Dave injected the dog with a sedative.

Then the vet and Brett carried the dog stretcher out to the vet's waiting van.

"I'll have to take a couple of X-rays and do the necessary fixing up."

Brett nodded. "Please do, Dave. I'll take care of the bill."

"Can you check if there's any ID on the dog? Tattoo or a microchip," Vanessa said.

"Will do. But I don't think you'd want to send the dog back, even if we do identify the owner."

"No, Vanessa wouldn't, but I'll want to have a word with the guy."

Dave shook his head. "Don't do anything stupid, now."

"I'll be darned if someone like that is going to keep dogs!"

Vanessa longed to smooth away the frown on Brett's hard features. "The dog could have escaped miles away and been injured after he got loose."

Brett looked thoughtful for a moment. "You don't believe that. I found the dog not wearing a collar and having such terror in his eyes when he saw my hand. I knew straight away he'd been abused."

Dave pulled on his gloves. "It does look like he was beaten. You've done a good job, both of you. I'll phone as soon as I found out the extent of the injuries."

The vet drove away. Brett turned to Vanessa. "That dog had grit and determination in his eyes. I know he's going to make it!"

"I hope so."

For a while, they stood close. Silent and still.

"Thanks for helping. When I saw the way he tried to drag himself over the trail, I didn't know what to do. You were the first person I thought of. Fortunately, I had the toboggan behind the snowmobile and we were on our way back."

"Yes, and luckily you happened to take your clients that way. He wouldn't have survived much longer."

Silence again built a wall between them. Turmoil raged inside Vanessa, but she wasn't going to let it show.

"Coffee?"

"Please."

They went back into the cabin. His wordless gaze enveloped Vanessa in a cocoon of heat. She wanted nothing more than to take his head in her hands and kiss him to relieve the prickling of her lips.

"Will that dog have to stay at the vet's?"

"Not for long. Once he's patched up, he'll be able to go home. Except he doesn't have a home." She lost herself in the dark velvet of Brett's eyes.

"That's what I'd like to talk to you about. As you guessed, I don't have a clue about dogs. Could you look after him until he's better? I'll provide everything he needs."

"Of course." She would have agreed, no matter what. But Brett's last sentence swept aside her first thought that having one more mouth to feed would worsen an already dire situation. The alarm bells ringing in her mind fell silent. The truth was that Brett could ask for the moon and she would gladly give it to him if it was within her power.

"I'll bring food for him tomorrow."

She served the coffee. "You don't have to." That was what one would say in the circumstances, but she was secretly relieved.

"But I want to. He's my dog, now."

They didn't speak for several minutes after that, yet now the silence was no longer awkward. He stood to go.

"Marcel around?"

"He's away in the Sawtooth Mountains, guiding a winter expedition."

"Really!"

"He couldn't pass up such a well-paying opportunity. So much more than I can afford to pay him."

There was a flicker of a frown on Brett's eyebrow. "I must go. Thanks again."

"You're welcome."

"I wish I were."

"We agreed to a truce, remember?" Vanessa's heart leaped madly. He was smiling at her and it was as though the sun had burst through the black clouds hanging over her. She wanted to scream and tell him that Marcel meant nothing to her, and that, more than anything, she wanted him, Brett, to love her. He said he did. She wanted to trust him.

But she didn't.

A few days later, Brett phoned to say he was bringing Buddy, as he had named his dog. Vanessa quickly put away the accounts and tidied the cabin, dusting furniture, fluffing the sofa cushions, and wiping the kitchen counters. It mattered little that she had done the very same thing not two hours before.

When she heard his truck approach, she was ready and waiting. Brett called to her. "Buddy's trying to walk and run as if he didn't know he has lost a leg."

"He'll get used to it. For now, you better lift him down and carry him inside the cabin."

"Will he be able to live a normal life?"

"Losing a rear leg is less of a problem than a front one. Dogs, especially huskies, are stronger and heavier in the front than the back. I'll teach him new tricks to cope with his handicap. He'll soon adapt."

She'd taken down the puppy pen in the cabin and had borrowed an extra-large dog crate from Jimmy. The crate, complete with blanket, stood near the wood stove, its door open. Buddy sniffed it and settled down in his new home with obvious pleasure. Brett watched Vanessa pour the coffee.

"Why do you put him in a crate?"

"Did you see how eager he was to get inside? He is recovering from trauma and the crate gives him a sense of security. In the wilds, an injured animal would seek shelter under a low-hanging branch, a hole in the ground or a cave and hunker down until healed."

"I learn something new every time I come here. I brought some dog food for him. I'll put it in the shed before I leave."

"Thanks. Did you trace Buddy's owner?"

"I did. You'll read about it in the *New Gazette.* The guy's been charged with cruelty to animals. He appears in court next week."

"Good! I trust he won't be allowed to keep dogs after that." Indignation brought a flush of color to Vanessa's cheeks.

"The Animal Shelter has seen to that in the charges, and I added some of my own."

"When Buddy is healed, he'll need a special home."

A playful smile floated on his lips. "Wolf Hollow has a wheelchair ramp for the less able. I've legally adopted him. Buddy's my dog." There was a note of pride in his voice.

Relief and happiness submerged Vanessa. "If you don't mind, I'll start work on a harness and a coat right now. I want to modify the harness so we can take Buddy out, yet support him until the amputation scar is completely healed. Like that, he'll learn to manage on three legs without risk of hurting himself."

Brett watched her work. He stayed long enough to witness the first rehabilitation lesson, as Vanessa led Buddy out onto the porch. In the pen, Lulik went crazy.

"Let her out, please."

Lulik was most interested. Vanessa let both dogs sniff each other. Lulik smelled the bandaged wound under the dog coat, then Brett took Lulik back to her pen.

Once she had the dog settled back in the crate, Vanessa straightened. Her head bumped against Brett's as he peered into Buddy's kennel.

"Ouch!"

Strong arms held her. "Sorry, my head is so hard."

"And so is mine." There was a moment of tension while their gaze locked, alive with awareness. Gently, he pulled her close. His hand moved slowly to cup the back of her neck. Feeble words of protest died in her throat. A muted cry escaped her throat as she pressed against him. Her hands moved up his chest to the broad shoulders, twitching under her touch. He opened the clasp of her hair and the shiny mass tumbled over her shoulders.

With one fluid motion, he lifted her in his arms and carried her to the bedroom.

Night was advanced when she half opened her eyes. He was watching her intently, his lips hovering inches above hers. She raised her head high enough to kiss him. "Do you want anything before you go?"

"I want a whole lot more of you."

"Let's stop here. I'd rather not..."

"Make love?"

She sighed deeply. "It's only sex!"

"Not for me, it isn't."

"Whatever its name, don't tempt me again."

Before he left, he kissed her and murmured, "Thanks... from Buddy."

Chapter Thirty-One

The intercom buzzed. "Ingrid, line one." Brett's voice made her start.

"You will excuse me for a moment," Ingrid said. Although she was no longer employed, clients sometimes requested her and Brett allowed her on the floor. She handed a photo album to the client and walked to her ex-office. Jon was busy. Who'd call her? Her parents didn't believe in spending money on phone calls when texting was free. Could it be one of the hotels where she had made an application?

"Ingrid speaking."

"Got an extra package."

She paled. "Dan, I told you not to call me here while I'm working!"

"I am the one who tells *you* what to do. It's in the shack. It must be moved right away."

"Send someone else. I can't leave."

"G has been detained."

Her contact arrested and in jail! A cold sweat trickled down her spine. "Change everything. It's getting hot around here."

"Who do you think you're talking to? Get that package. I'm working on something."

"I'll go after dark. But who do I give it to since Gene's not available?"

"You stupid or what? Hide it till it cools down."

"But if Gene talks..."

"He won't. Is that cop still there?"

"Weiman? He's back for the weekend. He's all over the place. Goes off on his own too."

"Then hide it in the garage."

"You're crazy! Brett, the mechanics and the clients are always in and out of the garage."

"Precisely. It's the best place."

"I've a better idea."

"Oh, man! Save me from women with ideas."

"I'll put it in our neighbor's shed."

"And the dogs will tell everyone you're lurking around."

"At night no one bothers if they howl because some deer go past."

"It better be good."

"My plan to make her leave is working."

"Not soon enough."

He hung up. Ingrid stared at the dead phone in her hand. Hatred boiled up inside her. She shuffled a few papers to calm herself time before she prepared to make what she swore would be her last run. Her month's notice at the lodge was almost over.

Dexter Weiman strode past the door just as she left the office. They almost collided.

He held her arm to steady her. "I'm so sorry. You look pale. Did I hurt you?"

She shook her head. "No, it's okay. I'm alright."

"Still, you look upset. Let me get you something to drink."

"Please, Dexter, you're a guest."

"But my charming hostess is upset on my account. Clumsy does not begin to describe it. Here, let me make amends. How about we go for a drink in town after work?"

For one mad moment, she wanted to accept and tell him everything. Maybe he wasn't a cop, after all. Perhaps it was just her fevered imagination. Her hand went to his chest, but he moved. That wasn't a normal reaction. Now she was sure he was carrying. In that instant, she no longer had any doubt he was a cop.

"About tonight?"

"There're a few people doing a night run to watch the northern lights. I'm not free."

He leaned over, all charm and smoothness. "How about if I tell the boss I need you to show me the nightlife in town?"

Ingrid laughed. "Brett's going with the party. I have to stay. Tomorrow?" She teetered on the edge of truth and lies. The man didn't know that she was no longer employed at the lodge, but she still assumed her hostess role when, and unknown to him, Brett was out. Clients were generously tipping in cash or costly gifts that she wasted no time reselling.

Dexter sighed. "Tomorrow it'll be."

After the small group had gone star gazing and other guests had retired, Ingrid went to her room and changed into her snowmobile suit. "Dam Dan and the others to hell! I hate driving at night. Why can't that stupid woman let us through!"

With her survival bag in her hand, she opened her door a crack and surveyed the hallway. No one in sight. Although she wanted to run, she walked to the back stairs and down to the snowmobile parking. The doors had been left open. Several spaces were empty. A light in the workshop part scared her. If someone was in there, they'd come out when she started her machine. She slunk to the Polaris Rush-Pro and deposited her bag on the seat. Taking care not to make the snow that was shoveled in with the tractor crunch under her boots, she peered through the small window in the door to the heated shop. To her relief, the shop was empty and the mechanics gone for the night.

Ingrid ran back and started her machine. She then drove at speed out through the garage's wide entrance. She liked the sporty snow-mobile. There wasn't much metal to it, but it was fast and easy to maneuver.

In an upstairs bedroom, a curtain fell back in place.

Dexter picked up his cell phone. After a moment, he got a signal. "She's on her way." Then he waited. Twenty minutes later, his phone rang.

"Yeah?"

"She's stopped at Gary Bird's and went up to his apartment. I saw him pull the drapes."

"Shit! She had got a call. I was so sure she was going to take a delivery."

"Want me to hang on?"

"No need to freeze your butt. She's been going to his apartment quite a bit since his wife went to visit her family in Whitehorse."

"Think he's involved?"

"Doesn't check out. I wonder if we've got the right woman. But I was so sure..."

"If not her, how about the Dog Lady?"

"She doesn't fit at all. But hell, who knows."

Chapter Thirty-Two

Vanessa waved farewell to the yellow bus carrying its enthusiastic load of elementary school children back to town. Alone at last, she flopped down onto a log to rest. It had been a delightful but exhausting morning. "Well, Lulik, I tell you I don't know how teachers manage the whole day, day after day, with a bunch of super active kids." Her sympathetic dog rubbed against Vanessa's legs, and Buddy sunning himself on the porch, watched closely. After she secured Lulik in the pen, she gave another lesson to Buddy on how to negotiate the steps. This time, he didn't waver. She pushed the door open, and he followed her inside.

Compared to the animation of the morning, the afternoon dragged by slowly. She was more than ready to abandon the task of updating her kennel records when Brett arrived.

Vanessa watched through the window as he gave his usual greetings to the dogs. A tightness settled in her chest. So tall, so strong and so gentle with her canine family! She reminded herself that what she felt for him was mere infatuation, a holiday romance, nothing more. Although her mind was convinced of this, the sensuous waves assailing her body told otherwise.

Brett finished playing with the pups. He walked straight in and playfully wrapped his arms around her. It was only a brief hug but sufficient to send the room spinning and sweeping her along on a tide of need. He peered into Buddy's small domain. "How's our patient doing?" At the sound of the voice, Buddy stood up and came out to greet his rescuer.

"Impressive! Coming along nicely."

Vanessa shook off the momentary paralysis. "I can put him through his paces if you'd like."

"I can't stay long. I'm off to the mountains for a two or three days run with a couple of clients that are more friends than clients."

"That sounds like an interesting trip."

"I need a breather. I've been on the go nonstop. It's so nice you've been home every time I've come to visit. Wait a minute! Shouldn't you be out giving sled tours?"

"Business is slow right now."

"Slow? Ah well, that proves people prefer snowmobiles over dogs, doesn't it?"

"The flu's playing havoc with my bookings. I'm surprised you're not affected at the lodge." Despite her self-control, her voice faltered.

He took her hand in a comforting gesture. A million electrical impulses shot up her arm. She made an attempt to pull her hand away, but he held it firmly.

"These are hard times for you. I guess I'm just lucky. Can I help?"

"If you can cure the flu so that people don't cancel their bookings, go ahead."

"You need to feed the dogs. That's costly, I know."

Vanessa wished she could unload her burden on him, let him share her worries. "We'll pull through."

"I'd like to help. It's not easy starting up a business. You've done well up to now. I'm sure it's only a temporary blip on the chart."

"That's what I tell myself."

His thumb drew circles on her hand. "You've helped Buddy without a second thought. Let me help you."

The tender pressure nearly undid her. "No thanks. I'm not bankrupt, not just yet." Her eyes moistened. She struggled to remain stoic. Before she put herself in his debt, she'd hunt wild game to feed the dogs. Although he hadn't mentioned the issue of the land recently, she had no illusion that it was still on his agenda. Too much in his debt and he would take it over. No, she would manage alone.

The phone rang. With a very sore throat, Patrick asked how she was doing.

"Patrick! You sound awful. Judging from your voice, I'd say I'm doing better than you right now."

"I'm back at work. Did Gary send you the bookings while I was away?"

"He did. Don't you worry about a thing. Did you hear from Alden?"

She asked that to divert attention from herself. Patrick talked about his son until finally his voice gave out. Vanessa took a deep breath. Brett stood up, ready to leave. She moistened her bottom lip with her tongue. He drew her in his arms. While her reason warned to her to step back, her being strained forward.

His lips brushed hers, so lightly that she involuntarily raised her head. Once more she felt her resistance crumble.

He dropped delicate kisses on her lips. "I want you so much," he whispered.

Want! A cold draft passed between them. Want! She was right not to trust him. This was not love, but *want,* a want born of lust. It couldn't be *want* her land, could it? Conflicting emotions, tinged with sadness, crowded her mind. Her whole body quivered. Abruptly, she tore herself away.

"You'll be late."

"Listen, we have something beautiful together."

"I don't deny it was good."

"Then we could——"

"No. I never meant it to happen, but I'm not angry with you. Only, I don't want it to continue."

The message was blunt. Brett bent over and stole one last burning kiss from her lips.

A heavy sense of loss settled over her after he left. Hopes that he really loved her battled with a certainty that he was manipulating her. Her heart wanted to believe him. Her reason didn't.

Her pain remedy was to take a team out and forget her troubles in the serenity of the wilds.

The third barren week drew to an end and still no new clients, save for some of the locals. A Jeep Grand Cherokee pulled into the yard. Vanessa rushed to the window. Would that be a client?

Dexter Weiman alighted. She remembered him as a good client. He stayed at the lodge. A brief thought surged. Did he not come with an Escalade previously? He must be wealthy to change cars at a whim. She opened the door on the first knock and smiled.

"Mr. Weiman, how nice to see you again."

"It's Dexter. I wasn't sure I'd find you home since I hadn't phoned."

"These days, I'm spending more time at home than on the trails. Did you come for a sled ride?"

"As a matter of fact, yes. I do enjoy dogsledding and being in the midst of nature. Is business slow?"

"The flu is making ravages through the population."

He frowned. It didn't add up. The lodge was fully booked. "You don't go to town very much, do you?"

While talking, Dexter's eyes took in every detail of the room. Nothing had changed.

"No, when I had daily bookings I had no time to run into town, and now... well, there's no point."

Still puzzled, he bent to pet Buddy. "Your dog?"

"No, Brett Lancaster rescued him. He was injured. I'm rehabilitating him, so he gets used to having only three legs."

"While you have no clients, you still have to feed your dogs, right?"

"It's only temporary, and I got a little help."

"Can I help too? I'm a consultant. Engineering."

"If you can cure the flu." She didn't want to dwell on her misery. "Do you work for yourself?"

One eyebrow lifted into a peak. "You could say that. My laptop is my office. It serves me well. Like that, I can spend more time enjoying winter."

"We have a few hours before dark. Where would you like to go?"

"No fixed idea. Where does that trail behind your cabin go?"

"It's part of the trail system on Tapiskoot. There's about fifty miles of winding trails. The previous owner cut them."

"Does it go to the Aishin forest?"

"Not directly, although it abuts my property. I'll need to cut a direct access in the summer. To get into the forest, I continue on my trail into the corner of the reserve and navigate through the pines up to the forest boundary. We can go that way if you like."

"Yes, that would be nice. Would I be able to see Lancaster's land from the other side?"

"Sure, once in the forest, I can take a trail that comes close to the boundary. Let's hitch up a team. Did you want to drive your own sled?"

"No thanks. I'll see more of the landscape as a passenger."

"True. How long do you want to ride?" *Please say four hours.*

"As long as there's daylight. I'm in no hurry."

She beamed. "Let's take carry along a picnic. It'll take no time to prepare."

Five minutes later, Vanessa had stowed food and thermos in the sled bag. Dexter helped harness the dogs and settled himself in the sled on the bison hide.

"Must cost a lot of money a hide like this." His job was to ask questions. If Ms. Riley had no clients, she must be short of money. Desperate people do desperate things.

"Marcel, that's my guide, gave it to me on loan when we had some clients from California. I couldn't afford one."

Once underway, the eager dogs bounded along the familiar trail.

"I suppose you have to feed the dogs, whether you have lots of clients or only a few."

"That goes without saying. The business started so well, I had to buy extra equipment. I was considering hiring a second guide when, suddenly, no clients."

"Your business is in the red?"

"I'm afraid so. But I shouldn't bother you with my problems."

"I asked."

"I have some kind friends. Jimmy Redhead brought me deer meat and Ranger Victor Ayupaq brought me a road kill. Stefan went ice fishing and dropped off his surplus fish." Her eyes misted over, but Dexter couldn't see them. "I think someone, maybe Marcel before he left, mentioned my predicament to a couple of mushers. Dog people help one another."

"Wonderful. That's what dogs do to people. Brings them together." He turned in the sled to look at her and smiled. "This is the Aishin forest now?"

"Yes. We've just left the reserve. There was a marker to your left."

"Yes, I saw it. Can we go along Lancaster's land to where his trail joins up?"

"Sure. At least, I hope I can find it again."

Vanessa wondered why Dexter wanted to see Brett's land. There was nothing there. Just a couple of markers. The snowmobile trail she had seen from the markers on one of her exploratory trips was little used. "I don't know if we can go right up to Brett's boundary. The trail might be choked with snow."

"No problem if we can't."

To her surprise, when the sled came in view of the trail going into Brett's property, it was open, packed down with recently made snowmobile tracks. "The trail has been broken. Someone must have gone past not long ago."

"Can we follow the trail?"

"No, sorry. I won't let his snowmobiles on my land, so I don't go on his. But I can take you to see the south markers from my side of the land."

"Yes. It's not a big detour, is it?"

"Not at all. We'll get back on my trail a little south of the boundary."

When they reached the markers, Vanessa stopped the team. Dexter got out of the sled and looked around.

"I wonder if Lancaster would sell me this piece of land."

"There's no road access."

He grinned. "That's what makes it an ideal spot."

"I guess the view onto the lake from anywhere must be as gorgeous as it is from my place."

"It's all beautiful around here. How long is this trail?"

"You mean, like along my boundary? Just under two miles. My boundary would be about three miles."

"I see. I'd definitely like to buy his land."

"I'd be delighted to have you as a neighbor. But Lancaster needs this land to access the forest trails beyond. He isn't likely to consider selling."

"So, let me figure this out. If there is no direct access to his parcel of land, and I were to come back with a snowmobile, how do I get here? On his side of the line, I mean."

"You'd have to go right round by the town or go along the shore of the lake until you cross his trail entrance. Brett is getting the snowmobile club to groom a trail in the ditch along the road to Donek. He's got maps of the trails. They all have a symbol easy to follow. Once on his network of trails, you can go wherever you feel like. Shall we go up to the lake and picnic there?"

"That would be great."

Ten minutes later, once the team tethered, Vanessa pointed to a fallen tree and brought out the food. She lit a small fire. They sat on the trunk and enjoyed the picnic cooked on the camp fire.

Dexter got back into the sled. After that, he had her go back in the forest and meander, following trails finally to reach the lake a short distance from Brett's north boundary. Brett asked her to stop. He climbed out, looked around and nodded.

"Yes, you could enter Brett's trail system from here."

"Right, I figure it out now."

They came back to Tapiskoot by way of the lake shore.

Vanessa's spirits rose, especially when she put his check in her folder. He had rounded up the fee despite her protests. Knowing why he did that, she swallowed her pride and accepted it.

Chapter Thirty-Three

After a long, lonely weekend, Vanessa went to the store to speak to Patrick. If the prospects showed no signs of improvement, she'd have to ask him for credit. That alone was enough to depress her. What would her friend Harold Glover have said about the situation now? Perhaps she should phone him and seek his advice. She had followed his business plan to the letter, except she'd not borrowed funds for the capital. Her savings were all gone. During those first couple of months, her business had blossomed like a runaway grass fire. On the brink of tears, she promised herself to phone him later that day to see if his offer to finance her enterprise still stood. Anything was worth trying, so long as it didn't involve Brett.

On the final bend before town, she was forced to brake hard to avoid a small blue car stopped on the side of the road. A young woman was peering under the raised hood.

Vanessa wound down her window. "Need any help?"

"D'you know how to start a dead engine?"

"I'm not an expert. My dogs never have a problem starting."

"You're Vanessa Riley, the Dog Lady."

Vanessa began to laugh. "Yes, I suppose I am the Dog Lady!"

"I'm Toni. I work part time at the lodge."

"Let me try to start your car." Vanessa climbed into the driver's seat and turned on the ignition. The engine coughed and died. After several futile attempts, it still refused to fire. "We're draining the battery. I'll give you a ride to the garage in town. They'll be able to give you a boost. Climb in."

A look of gratitude came over the girl's face. "Gee, thanks! I was on my way to Pathfinder. Now that you're going that way, you can collect your stuff yourself. Still, Ms. Lancaster is going to be mad at me for taking so long."

Vanessa raised her eyebrows, unsure of quite what the girl was talking about. "It's not your fault. Ms. Lancaster knows about cars breaking down."

"She's been in a bad mood for a while."

"The winter blues, I guess. She'll get over it."

"I guess so."

They fell silent for the rest of the journey. Vanessa dropped Toni off at the garage and drove on to Pathfinder Outfitters.

Patrick got up from his desk as she walked into his office. "Vanessa! Long time no see. This is my first real day back at work. Damned flu! Come feast your eyes on this list of bookings."

Her surprise smothered her mind and left her speechless. With a flourish, Patrick pulled out a double sheet from the Tapiskoot folder.

"Now, look at that! Mind you, I don't understand why some of the people asked if the guide was better. The messages were taken by the girls, and I'm not sure what they mean. Gary's off, taking a bit of a vacation with his missus."

Vanessa's eyes bulged as she stared at the paper.

Patrick looked at her. "Are you okay?"

She nodded. "Some of these names were on the last schedule, but they were canceled."

"What do you mean, canceled? I don't understand. What's going on? Look at this, it says *Hope guide is better.* Have you or Marcel been sick?"

"Not at all. These people canceled because they, not us, were sick."

"Not according to this."

Patrick and Vanessa stared at each other in utter incomprehension. He let out his breath.

"Bookings canceled. Tell me what happened. From the beginning."

Over the following couple of minutes, Vanessa filled him on the mysterious cancelations. "Three weeks ago, you sent all the bookings, except a few, canceled because of illness. Then last week, same thing."

"Three weeks. No, I remember emailing you a complete list before I left for the trade fair. I know because I prepared that schedule myself. Apart from the occasional phone call Gary takes, and the in-store bookings from locals, all calls and website bookings come here to this computer."

"Strange. The emails I received stated 'no bookings.' One in-store booking list was in your handwriting, but was stamped *canceled*."

Patrick scowled. "Do you have it here?"

"No, it's at the cabin. I only brought back the empty folder."

They look at each other in dismay. Patrick shook his head.

"I have the horrible feeling someone has been tampering with your business."

"It's evident. But why would somebody do that?" A load of depression washed over her.

"Let me ask my staff. But first let me check the computer." He downloaded the mail. "Here we have some more. Hang on! From California. *Is the flu epidemic over? We've re-arranged our vacation for the end of the month and still would like a camping trip by dogsled."* Patrick rubbed his neck. *"*I don't like this." He left the office.

Vanessa picked up the new schedule and scanned the names she recognized from the previous one.

Patrick came back, shaking his head. "Nobody here knows anything about any cancelations. I wonder if Alden would know."

"I believe he left the day after I collected the schedule. No, as a matter of fact, I didn't come to pick it up. I found it hanging on my door."

"I'm almost sure Alden didn't go up to your place. We were too busy. The kid barely had time to pack."

"He came to say goodbye the day before... Somebody had access to the file and must have put it on the door."

"There's no doubt about that. I'm just trying to figure out who could have tampered with it. None of my staff would do such a thing. They're your Number One fans."

"What about the website direct bookings? Is there something there?"

"I'm baffled." He pulled up the *sent* folder. "Look here, everything deleted!" He let out a few choice expletives, then immediately apologized. "Don't worry. I'll get to the bottom of this. Someone wants to create trouble for you. And for me. That's for sure."

"Somebody who wants me gone?"

"Looks like it. Who's your enemy?"

For a fleeting moment, Vanessa thought Frances would have access to the office, but she had been very sick. "The only one who'd like to see me gone is Brett."

Patrick straightened. "Brett? Absolutely not! We've known each other from the cradle. He never, never would do anything like this."

She blushed. "Actually, no, I don't believe *he* would resort to such tactics."

"I'll tell him. The storm delayed his party, but he's due back tonight."

"Thanks. I better go and start preparing for this tidal wave of business."

"You must have been pretty depressed when you saw the cancelations."

"That's an understatement."

"I'll have one of the boys deliver the dog food tomorrow. With the loss you've taken, I reckon you must be hurting. So take your time paying. It's okay."

"Thanks, Patrick. I'll make up for it." She thought for a minute. "Do you think it would be a good idea to phone back all the people on the previous schedule and offer them another booking? Maybe even add a small incentive?"

"That's a great idea. You have nothing to lose except a few phone charges."

Her mind worked furiously. "I'll do that."

"Forward me half of the cancel emails. I'll call them."

They discussed the incentive and settled on an extra hour with a picnic.

"You won't get much profit with those, but it will create goodwill and keep the business afloat."

In an elated mood, Vanessa finished her shopping and hurried home. The plan they had formulated to make to the 'canceled' people delighted to hear from her or Patrick was a good one. Now, she had to start baking. For the moment, her desire to find out who had sabotaged her business was pushed at the back of her mind.

The clients were indeed happy to hear from her and to learn that her dogsled excursions were again available. Longer daylight hours meant everything would run smoother. Soon, she had doubled up every sledding tour. She lost no time calling on her helpers, Janine and Taylor. The pair had no job and were more than happy to work, and after hearing there had been a problem with bookings, they protested they didn't want to be paid. Later, they said, later. Jimmy turned up early in the morning.

"I heard you're alone with the girls to do a whole lot of tours. Can I help?"

"Thanks so much, Jimmy. I'll pay you from the fees——"

"No, you are not. I have been wanting to drive those dogs again, and this is my chance. I love taking people out and showing them the land we share." He was all smiles.

After her period of enforced inactivity, Vanessa welcomed the bustle. For one thing, it kept her mind off Brett. Janine took over the kitchen and prepared lip smacking picnics for the stream of guests, whose appetites were sharpened by the crisp air. Her bannock soon became a favorite of the guests. Taylor worked in the kennel, hitching, unhitching dogs, loading the sled, her long black braid dancing around her head, all the while smiling and making the clients laugh with her self-directed humor.

It was late evening when a knock on the door roused her from a doze in the armchair.

"Ah, Patrick. Come in. You've got news for me?"

"I have. I spoke to Alden on the phone. He remembers handing the schedule to Toni. For some reason, she was supposed to deliver it to you."

A sudden pallor drained the blood from Vanessa's face. "Toni? Toni works for Wolf Hollow Lodge."

"I know. Apparently, Toni asked for it, saying it'd save you a trip."

"She couldn't have tampered with the computer list, though."

"Or phoned the clients. No, but I know someone else who could have."

"Who?"

"That scheming bitch, pardon my Latin, of a manager. Her boss."

"Ingrid? You don't believe..? Yes, you do. But why? My business doesn't compete with theirs."

"She's jealous."

"But to go to that extent!"

"Who knows? Anyway, I've given strict instructions that the list had to be given to you, personally, if you're in town. If you're not, I'll bring it to you myself. I'll put a password on the office computer. Never had the need of one until now. My staff would check on orders, when I was out of the office. Alden feels bad about the whole mess up. He wanted to come back, immediately."

"What for? He's not responsible."

"Oh yes, he is. He didn't have to get starry-eyed over that girl Toni. When I see her, I'll have a word with her."

"Don't be harsh on her. She's only sixteen and only doing what she was told. Incidentally, I gave her a ride into town today. She did happen to mention something odd about collecting my stuff from you. At the time, I didn't understand. I do now."

"My hunch is she was on a follow up mission for her boss."

Vanessa passed her hands over her face. "What did I do to that Ingrid to make her hate me so much?"

"You're standing between her and Brett. Though, I've a hunch there's more to it than that."

"Between her and Brett? I'm no threat to her. I hate the man." She checked herself and blushed. "Well, no. I don't, but we've had words. Sort of..." The more she tried to explain, the redder she became.

A smile floated over Patrick's lips. "I should also have a word with Mr. Lancaster himself."

"Don't! I don't want him to know."

"Toni is one of his employees."

"I have enough problems as it is without him getting involved too. Besides, we have no definite proof."

Patrick shrugged, clearly unconvinced. "How are you managing all the extra work?"

"No problem at all. Okay, loads of problems!"

He shook his head. "Ask Jimmy Redhead to lend a hand. He doesn't train every day."

She smiled. "He already heard and came to help out. Before that, he brought me deer meat for the dogs."

"That's the guy, alright. See you later."

Chapter Thirty-Four

Late next evening, Brett came back. It wasn't long before he became aware of a buzz in the air. He saw Jimmy leave with Janine and Taylor. Since no one mentioned anything, he didn't stop to ask. His mind focused on his next visit to Buddy. At the cabin, he knocked and pushed the door open at the same time. Vanessa's pulse quickened. The wild idea crossed her mind that perhaps they could start afresh.

She leaned against the back of a chair, her hair a shimmering pool of burnished copper. Brett studied her with a blatant look of longing.

"I missed you those last few days."

"You had a good time?"

"I thought and dreamed about you nonstop. You're so much more beautiful in person."

Fatigue lines creased the edges of her eyes. She blinked. "Flattery!"

"Are you not feeling well?"

"I'm perfectly well, thank you. Just that it's been a long, hectic day, after a long hectic week."

"I thought you said business was slow."

"It was artificially slow. Some person or persons unknown played a dirty trick on me."

"A dirty trick? What do you mean?"

Vanessa didn't want to tell him, but his closeness and the concern in his eyes compelled her to.

In a voice, faltering at times, she recounted the incident, omitting the names, not to protect the guilty, but to prevent Brett's angry reaction. Already anger distorted his face. He began pacing the floor.

"Stop that, Brett. You're disturbing your dog."

"Sorry."

He went over to pet Buddy who, now perfectly at ease, lay on a mat in front of the stove. His mind raced. "Just who would do a thing like that? And why? Everyone here respects you. And you've no idea who hung the bag on your door and tampered with the bookings?"

It hurt her to lie. If she accused Ingrid, Brett would rush to confront the woman. Then he'd be back, full of compassion. Brett's compassion was the last thing she wanted right now. There was also the fact that someone other than Ingrid could have been using young Toni, though she doubted it. There was no denying that someone had accessed Patrick's computer. So far, she didn't know who or how.

"No. I have no idea how that red bag came to be there or how someone deleted the emails from Patrick's computer. All the employees at Pathfinder have been cleared and are actively trying to remember anything unusual." That was the truth, as far as she knew.

"I'll find out. In the meantime, I'll send you help."

Vanessa saw him to the door. His hands cupped her face. When she opened her eyes, she saw warmth in his gaze. It shone with love, and promises, too.

On the question of help, Brett was true to his word. He proved it the next morning. Vanessa was still eating breakfast when Stefan Browne arrived.

"Brett sent you?"

"Sure did. Said Marcel was away, and you had too many clients to handle on your own. Jimmy can't come everyday seeing he has dogs to train."

"One problem, I can't pay you as much as Wolf Hollow. But I'll pay you the same as Marcel."

"Don't worry about that. I'm still on Mr. Lancaster's payroll."

Vanessa bristled at the thought that Brett was once more using his wealth to worm his way into her good graces. Or, was it a real concern brought about because he truly did love her? It wasn't something she could discuss with Stefan. So she simply nodded.

"What about your work at the lodge? You're busy there, too."

"Plenty of others who can take care of snowmobile end of things. I'm the only one there who knows how to handle a dog team."

"You have experience?"

"I used to race." A wistful look came into his eyes.

"You don't anymore?" She slapped herself mentally. It was obvious.

"The wife's not too keen on me traipsing around the country with a bunch of dogs. I was a good race musher, mind you. I always ended the season in the money. But now with the kids, that's not enough."

Vanessa's eyes sparkled with tears she was trying to contain ever since he stepped in through the door. "You know my dogs aren't racers?"

"That don't matter. It's being out with a team that I love."

"Great. When can you start?"

"Right away. I brought my gear with me. Lancaster mentioned you had an overnight trip planned. He's aiming to go with you while I take care of the day trips back here. And Jimmy will be back again tomorrow."

"Brett? Coming with me? But he can't!"

Stefan gave a laugh. "You'd best tell him that yourself." He jerked his thumb toward the yard. "He's here now." He walked away, a deep chuckle still rumbling in his throat.

Brett parked his truck in the yard and lifted several bundles from the open box.

Vanessa waited for him, her hands on her hips. "What this all about, Brett?"

"What's what about? You need a second driver for the camping trip. So, here I am."

His boyish grin sent her pulse racing.

"Why don't you go with Stefan and I'll stay to take care of things at this end?"

"Nah, Stefan hates camping."

"Tell me why I somehow don't believe you."

"Never mind. We've got a lot to do. Our first guests are on their way as we speak."

Her ears pricked up at the easy way he referred to *our guests*. She liked it. It sounded so natural on his lips.

In the midst of the preparations for the departure, there was no time for argument. The matter of paying Stefan would have to wait. A young couple and a family with two children had signed up for an overnight camping trip. Vanessa allocated a sled to the mother, who was determined to drive dogs. Ken, the young man, was equally keen and asserted he had studied videos on sled dog driving. He and Jean practiced gliding with the basket sled and putting the brakes on. To make sure they would be successful, Vanessa gave each novice two of the most stable dogs with a small box of dehydrated food lashed to the basket to make weight, not that it weighed much. It was psychological. The two-dog teams would be most manageable. Then, she assigned Lulik, the alpha female, and Nukatuk to Brett's team of five as he would be breaking trail. The two dogs liked each other. Lulik's adoring eyes was the assurance she would not only obey his voice but that she would keep the gangline taut. He also carried Laura, who preferred to sit in the sled on top of the sleeping bags. Finally, Bill and his children settled in her sled, with the rest of the camping equipment. They set off, Brett in the lead. She brought up the rear to keep an eye on the apprentice mushers.

She discovered just how charming Brett could be when a mishap resulted in his woman passenger being ignominiously ejected from the sled when it hit a bump in the trail. Laura rolled into the deep snow, laughing. She laid on her back and made a snow angel. The hilarity made everybody's sides ache. A round of chocolate bars calmed the travelers.

Brett needed to gain a lot more experience with handling a dogsled to avoid such accidents, but he was making progress.

To the great excitement of their guests, they traveled through the darkness before pitching camp beside a lake, asleep under its thick cover of ice. A high, tree-covered bluff sheltered the tents from the wind. Brett erected two tents for their guests before helping Vanessa with the dogs and the dinner.

After an enjoyable time around the campfire, Brett and Vanessa lit the Coleman^{TM}, the only reliable lantern that wouldn't freeze in the cold like battery powered lanterns. The clients retired to their tents, Brett and Vanessa sat a while longer, yawning and drinking the last of the hot chocolate.

"We'd better put up our tents," Brett said.

Vanessa was about to agree when a scream ripped through the air and the tent of one of the tourist couples burst into flames. The dogs set out frantic howls. Brett dashed forward and dragged Laura out of the burning mass. Vanessa seized an empty cooking pot and threw snow on the flames. Brett then helped Ken extricate himself from the smoldering remains. He wrapped both victims in blankets.

"It's my stupid fault," Ken said. "I wanted to relight the lantern and knocked it over. The fuel spilled. I dropped the match. I'm sorry, I'm such a klutz." His teeth chattered.

The commotion roused the second couple and their children.

Vanessa was the first to react. "Don't worry. You're safe. That's the main thing. Did you burn yourself?"

"My hands are a bit singed."

"Just a moment." She pulled the first aid kit out of the sled bag and examined his hands. They were red, but no blisters were forming. "I don't have ointment because it would freeze, but I have an ancient remedy for burns."

He looked at her quizzically.

"Bicarbonate soda." She sprinkled it generously on his skin, dipped a gauze bandage into the snow and wrapped his hands.

"Thank you. It feels cool now. I'm sorry for the trouble I've caused. I'll pay you for the tent."

"Don't mention it. Let's get organized. I see your wife has sorted out your clothing and the sleeping bags. They don't appear to have suffered too much damage. They're fire resistant, but the tent isn't usable."

"The packs are okay, so are our clothes, superficially burned. It's only a big hole in the tent," Laura said.

Vanessa comforted her shaken guests while Brett finished pitching his tent.

"Take my tent. You'll be okay. The sleeping bags are fine. Just a small patch of melted nylon which won't interfere with the insulation."

Vanessa rekindled the fire and made more hot chocolate to soothe everyone's nerves. The northern lights exploded in the sky, leaving the guests speechless. The green train of some mysterious fairy floated through space, disappeared and sailed down again, brushing against the red silk of an ethereal cloth before sweeping the sky to leave only twinkling stars in its wake.

Brett produced a harmonica from his pocket. Vanessa was intrigued. So it was he who had played during that other camping trip. The guests gathered around the campfire and began to sing along. The impromptu concert helped to erase the shock of the accident. Soon afterwards, they retired for a second time that night.

Vanessa looked at Brett. "Those tents are not supposed to catch fire."

"We'll call the company and complain. It shouldn't have caught fire with just a match and a little fuel. We'll return all of them and switch to a better brand. Maybe even an old-fashioned prospector tent."

She sighed. "Nothing's perfect. We're going to have to double up in my tent."

"I'll sleep under the stars. I often do."

"Sleeping out isn't a great idea. Far from toughening you up, it actually weakens the body by using extra energy to keep warm. Tonight is exceptionally cold."

"I like seeing the stars over my head. And look, more northern lights."

They watched for another minute.

"Suit yourself." She lit her lantern and unzipped the entrance to creep inside. A dual thickness sleeping bag over a foam mat and an insulating layer of tiny pine branches the children had gathered when they had arrived provided a comfortable bed. The catalytic heater took the chill off the air. She made doubly sure her lantern was stable and hung her mitts and socks she'd been wearing on a line strung between the poles.

The inside temperature had risen a few degrees with the addition of the lantern. She undressed in comfort. She put on fresh socks, underwear and her thermal outfit. The feel of the silky cashmere against her skin was a comforting experience.

As Vanessa sat on the bedroll and toasted her toes against the tent heater, she reflected on how nothing keeps a body as warm as silk, except, perhaps sharing a sleeping bag with someone... A sigh of regret trailed from her lips.

She was startled by Brett's whisper outside the tent.

"Vanessa?"

"Yes?"

"Does your offer still hold?"

"Sure. Come on in."

She dragged her bedroll to one side, and he crept through the tent door, holding his bedroll under his arm. His muscular presence filled the tent.

"I took your advice." His voice was so humble she almost laughed.

"Watch your head against the lantern."

Hardly had the words been spoken when she realized that in undressing in front of the light she must have put on what must have been a wilderness striptease act exclusively for Brett's enjoyment. Which was probably why he changed his mind about sleeping out in the open. "You weren't watching me undress, by any chance?"

"I didn't look. Scout's honor! I didn't need to. I've seen more than your silhouette before now."

"Bastard!" Vanessa kicked the infuriating man with her stockinged foot. "You were enjoying the show."

"Okay, I admit it. Out there in the cold, it was divine. But the cloth of these winter tents is so much thicker, the picture was rather blurred. I won't complain if you want to make a repeat performance."

"Didn't we agree to forget about my moments of folly?" She drew up her knees and wrapped her arms around them.

"*I* didn't make any such agreement. I never hid the fact I want you."

The rasp in his voice affected her in ways she couldn't resist. "Be reasonable."

"Why don't you admit you want me, too?"

"That's not the point." She fought with herself.

"Just relax, can't you?"

"For me, a relationship has to be meaningful."

"Women are supposed to be creatures of love and passion, yet they seem incapable of enjoying themselves."

"Thank you for sharing your worldly experience. I'm sure many women do give in to their passions. I happen to be different. I don't even understand why you're interested in me, not when you have the delectable Ingrid waiting for you back at the lodge." Vanessa battled the rising heat that threatened to engulf her.

"That's where you're quite wrong. One, she means nothing to me, and two, I find you a very beautiful and lovable woman."

"She's good-looking and has a stunning figure."

"Forget Ingrid. She doesn't appeal to me, never did. By law, she's my step-sister, and that's exactly how I treat her. Anyway, why do we have to talk about her? She's been fired, and it's you I'm with."

"I'm just a trim athlete."

"Your curves fill my hand perfectly. I don't need anything more than that."

"You've got a one track mind."

"Look who's talking! Women want romance, marriage and babies, in that order. That's a pretty single track."

"There are many men who feel that way, too, about marriage." Vanessa spoke wistfully.

"Like Marcel?"

Now was the moment to tell him that Marcel meant nothing to her, but the devil within prevented her. "Why not Marcel?"

"I know Marcel well. Nice guy, but he's got other ideas in his head than settling down."

"Whereas you have a different goal?"

"I do. What about you? What's your goal in life?"

An inner voice urged her to say to win his love. Instead, she said, "Developing a successful dogsledding tour business."

Brett thoughtfully digested her reply before answering. "Then what?"

Vanessa knitted her brow, guessing he was leading her into a trap. "More involvement, I guess. Maybe a couple of lodges."

"Take it from one who's been there and done that. Success in business can be a lonely path to tread."

With a shake of her head, Vanessa tossed back her hair. "Loneliness isn't something I fear. When I want company, I always have my dogs to talk to."

"I love it when you get angry. Your eyes flash fire."

"I think we'd better switch off the heater and keep our sleeping bags firmly zipped up till tomorrow morning." The quaver in her voice betrayed her emotions.

Bret edged slowly over to her. Defensively, she rested her chin on her knees. His kiss became more insistent. Somewhere in the distant reaches of her brain, warning bells, very tiny ones, sounded. For a while, she resisted the inevitable. "No, we mustn't." Drunk with emotions, Vanessa slurred her words.

"Why not? You want this as much as I do."

"Please, let me go." The fear that trembled in her voice was directed not at him but at herself. She knew she would weaken if he kissed her again.

"If that's what you really want. I'd never force myself on you."

As soon as he released her, Vanessa sought the sanctuary of her sleeping bag.

With a low growl of barely contained frustration, Brett doused the lantern.

Chapter Thirty-Five

V anessa went about the morning task of watering and feeding the dogs. The sight of Brett's face shadowed by a day's growth tugged at her heart. Sleep had eluded her for hours after rejecting him. In the eerie light of a north country night, she now wished she hadn't.

The guests stirred in the tents. Duty called.

The trip continued smoothly, and the party took a mid-morning break. A late dawn burst through the gray night with red streamers. They stretched and stretched until they were so thin the sun could bound through. It touched the top of the mountains, crowning them in a glory of light. For a while, down below, the ground remained wrapped in darkness. Shards of light stretched the trees' shadows over a frozen lake. This serene hour was Vanessa's favorite time of the day. Brett, too, straightened to watch night metamorphose into day. He came to her, subdued and unthreatening, while the clients watched in amazement.

The sledding party was in a buoyant mood when they skirted Eagle Point.

Ken called out, "Brett, I'd like to treat everybody to dinner at the lodge."

"That's fine with me, if it's okay with Vanessa."

"If that's what everybody wants to do, I'm agreeable." What troubled her was having to meet Ingrid face to face, but she didn't voice it. The party continued on to the cabin and the end of the tour.

She was hoping her guests and Brett would climb into their cars and go to the lodge right away, while she could take her time, lots of time, to water and feed the dogs. Much to her dismay, everyone wanted to help and Brett gave her a ride to the lodge.

Panicked at seeing Brett and Vanessa, Ingrid who wasn't supposed to be on the floor, tried to escaped, but failed as another set of clients called her. Ingrid's unctuous charm with the guests wavered. Fearing Brett's wrath, since he'd said her services were no longer needed, she quietly retreated.

Brett motioned to Vanessa to sit down next to him. The dining room buzzed with animated conversation. He leaned over. "Did you find out who tampered with your bookings?" He whispered.

"I have my suspicions. Patrick has too."

"Tell me about them."

She toyed with the food on her plate. "I don't want to risk accusing an innocent person."

"Did young Toni have anything to do with it? Despite Ingrid no longer being the manager, she fired the girl a couple of days ago."

"The poor kid knew nothing about the scheme. She was used."

"People are always sacked for a reason. Apparently, she was spending more time thinking about her boyfriend than her work. By the way, who is her boyfriend?"

"Alden Carrigan."

"Then you're right, she wouldn't be responsible since Alden is away in Alaska. That leaves only one person."

She shrugged. "Someone who hates me enough."

"When you finish dinner, come with me to my office. We've got to get to the bottom of this."

Moments later, unnoticed by the guests, they slipped out of the dining room.

Brett motioned to Jon. "Ask Ingrid to come to my office, please."

"Sure thing, boss."

Vanessa seated herself in Brett's leather armchair. Before they could speak, Ingrid burst in.

"Ah, Ingrid! Just the person I want to talk to."

Ingrid's face tightened at the sight of Vanessa. "What is it?"

"We have some unfinished business to deal with." Brett's features hardened. "Did you sabotage Vanessa's business?"

His former manager paled under her makeup. Her lips compressed into a thin white line. The silence stretched into the uneasy calm before a storm. Under Brett's baleful glare, Ingrid retreated to the door.

"You may as well confess."

Ingrid's voice was barely audible. "I did it for you."

"For me?" His incredulous laugh reverberated around the paneled room.

"I wanted her away from here. She's interfering with your plans."

"*She* has a name! Whatever your motive was, tampering with her bookings was a most despicable act, a criminal act, in fact."

"I wanted the best for you."

A rictus at the edge of Brett's mouth was the only outward sign of his anger. "Best for me? You've always done what's best for yourself. So explain."

Ingrid raised her chin in defiance. "We're losing business since we've been obliged to go through town to access our other trails. She's too stubborn to let us use the direct trail, like we always have."

Brett's face darkened. His features hardened menacingly. "Leave the lodge immediately. Your month's notice is over. And be thankful I'm not calling the police."

"Brett…"

He slapped the desk. "Now!"

His glacial tone cut short her pleading. Ingrid averted her eyes. Then, shooting a murderous look in Vanessa's direction, Ingrid fled muttering, "He's going to kill me!"

Vanessa's head swiveled. Brett stretched his neck, half standing to go after Ingrid.

"What does she mean by that?" Vanessa said.

He fell back in his chair and propped his head on his hand, a picture of weariness. "I don't know what's got into her."

Vanessa walked over and placed her hand on his shoulder. "Ingrid's not a bad person deep down. She only behaved rashly."

"You must have thought I was behind that scheme. You had every right to."

"I didn't really believe you had anything to do with it. It just wasn't like you, but when you get fed poisonous information, it's hard not to wonder if maybe there's some truth in it."

Vanessa saw the torment in his dark eyes battle with a sea of conflicting emotions. Brett broke the spell. The inner struggle was over. He looked calmer than she had ever seen him. Humbled, too. "Let's get back to our guests to thank them. It's time I took you home."

A smile formed on her lips. Home, he'd said. She hoped he meant it for them both. It was a contented but weary group of clients that thanked Vanessa and Brett for the backcountry adventure. Since no one was hurt, the flaming tent became something to laugh about, one they would enjoy recounting to their less intrepid friends.

***

The truck glided into the silent yard. "The dogs must know the engine. They don't even bother to say hi," Brett said.

"That's correct. They recognize sounds and decide whether or not it deserves a greeting. Let's check them. I'll be glad when I can build proper pens in the spring."

A while later, they relaxed in front of the wood stove.

"Vanessa..."

"Let's not talk."

He gently pulled her into his arms. "Tomorrow, I'm off to Tamarack Lodge. It's barely three hours ride by snowmobile from here. I'm thinking of buying the place and promised the present owner, Willard Holt, I would drop by to inspect the place. When I come back, there're things we should talk about."

She snuggled closer. His hand freed her hair. He tasted of coffee and the outdoors.

"I'll be waiting for you."

"Remember, the day after tomorrow is reserved for us."

Vanessa sat cradling her chin in her hands long after he'd gone. "The day after tomorrow!" The words sang in her heart, stirring the hope she'd kept bottled up for so long. Now she had recognized that he had not tried to run her out of her land, she was tempted to look at the future. Would he tell her again he loved her? The question kept dancing in her mind. This time, she was ready to believe him, ready to release all that love she had so firmly compressed into the deepest recess of her heart. She closed her eyes to dream.

Even the heavy overcast sky the next day couldn't dampen her spirits, nor did it deter the enthusiastic people who crowded into her yard.

"Ms. Riley, I hope it'll be alright. We've brought two friends with us."

Vanessa eyed up the young people. Obviously athletic and used to the outdoors, they were wearing the right winter clothes. "We'll manage fine. You are Lew, aren't you?"

The young man grinned. "That's me."

"Didn't you say you wanted to try driving a sled?"

"I did. Is it possible?"

"Of course. Especially now with eight people."

"Can I drive too? I'm Mara. I'm a figure skater and I consider myself pretty strong."

Chuckles greeted her words.

"What's important is that you have a good sense of balance and coordination. You need it behind dogs. I'll give you Singarnak for lead. She's unflappable."

"Yay!"

Vanessa and Stefan conferred on the choice of dogs for the teams. At that moment, all the dogs started a deafening ruckus. The guests smiled while Stefan and Vanessa looked toward the road. Such howling signaled the arrival of a vehicle. As fast as they started, the dogs stopped. There was no sound of engine.

"False alarm," Vanessa said.

Stefan picked up the harnesses. "I wonder though. I've seen shadows around the lodge. Marcel told me you had met snowmobilers by Mercy Lake."

They walked into the pens, followed by their eager guests. Vanessa sorted the harness for each dog. "I don't think there is any connection."

"Just a few strange things going on. I think there may be some traffickers in the area."

Jimmy arrived to take care of a later ride.

The lesson on how to harness the dogs began. *There may be some traffickers in the area.* Stefan's words stuck in her mind, but right now she was teaching her eager students the finer points of keeping the sled upright on its runners in a tight turn.

She told Stefan to take the lead so she could watch over the novice drivers from the rear.

Soon the teams were trotting down the Tapiskoot's trail to the accompaniment of the young people's cries of delight and the pups' wails filling the air because they had been left behind.

Dusk changed to night by the time the party got back to the yard, much later than planned, as everyone had clamored to take a turn at driving a sled. There had been so much laughter that Vanessa's sides still cramped.

They fed the dogs, cleaned up and played with the pups. Finally, the young folks went on their way.

"Staying for a bite to eat, Stefan? I see Jimmy put a stew on the stove."

"I'm ravenous and I'm not expected home till much later."

"It smells delicious."

"Anything to fill the hole in my stomach." He put plates on the table. The phone rang.

"Hi, Brett. How was your day?"

"Successful. And yours."

"We had fun."

"Does Buddy want to see me?"

"If he doesn't, I know someone who'd like to."

"Must be Lulik, then."

"Yes, sure." They laughed. "See you."

"Lancaster coming over?" Stephan stirred the casserole.

"Checking on his dog."

He winked. "Sure, I believe that!"

Soon after, the dogs greeted Brett's arrival with a long howl. A blast of cold air came in with him. He peeled off his outer clothes. Buddy came to him wagging his tail. Brett hugged him, then sat down, Buddy at his feet. "It's smells delicious."

"Want some?" Vanessa put a plate in front of him.

"Thanks. So Stephan, you're enjoying yourself?"

"Yes, boss. You should try it sometimes."

His mouth full of casserole, Brett nodded. Vanessa chuckled.

"How about your kids, Stephan, would they like another ride?" Vanessa said.

"You bet. Carine's been bugging me. She's my oldest."

Vanessa tilted her head. "Carine, Bobby, Justin and Savanah. Your wife's Aline?"

Stephan grinned. "That's them."

"They came for a ride during the... how shall I say... the dry period."

Brett put his hand on hers. "I heard they had a good time."

A moment of hesitation. She looked at Stefan. "Thanks for sending them." He hadn't done it out of pity, but as Marcel had said, to help in time of need. A serene smile came back to her lips.

"I have more work for Aline. All the dogs need new collars, and I need a stack of harnesses in reserve. Some dogs are not above taking a chew on their harness when they have to wait."

"She'll be pleased."

"Are the kids interested in racing?" Brett asked.

"Carine and Bobby used to come to the races. They loved it." A tender smile floated on his lips. "Anyway, should we go out and check around the place in case there'd been someone this morning?"

Brett lifted his head and swallowed quickly. "What d'you mean?"

Vanessa shrugged. "The dogs sounded the alarm, not a greeting like they do when a vehicle pulls in. There was nobody, but then they'll also howl if a mule deer comes near."

Stephan shook his head. "With the noise our young people were making, no respectable mule deer, not even a rabbit, would have come close. I say that, because twice I've seen a shadow around the storage sheds at the lodge."

Brett frowned. "You didn't tell me."

"Was about to. I just wanted to make sure I wasn't imagining things."

They exchanged glances. Unease permeated the atmosphere. Vanessa stood and went to the bedroom. After a quick check in the closet, she glanced into the pantry. "It doesn't look like anyone came in here. Nothing has been touched."

The phone rang again.

"Marcel! Good to hear from you." When the conversation ended, Vanessa turned to the men. "Marcel is back. He's reporting for duty in the morning."

"Good. It'll ease the workload. Now, I better get home. See you tomorrow." Stefan left.

"I should go too, but I'm not too happy about what Stefan said. What's going on?"

"There must be a logical explanation."

Brett pulled her into his arms. "I'll get to the bottom of this. Tomorrow is our day." His mouth imprisoned hers.

For the next few minutes, the world spun into outer space.

"I'd like to stay."

"But you've got to check things over at the lodge. And Buddy is going with you to his new home tonight."

He pulled away from her. "Lock your door."

"If it's a burglar, the dogs will let me know."

"Lock your door, all the same, and don't go out. Phone me. I'll keep my cell under my pillow, but call on the landline in case you have no connection. By the way, I'll ask the IT for more coverage on my tower so you can run your business without having to rely on Patrick's connection. I'll give you a password as soon as they bring you a modem."

Her hand reached his cheek for a soft caress. "Maybe I'll phone, anyway."

He grabbed her hand, turned it over and kissed her palm.

"Do."

"I won't though. Let's keep that for an emergency."

Regret showed on his face, he braved the cold, Buddy in his arms. Moments later, the sound of the diesel engine died away. Nobody locked doors in the area and she never did. Vanessa sighed and slid the deadbolt in place.

CHAPTER THIRTY-SIX

Brett bent to unlace his boots. A movement caught his eye by his office door. "What are you doing here?"

Ingrid flushed red. "Packing."

"I don't see any suitcases."

She took a big breath. "My things are in my room. I was going over the accounts with Jon."

"How long does that take?"

"Not long. Look, Brett, I'm sorry. I'm deeply sorry. I've been under a lot of stress. How can I apologize? I should never have done what I did... but it seemed to be the..."

As stern as a judge, he waited. Tears pooled in Ingrid's eyes. A sigh escaped Brett's chest. Vanessa didn't bear a grudge. How she could be so forgiving was beyond him, but she was. He'd follow her lead. After all, Ingrid was his sister. The sled dog tour business was rebounding. The scar of that unsavory incident would soon disappear.

"I accept the apology. Perhaps you could also apologize to Vanessa. But be gone as soon as everything is in order."

Her voice thinned to a whisper. "Thank you, Brett. And thank you for the check."

He waved her on and mounted the steps to his office. With a powerful flashlight and a bunch of keys in his hands, he was outside in seconds. He went straight to the bigger storage building, inserted a key in the lock and switch on his flashlight.

The beam lit up bundles of sleeping bags and parkas on wide shelves. On the floor, boots were lined up by sizes. To the side, mitts, hats and snowmobile suits hung from pegs. Brett couldn't see anything different from the last time he looked in.

He carefully relocked the door, then moved on to another building. It was unlocked. Inside, paddles and life jackets stood in neat rows. Waterproof bags and other camping gear were stacked up neatly. Nothing had been moved since the summer, if the dust was any indication.

With relief, Brett locked the door. When he turned round, he almost bumped into a solid body.

"What the hell..!"

"Sorry to startle you," Dexter said. "I saw the light and wondered."

"My staff reported seeing shadows around the sheds."

"Anything missing?"

They walked toward a smaller shed.

"Not as far as I can see. We store all the extra gear in there."

Dexter pointed downward. "Lots of tracks."

Brett directed the beam onto the snow. "Must be staff. We keep some clothing equipment for the guests in the lodge, but depending on the numbers, we often need more. This is the wood shed."

They both looked into the shed. Brett trained his light beam into every corner. There was nothing except rows of neatly stacked logs.

He opened the door of the tool shed and flashed the light inside.

Dexter stepped in. "A nice ride-on snowblower."

"A much needed item. Then we've got a couple of handheld blowers and brush cutters, trail mowers, sickle bar mowers. That sort of thing."

"Everything you need to maintain the grounds summer and winter."

Dexter trailed a finger over the edge of a shelf. His finger showed a thin gray, powdery substance. He rubbed it with his thumb. "Dust."

"The shed's used quite a lot, but no one does any housekeeping in here. Hey, just a moment! The door was unlocked. It's a rule that it must always be locked. Not that we fear burglars, but we don't need curious kids looking into the sheds when they play."

"Do you get many kids?"

"Some, mostly older kids with their parents."

Dexter shook his head. "Indeed, they see nothing wrong with looking around private property."

"Right. I'd better check the gas shack. If anyone wants to steal something, it's more likely fuel." He locked the tool shed and shook the door to make sure it was secure. They walked to the end of the yard where a small shed, next to a tank high on a steel cradle, stood away from the trees and the other buildings.

Dexter walked round the back and stopped. The snow hadn't been cleared. "It doesn't look as it's been tampered with."

"Only the mechanics and I have the keys to this shed and the gas tank." Brett opened the door and pointed to jerrycans. "Bob fills them."

"Hardly worth stealing, really."

"Never had a problem that way."

"Do you mind if we go back and do a closer inspection of the buildings?"

"No need to. I've just done it. You should be back with the other guests taking in the evening entertainment."

"I'm working tonight."

A look of incomprehension spread across Brett's face. Dexter reached inside his parka and flicked open a wallet.

"Police Inspector?" Stunned, Brett's eyes widened.

"In short, the narcotics branch."

"What's that got to do with me?"

"We've been following leads right to this area."

"Surely, not here at the lodge!" Brett's voice rose with outrage. "My business would be ruined! Are you going to arrest somebody?"

Dexter shrugged. "Not until I find evidence. That's why I'm asking for your cooperation."

A subdued Brett reopened each building, while Dexter produced a small but powerful LED headlamp to inspect the contents in detail, moving, lifting and replacing each item.

"Glad to say, Lancaster, that I don't see anything hidden in here."

The anxiety disappeared from Brett's brow. "Let me make sure everything is locked."

"Some footprints are very small. Maybe, women's tracks."

"I have female staff. Anyone could be sent out to fetch some item or other."

"Of course. Keep mum about all this, would you?"

A dusting of snow started falling. Brett brushed flakes off his face. "Shouldn't I tell my employees to be on the alert?"

"No, not a word. It'll be easier for me to do my job."

"So all the times you've come here was for the investigation, not for fun?"

Dexter laughed as they walked back to the lodge. "I've had fun, too."

"Good!"

"Is that snow going to fall hard?"

"This piddle? Won't last more than a few minutes. Why?"

Dexter held the door open for Brett. "I'd like to take a machine out on my own tomorrow morning."

"Go ahead. It won't make a dent on the trails. Just be careful in the ditches to town. The groomer will continue smoothing the trail in the morning, but it'll take all day. We're putting it through the municipal woods and east of the narrows."

"That's sounds interesting."

"May as well make the most of it."

"I heard this is because Ms. Riley won't let you through her land. Is that correct?"

Brett shrugged. "It's her right. I can understand that." He went to his office, his mind still reeling from Dexter's disclosures.

***

Night had barely lifted when Dexter bounced along the partly groomed trail in the roadside ditch and the new detour around the town. Finally, he joined the trail network in the Aishin forest. He checked his map and a piece of paper with the hand-drawn map he had made from memory after his trip with Vanessa. He soon arrived on the edge of Brett's property, where Vanessa had taken him and had been surprised to find the trail had been used in recent days. Cautiously, he followed the tracks.

With the machine in low gear, Dexter cast glances left and right to try to see through the curtain of spruce and denuded larch. Then, as the tracks petered out, he saw something ahead. He pulled his binoculars out. A small weathered shed stood in the midst of the trees. Using the utmost caution, he approached a little farther. Almost derelict, with its shingle roof and boarded-up windows, it had endured the ravages of time.

Dexter turned the machine and killed the engine. He looked at the mileage, then at his map. An eyebrow went up. He pulled out his GPS. Pencil in hand, he wrote down the coordinates. A moment later, he gave a low whistle. The shed was indeed inside Vanessa's boundaries. He was actually standing on her land.

As he came close to the structure, he saw a shiny padlock on the door. *Bingo! Who would put a lock on an old shack in the middle of nowhere? Not Vanessa? It didn't fit, but...* He kicked through the deep snow around the shed and noticed the presence of prints, some small, others larger. There was no other entrance than the padlocked door.

A throaty laugh escaped him while he selected a tool from a key ring. Ten seconds later, the padlock sprang open. He fished his headlight from his inner pocket and cast the beam around. A bunk, a stove without a chimney pipe, a rickety table and two dilapidated chairs under the boarded window. Not much, but enough for a man to have lived in moderate comfort in times long past.

Dexter trailed a finger over the tabletop. No dust. His blood coursed faster in his veins, as it always did when he was closing on his prey. He opened the door of the only cabinet on the wall opposite the window. A few cans, some spices and a ten-pound bag of flour sat on the shelves. As he examined the shelf, he noticed some floury drag marks and wondered if sometimes there had been more than one bag of flour.

The remote whine of a snowmobile engine caught Dexter's ear. He went and stood by the open door. The sound moved away. He returned inside the shed. Before touching the flour bag, he took his camera from its insulated case and took pictures. With latex gloved hands, he retrieved the bag of flour and sniffed it. *I'm no dog. Too bad.*

He put the bag on the table and examined it. It was just an ordinary flour bag, properly sealed. He attached the headlamp over his woolen cap, adjusted the beam, and took out his survival knife. With slow and deliberate movements, he slid the knife under the top flap until it came unstuck.

Adrenaline pumped in his body. This was the heady rush he got when he finally reached a goal. A sealed plastic bag of white powder was embedded in the flour.

"My lucky day!" He took more pictures. When that was done, he pulled his satellite phone and dialed a number praying for a connection. Luck was with him. The shack stood at the top of a low ridge. He breathed with relief when the phone dinged.

"I've got just under 10 lb."

A voice at the other end replied, "Speak up."

"I'm in the bush." He twiddled with the phone. "Better?"

"Clear. Go ahead."

He related his find. From the survival bag on his wide-track snowmobile, he withdrew a yellow, waterproof canoe bag. After placing his booty inside, he deposited the canoe bag in the snowmobile's carrier and secured it with bungee cords as an extra precaution.

Chapter Thirty-Seven

D exter and Ron Larsen got out of an innocuous SUV on the road. Tapiskoot yard already housed two vehicles. With the clients settled in the sled, Stefan waved goodbye. Through the jack pines at the entrance of the yard, Dexter observed Vanessa showing the dogs to a couple of children.

He approached. "Hello, Vanessa. I see you're busy."

"And happy to be. Did you come for a ride?"

"No, just hanging about, but maybe later. I wanted to discover your operation with all these children. I meant to ask you the other day, what do you keep in the sheds?"

"Dog food, spare clothing, wood. They're unlocked if you're interested. Make yourself at home. I have to go before the dogs decide to take the little ones out on their own." Her visitors always asked all manner of questions. She didn't think his was odd.

He watched her, smiling, gentle and efficient. He wasn't surprised when Brett walked in just as he was about to check the dog food shed.

"Dexter. What are you doing here?"

"My job."

"Sorry I asked. Though, I understand your lead brought you to my business, but Vanessa is too far away from Wolf Hollow to be concerned."

"What if I told you I found something of interest on Ms. Riley's property? In an old shack out there in the middle of the forest?"

"You've got to be kidding me."

"Alas, no."

"Where?"

"In her shack."

Eyebrows high on his forehead, Brett scoffed. "What shack? I don't know of any shack. I'm pretty sure she doesn't, either."

"The shack that is located close to the northern edge of her property."

"I never saw a shack there. We used to go right through to get to my property."

"It's not too far from your south boundary line."

Brett realized that Dexter gave out information with an eye-dropper. "Honestly, I never knew of the existence of a shack where you describe. What use would it serve? It's too far away from her cabin."

"There're fresh snowmobile tracks around it."

"But not dogsled tracks."

Dexter crimped his lips to prevent a smile. "You're quite correct."

"So that leaves a connection to the lodge. As you doubtless know, we have the most snowmobiles in the area."

"We'll make a detective out of you, yet. Ms. Riley could have got there by snowmobile."

Brett mocked him. "She doesn't own one and would never even drive one. I tried to convince her to try, but failed."

Vanessa's return cut short their conversation. Brett remained puzzled.

The excited children tumbled out of the sled and watched the un-hitching of the dogs, all the while bombarding Vanessa with questions. She busied herself with returning the dogs to their pickets. When she was finally free, and the parents gone with their children, she invited the two men inside. Sergeant Larsen paced outside until they were gone, then walked to the dog food shed.

"Coffee for you both?"

"Yes, please."

She served the coffee and added a plate of cookies to the table.

"Ms. Riley, I'm going to ask you to remain at Tapiskoot."

"What do you mean?"

"That you are not to leave your house."

She was stunned. "Remain, why?" The sudden realization of the significance of the few unusual remarks from Dexter came flooding back to her. "Who exactly are you, Mr. Weiman?"

He showed her his badge and police ID. Vanessa, not fully comprehending, looked up at Brett.

"The inspector here has found some illegal merchandise in your shack at the northern end of your property," Brett said.

"What shack?"

"The one near your boundary with my land."

"There's no shack there."

Dexter nodded while looking into her eyes. "Yes, there is."

"Could you, one of you, be a little more explicit? I don't know what you're talking about. What shack, what illegal merchandise? Besides the dog food, the sled equipment and spare clothing for guests, there's no other merchandise here in my sheds... What other shack did you say?"

Dexter glanced at Brett. "There's a small shack on your property, four or five hundred yards inside the northern boundary."

"I've never seen any shack. Edmund never told me there was anything else on the land. There was nothing in the real estate description or the land title deed. I must have followed every one of the trails he has cut. In fact, that's where I take the children on tours, but I never saw a shack or shed or anything except trees and marshes and two beaver lodges."

"That's becoming obvious. However, it is on your property. And presently housing an illegal substance."

Aghast, she tried to enunciate her words clearly. "That means someone knew about it and has been using for some traffic while I didn't even know it existed."

"It still is evidence. Therefore, I'm asking you to remain in your cabin."

"No. First, I have to feed and care for my dogs. Then I have a business to run, and the next few days are booked solid. After the disaster of the past three weeks, there's no way I'm going to lose anymore business. Sorry to be contradictory, but I have nothing to do with that mysterious shack and whatever traffic you found."

Brett slapped the table with his hands. "Weiman, you know Vanessa isn't involved. For goodness' sake, she didn't even know there was an old shack on her land. You can't put her under arrest for nothing."

The dogs howled and soon after, Stefan returned. Without a glance at the inspector, Vanessa went out to help her guide and their guests. She waved them goodbye, while Stefan gathered up the equipment. Before he had time to put it away, it was Marcel's turn to show up.

They greeted him as did the dogs in the pens. They soon took care of the dogs and waved goodbye to the clients.

"Come in, you two. We're about to have dinner as soon as the inspector leaves."

While Vanessa busied herself with dinner, the men brought the guides up to date on the latest events.

Marcel frowned. "All this fits with the snowmobiles Vanessa spotted at Mercy Lake."

Weiman shot her an inquiring look. Brett just stared. She recounted her trip and the discovery of the snowmobilers.

Brett raked his hand through his hair. "How can you be sure it was Ingrid?"

"I've had the displeasure to meet her on a few occasions. I think I can recognize her from a distance. Who else has platinum blond hair?"

"The woman was riding a canary yellow snowmobile. I reckon it was a Polaris 850 Rush Pro-S, from Vanessa's description," Stefan said. "How many yellow snowmobiles of that particular make and model are there in Donek?"

Stunned, Brett was tearing at his hair. "Yes, we do, in fact, have a yellow 850, but the notion of Ingrid riding a snowmobile is beyond anyone's imagination. It's a powerful snowmobile! Not one for a novice rider. It doesn't make sense. I fired her because she was harassing Vanessa, but that incident took place long before me firing her."

"Actually, I've had her watched for some time. I saw her twice on that Polaris. In addition, one of your employees mentioned she has a rather unsavory regular visitor. We're watching him too."

"Was it Karl?"

Dexter nodded. "Karl did mention that Ingrid has an occasional visitor. He never stays more than a few minutes."

"He didn't tell me anything."

"Maybe he didn't think appropriate to comment on Ms. Lancaster's movements or who she meets. After all, she was his boss."

Sergeant Larsen knocked and let himself in. He looked at the inspector and shook his head. Dexter stood and took his leave. Only when the sound of their vehicle died away did Brett explode with anger. Vanessa had remained silent, too upset to speak. Stefan served the stew which simmered in its pot on the stove.

"We'll sort it out, don't worry," Marcel said. "The wind has picked up. It's going to blow hard. We should leave as soon as we do justice to this delicious stew."

"I'm staying here." Brett's forceful tone didn't surprise anyone. "And I think you two should stay at the lodge."

"Okay, I'll stay at the lodge, just in case," Stefan said. "May I phone Aline?"

"Please go ahead."

Marcel nodded. "Agreed, I'll stay. I don't like this turn of events. I'll bunk with Stefan."

They all went out in the blowing snow to ensure that the dogs were secure. The two guides left. Back in the cabin, Brett pulled a blanket from the closet.

"I'll take the sofa. Go ahead to the bathroom. I'll wait."

"I'm trying to make sense of it all. Why would Ingrid... No, I know why. But to stoop to putting drugs in that shack to have me arrested goes beyond malice. You don't have to stay over, Brett. I'll be fine and I'll lock the door. "

"When drugs are involved, danger is close."

"I have a thirty-two security alarm outside. No one will sneak in. You should really go home and keep an eye on your manager."

He sighed. "Which she no longer is. You're right, I ought to make sure she isn't up to something. I'm pretty sure Stefan and Marcel are staying over to do just that, but she isn't their responsibility. They can't go into her room, and I intend to search it."

When he kissed her, he reined in his passion and let tenderness take over.

The wind blew all night, rattling the cabin's triple-pane windows. Morning brought Stefan and Marcel. Soon after, the first clients arrived. Stefan tugged Vanessa's sleeve.

"Have you seen the sky? We're in for a big storm, a blizzard actually. It blows hard around here with the lake acting as a funnel."

"Strange that the forecast didn't mention a storm."

Stefan gave a gruff laugh. "They never do until it drifts over the radio station window. We have to cancel the trip. We can't take them as far as Leech Portage as promised and camp overnight. There wouldn't be time to make it back before the blizzard hits full blast."

Despair colored her voice. "I can't cancel! These people were already canceled and have booked a second time. They've driven all the way from Calgary."

Marcel was showing the dogs to the clients and preparing the sled. They came into the cabin. Stefan took his friend apart to talk quietly out of earshot of the guests.

Marcel signaled to Vanessa. "We're switching. Stefan will take the clients. He'll drive to Tamarack Lodge and hunker down there until the weather lets up. The guests will realize that camping out isn't a good idea. The lodge is well-equipped to entertain visitors."

"Are you sure you can make it safely?" Vanessa murmured.

"Positive. Let's leave."

Vanessa did a quick check of her guests' clothing and ushered them out. Excited, they left without wasting time. Vanessa had no reason to worry. They were safe in Stefan's hands. He was familiar with the snowmobile trails, which would be hard and would make the going easier.

She turned to Marcel and cast a glance at her notebook. "This doesn't look good. We've got four people coming between eleven and five."

"It'll start blowing hard before then."

"But I can't cancel. They must already be on their way."

"I'll tell you what. Let's take them in a snake pattern along your trails and perhaps the lakeshore."

"Snake pattern? What do you mean?"

"We start down there at the edge of the lake, go away from the lake, make a one-mile loop on your trail and come back almost to the starting point, and back out again just a little farther."

"This is really ingenuous."

"The clients won't know the difference. I don't think so anyway. If the storm begins to hit hard, they'll be happy that we can get back home in fifteen minutes."

"Marcel, you're a genius! Old Ed's trails do wind around a lot. He drew a map for me." She handed him the crinkled map.

He chuckled. "Good. Like that, there's no chance for the guests to recognize the way. We'll slalom our way through the trees. This is a fantastic trail network."

"When the kids ask how far we've been, I tell them we're close to the North Pole. You take the lead with Neviartok team and put Upingak at the head. She'll find her way anywhere. She has the nose of a bloodhound."

Laughter relieved some of the mounting tension.

The clients arrived on the dot of one. They were a young couple with their two small children. They eagerly piled into the sleds, but not before insisting on petting the dogs. Snow was falling thickly by the time the party was ready to set off, but the wind had not yet reach full strength, and the trees offered good protection.

Just before releasing the brake, Marcel leaned over and whispered in Vanessa's ear. "This snow will cover our tracks. Like that, we'll be able to backtrack even closer to home without anyone being any the wiser."

The excursion was a resounding success. Snow was coming down even thicker by the time the dogs made the final dash to the cabin. Blinded by the thick flakes, Vanessa barely saw her lead dogs until she reached the shelter of the yard. Driving through the forest in a snowstorm was a magical experience and had only heightened her clients' enjoyment.

Vanessa was still worried about their safety. "I hope you're not heading back to Whitehorse in this. I suggest you stop at Wolf Hollow Lodge until it's over. Marcel will lead the way for you in his truck."

The chores finished, Vanessa stretched out on the sofa with a book. Harold Glover had sent her a copy of his latest work: *The Guaranteed Path to Financial Success*, along with a long document relating to her business' losses and ways to mitigate them should it happen again. Try as she might, her mind refused to concentrate on the words. Her thoughts were with Brett. He hadn't phoned. Maybe he'd brave the storm and come to her cabin. She berated herself. Even two miles in such a storm could be dangerous.

CHAPTER THIRTY-EIGHT

The storm still had not abated by the following morning. By now, snow had piled knee high in the yard. She had to don snowshoes to feed the dogs. The hardy Arctic dogs shunned their snug houses, preferring instead to curl up in the open and let the snow settle over them. Painstakingly, she checked all the collars and made sure all the chains were free of snow. There was just enough wind through the open yard to blow most of the snow beyond the pens.

There was no need to wonder how she would be spending the day. Everything over a vast area was at a standstill. Her bookings for the day were all local, so she didn't worry about those. They'd return another day.

Waiting for the storm to pass was a test of endurance. To occupy her hands, she cooked.

From time to time, she peered through the window. It was still snowing, but she knew nothing would prevent Brett's snowmobile from getting through.

The shrill ring of the phone made her jump. She expected it to be Brett, but it was Jon' voice on the line.

"Hi, Vanessa. Is Brett with you?"

"No, he's not here."

"He left last night. I wondered if he was at your place."

"No. I expected him to call this morning."

"Where did he go? Any idea?"

"None. Why would he go out after he told the guides to stay at the lodge, instead of driving home in the storm?"

"I was wondering why he set out with the storm threatening and assumed he was going to you. It's only a short distance."

Anxiety mingled with fear churned in Vanessa's stomach. "What about Ingrid? Is she there?"

"No. I think she left yesterday."

"Did they leave together?"

"I don't know. It's been so hectic here, what with guests staying over and drivers caught out on the highway and being directed to the lodge by the already packed Donek Hotel."

Dexter came on the line. "Ms. Lancaster was spotted on a snowmobile on a trail south of the lodge."

Desperation washed over Vanessa. "Brett must have gone after her."

"Very likely. By the way, we arrested a certain Dan Cipolla."

"Who is he?"

"You don't know him?"

"Never heard the name. If he had been a client, I'd recognize the name."

"He's a cog in a drug trafficking organization. He confirmed using Ms. Lancaster to ferry parcels that came over the border." He paused. "Cipolla said he was grateful to you for letting him use your shack."

A cry sprung from her chest. "What? It can't be. This is ridiculous. As I told you, I didn't even know there was a shack on my land."

"I know. Don't worry for the moment. I'll talk to you later."

Marcel came on the phone. "I believe Brett's gone after his sister. The wide track Polaris is missing."

"Do you know if he had survival equipment?"

"Must have. He's very fussy about safety. Jon thinks he was traveling light. No toboggan. So he wouldn't have much in the way of supplies with him, but he'll have an essential emergency pack. I'll call the rangers. Not that it'll do much good. Even they aren't moving in these conditions."

"My dogs can. I'll find him."

"Vanessa! Don't you dare go out, it's still snowing hard!"

"I can handle myself."

"Please! When it's safe, we'll mount a search and rescue mission. We don't want to have to search for two missing persons, or three."

"I once drove a team in a raging blizzard up near Kuglutuk in the high Arctic. I know what my dogs can do."

"Vanessa, Listen! Brett is no fool. He'll have dug himself a snow shelter for the night."

"According to you, he has little in the way of equipment."

Marcel sighed. "As I said, he'll have a basic survival kit in his machine. He'll have a space blanket, a folding shovel and plenty of high energy bars."

"Which trail south was Ingrid seen on?"

Vanessa knew from the tone of his voice that he had pulled a grimace. "The trail toward the park, but it stops at Beaver Lake, a damn big lake too, on the boundary. Then it turns south again. Look, it's a folly to try, even though I'm sure your dogs can travel in this mess. Snow piles up high quickly around here."

"I know. I've already prepared my stuff. Bye, Marcel."

"Vanessa, don't hang up! Listen, you're more stubborn than Brett himself. I can't tie you up. Keep off the lakes. Out in the open, the wind will blow you off course and you'll just travel in circles. Stay in the trees. Whatever you do, trust your compass. And use that damned GPS!"

He made her write down the map references of the route.

"And if Brett left soon after we got here, I reckon he would have reached the head of the lake by the time it became unsafe to travel. But I'll say it again. It's madness to venture out until the storm abates."

"It's already lessening."

Inwardly calm but with a runaway pulse, Vanessa quickly packed food and clothing for herself and an extra parka, socks and mitts for Brett. She wasted no time putting her winter clothes over her thermal underwear. The fine wool proved an excellent insulation next to her skin. The ever-ready bag for dog care over her shoulder, she went out.

Methodically, she readied the big sled and collected the harnesses. For her team, she chose Neviartok and nine of his more robust companions, including Lulik, whom she placed in the lead with stalwart Amaruq. Those ten dogs made for a powerful team. The restraint and toughness of her northern dogs never ceased to amaze her. Of all the dogs that could take her to Brett, these were the ones. They must have understood the serious urgency, for they didn't exhibit their normal exuberance, but leaned into their harnesses with determination.

A last-minute check and she gave the signal to start. The dogs set off, pulling hard, heads bent to the wind and falling snow, plodding slowly through the deep powder. At every turn, piled snow blocked the trail, hard-packed upwind and miserably soft on the lee side. Although the pines broke the strength of the wind, snow swirled about her whenever she crossed an open space. So intense was the storm, she could scarcely keep sight of her leaders. Her world had been reduced to a swirling vortex of white.

Snow soon clogged up her goggles. She tore them off and pulled her hood, edged with fur, low over her face to protect it. At intervals, she faced away from the wind to check her compass. By some miracle, she and her team were still headed in the right direction and, according to the GPS, not so useless after all, still on the right trail.

Vanessa knew when they reached Beaver Lake. Without the trees to shield her from the storm, she found herself in a featureless landscape. Sky and land blended seamlessly. Nowhere could she discern the vaguest landmark. Up in front, Lulik lifted her muzzle and whined. Vanessa ordered a halt. She needed to find her way back into the trees, where the trail turned south to skirt the lake. Only there would they be protected. Since day or night made no difference in the moving snow, she'd continue until the dogs started to show signs of fatigue. She smiled inwardly. That wouldn't happen for a number of hours yet.

Lulik infuriated her by refusing to obey the halt command for more than a few seconds. The lead dog set off in a direction of her own and dragged the other nine snow-encrusted huskies with her onto the lake.

Fear gripped Vanessa. Just what she didn't want to happen. The sled brake scraped uselessly on polished lake ice stripped clean by the wind. Her futile attempts to stop the sled had no effect on the dogs. The glare ice offered them a firmer footing than the loose snow. They hurled themselves toward the mysterious destination known only to Lulik.

A musher's worst nightmare is to lose control of the sled and the team, particularly on a frozen lake. Vanessa's stomach churned as she realized this was just what was happening to her. She prayed that Lulik and Amaruq could maintain a straight course toward the trees and hopefully pick up the trail beyond. After an interminable period of moving through a blind void, she felt the ground rise beneath the sled runners. A solitary tree came in sight, bent low by the weight of the snow. Then another, and another. She had made it across the lake and into the buffer of the forest.

At one point in their relentless march, she thought they crossed a marked trail. All her efforts to turn the team onto it were in vain. Lulik was bound for a mystery destination. Tears of helplessness welled up in the corners of her eyes and left her eyelids encrusted with ice. In the deep snow, she had no hope of stopping ten powerful sled dogs hell bent on pursuing their own goal.

Her lead dogs halted so abruptly that the rest of the team collided with them. "Oh, no!" Vanessa expected a big dog fight. Lulik began pawing the snow at the base of a drift. The rest of the pack joined in.

"Lulik! Stop! For heaven's sake! It may be a bear's den." Lulik paid no heed to the warning. The other dogs were now frantically digging. Sick with fear, Vanessa waded through the drift to pull them away. She had enough problems on her hands without rousing a hibernating bear. After a couple of clumsy steps, Vanessa lost balance and pitched forward into the drift. In an instinctive gesture to break her fall, she threw her hands forward. They struck a hard object buried under the snow. A hard object? Certainly, no bear. That was a relief. By scooping with her mittened hands, she uncovered something which definitely did not belong in a bear's den. A few seconds later and she exposed the rounded contour of a snowmobile windshield. Emotions swirled through her. It had to be Brett.

"Brett!" He had to be close by.

The thick snow stifled her yell. Her sled bag contained a folding shovel, but she was too alarmed to wade back to get it. First, she must find Brett. Still pawing furiously, Lulik had obviously detected something. If Brett was unharmed, he would have dug a snow shelter. And if he was in there, why wasn't he answering? Her calls and the dogs' scratching with an occasional short howl made enough noise despite the wind.

All the dogs were still digging.

After much clawing at the snow, Lulik enlarged the hole and fell through on top of an inert figure, wrapped in a gold space blanket, in the cavity she had exposed.

"Brett! Wake up! Wake up!"

He stirred.

"Move, Brett! Answer me! Are you alright?"

As she crawled in to help him, her nostrils caught the fetid, stale air of the narrow snow shelter. Brett had been in danger of suffocating from lack of oxygen. He would have cut a vent hole in the roof, but under the heavy snowfall, it must have been blocked.

With renewed strength, Vanessa managed to drag him out. Lulik pawed him and licked his face with her soft, pink tongue. The whole team crowded round him, licking, nosing between yips and yaps. It dawned on her how much he had become part of the pack. The dogs really dug one of their own.

Brett's head lolled on his shoulders. A hiccup raked his chest. Vanessa brushed the falling snow off his face. He groaned and his eyelids fluttered. "Wha..? What's going on?"

"Welcome back to the land of the living. You passed out."

"I did?" He eased himself to a sitting position and rubbed his legs. "How did you know where to find me?"

"We figured you must have followed this trail. But it's thanks to Lulik we found you."

At the sound of her name, Lulik sat back and brushed the snow with her bushy tail. Her dark, intelligent eyes gleamed with happiness. She expressed her loyalty by leaning against the man she had saved from a slow, certain death.

Brett rubbed the dog behind the ears. "I'm proud of her and her teammates."

Now that the man was sitting up, the team curled up and covered their noses with their tails. They were the most economical of dogs, resting whenever they had the chance.

"You must be hungry. The dogs won't go anywhere just now. I have broth in a thermos."

"Thanks, I am starved and light-headed."

Despite the impossible conditions, Vanessa succeeded in securing the sled line to a tree, not that the dogs showed any intention of running anywhere. She also gave each dog a generous chunk of hard fat as a reward, a favored treat. She abandoned hope of setting up the tent and took two thermos flasks out of the sled bag.

"I guess you arrived just in time. You saved my life." Brett was subdued, emotional.

"Not me. The dogs."

An unbearable urge to nurse him in her arms and kiss him overwhelmed her. Common sense prevailed. She grabbed his folding shovel and enlarged the hole's opening.

"Actually, as incredible as it sounds, Lulik scented you from the other side of the lake. She led the team across, despite my attempt to get back into the trees."

"She must have followed my trail. I came straight across the lake."

"What about Ingrid?"

"I lost her tracks even before the lake, but that was the most likely route."

"Put that parka on top of your suit. You're shivering. How are your feet?"

"I can't feel them."

She bent and began to untie and remove his boots. The amended shelter offered them some protection. She unzipped her parka and put his feet against her chest. They shared one thermos.

"Feel better?"

"Definitely."

"Have the second thermos. I'm fine."

"My feet tingle. They're cold but not frostbitten."

"Good. We can leave as soon as you finish eating."

"How can you travel in this storm?"

"Superiority of the dogs."

"*Touché.*"

"What about your snowmobile?"

"Nothing to worry about that. Stefan and I can come back later and dig it out."

"Sled dogs never break down. Have you thought about that? They just shake off the snow and start. Even in the dark, in the thickest storm, they never fail to find their way home."

"You're preaching to the converted. Machines don't have a nose, either, to sniff out lost souls."

"Tell me, why did you go after Ingrid?"

"Her life was threatened. Although she's my sister, I had fired her for what she did to you. When I saw she had taken a snowmobile, I couldn't leave her to her fate. We thought she couldn't handle a snowmobile. What a lie. But she really has no experience surviving in the wilderness and Dexter told me some thug was threatening her life. No matter what, nobody deserves to die."

"Were you ever lovers?" There, the question that had bugged her for a long time was out.

He looked indignant and sad. "No. She did her best, though. I thought at one point years ago maybe we could consider a future together. But I was into snowmobile racing. It took me away a lot, then she took off with a guy. In a way, I was relieved."

"Poor woman, she took up with the wrong man. We can't go after her now. You're in no state to plod through this storm. Put these extra socks on." She pulled them out from under her sweater.

"Oh, marvelous, they're warm!"

With a smile she handed him his boots. "We'll take you home now."

"That's on the condition you agree to be my wife."

Her love, held in restraint for so long, surged up from deep within her. "Do you mean that?"

"I mean it. I love you. I want you to be my love, my wife, my friend, my everything."

She flung herself on his chest and squeezed him tight.

"That's what you really said? About wanting me to marry you?"

"I've never been more serious about anything. Will you marry me?"

"Oh, Brett, I love you. Yes, I will."

They sealed their future with a kiss.

Still shaky, Brett got to his feet, while Vanessa, with some difficulties, turned the dogs and sled round.

"Let's share the runners, the exercise will keep you warmer than sitting in the sled. It gets bogged down in soft snow and makes it hard to handle."

"Yes, it'll prevent me from going to sleep."

"You're sleepy? Are you too hot? Those are signs of hypothermia."

"No, I'm fine now, thanks to you."

"I think you're on the brink of hypothermia." She pulled an energy bar out of her pocket. "Eat it."

"Lulik, Amaruq." The dogs looked at her. "Home."

On the return trip, the sled made slow progress through a landscape transformed by the heavy snowfall, but the storm was slackening. Clouds tore apart to reveal a shard of pink and blue sky. The sun hurried to set for the evening, painting the sky blood red. As they neared

Donek, Vanessa sighted a rescue posse of snowmobiles gathered at the trailhead.

Cheers went up from the drivers when someone spotted the approaching dog team. Vanessa turned to Brett. "That looks like your welcome home committee. Though, I suppose they were on their way to find you. They didn't believe my team could do it."

"Before we get mobbed by these good people, there's one thing I have to tell you. Back there, was the most incredible experience of my life."

Friendly shouts and cheers drowned out the rest of his admission. Vanessa was left to wonder if Brett's incredible experience was his being stranded in the storm and almost dying, or proposing marriage to the woman he loved. That tantalizing question was one she intended to take up with him at a more opportune moment.

Plastered with snow, Dexter elbowed his way up to the sled. "You're a fool, Lancaster, we picked up your sister by the Alaska Highway last night. She was seriously hypothermic, but she's going to be okay."

"Are you going to put her in prison?"

"Not my department. The judiciary will take over. She's really more of a victim."

Brett swayed. "Thank you."

"Let's get you home," Vanessa said.

He made no objections. They had a lot to discuss, but talk could wait.

CHAPTER THIRTY-NINE

The ensuing summer saw a flurry of activity between Wolf Hollow and the Tapiskoot cabin. Dog pens were built to the side of the lodge, which now only offered dogsled touring in winter and canoeing in summer. The new snowmobile club held classes to teach snowmobilers to ride safely, along with survival courses. A few snowmobiles were retained to pack the sledding trails, and as Brett said, for old times' sake.

The two parcels of land were joined and more sledding trails established. His arms around Vanessa's waist, Brett watched hundreds of birds flit about the yard. "Are you happy, Mrs. Lancaster?"

Her radiant face turned upward. "Total bliss, my love." Though now and then, she longed for the tranquility of the cabin, away from the animation of the lodge.

"I'm also happy that Ingrid received only a suspended sentence. House arrest under the supervision of our parents and takes online courses to gain a degree in the hospitality industry."

"Yes, that's good."

"You know, from time to time, we should escape and come to *the little cabin in the woods*, just the two of us, to escape the bustling atmosphere of the lodge."

Full of mirth, Vanessa confessed she had been thinking the same thing.

****

ABOUT THE AUTHOR

Born and raised in France, she was involved in writing from an early age, Geneviève has written a score of books: children's fiction in French and English, romances and historical novels published in France, Canada and the US, non-fiction books and numerous articles for Dogs in Canada. Her poetry has appeared in the Anthologie de la poésie Franco-Manitobaine, andin several short stories anthologies. She also worked as a translator.

In 2003 she received the Queen's Jubilee Medal

In 1983 she was nominated for YWCA Women of the Year

About the Author

ROMANCES

Untamed North Country Series

- RacingNorth
- To LoveAgain
- NorthernVet

Heart of the Prairies

- The Magicof Music
- Pizza forTwo
- The longTrek

HISTORICALNOVELS

All the Silences Series

- The Tears
- The Rage
- The Hope

NON-FICTION
- WWIIFRANCE: A Writer's Guide
- The InuitDog of the Polar North

CHILDREN
Tezzero,French edition
A Dog NamedTezzero

TRANSLATIONS
L'héritage dela guerre, translation from A Touch of Magic, June Gadsby.

OTHERS
Where theRiver Narrows, with Kathy Fisher-Brown